THE 36TH
EAGLE

ONE MAN'S STAND AGAINST CHINA'S
INVASION OF AUSTRALIA

Printed in Australia
Cover and internal design by Shawline Publishing Group Pty Ltd
Images in this book are copyright approved for Shawline Publishing Group Pty Ltd
Illustrations within this book are copyright approved for Shawline Publishing Group Pty Ltd

First printing: October 2023

Shawline Publishing Group Pty Ltd
www.shawlinepublishing.com.au

Paperback ISBN 978-1-9231-0102-9
eBook ISBN 978-1-9231-0108-1

Distributed by Shawline Distribution and Lightning Source Global

 A catalogue record for this work is available from the National Library of Australia

THE 36TH EAGLE

ONE MAN'S STAND AGAINST CHINA'S INVASION OF AUSTRALIA

JEFF MULLER

DEDICATIONS

The real Dave Pentreath wasn't a pilot, but he was the sort of person who'd carry out the deeds I've attributed to my lead character. He was my best friend, and he died too young.

ACKNOWLEDGEMENTS

My wife Liz, sharer of numerous adventures, including aerial ones, is my number one supporter. Long may our adventures continue.

Tony Park, highly successful author of many novels, gave me much guidance and encouragement. Without it, the novel wouldn't have progressed beyond first draft.

Editor Aidan Demmers waded through my technical stuff to make it readable, and hopefully entertaining.

Bradley Shaw of Shawline Publishing, who gives novice authors like me a chance.

The F-15 Eagle, a legendary fighter that in the real world has never lost a dogfight. The type has 104 victories versus zero losses as at September 2023. My apologies for spoiling its perfect record.

Finally, my friends in the aviation world who have, shared with, helped and encouraged me during fifty years of flying. Trevor, Patrick, Col, Charlie, Norm, David, Bruce, Pete, Phil… you know who you are.

AUTHOR'S NOTE

A few acronyms and specialised terms are inevitable when dealing with the military, although I have tried to minimise them.

AGL: above ground level

AIF: the Australian Infantry Force

ASI: the airspeed indicator in an aircraft

ASL: above sea level

AWACS: an Airborne Warning and Control System, a large radar fitted in military aircraft to detect other aircraft at long distances

CAP: a combat air patrol, usually consisting of one or multiple fighter aircraft over a ship or stationary potential target

Chaff: small strips of aluminium ejected in a cloud to confuse radar guided missiles

DOD: the Department of Defence

Flares: decoys to counteract heat-seeking missiles

IFR: instrument flying, as in conditions of zero visibility

Jet A-1: the kerosene-based fuel used in jet engines

NATO: the North Atlantic Treaty Organization

No SAR: no search and rescue watch required

Ordnance: a term that covers bombs, missiles, and bullets

PLA: the Chinese People's Liberation Army

PLANAF: the People's Liberation Army Navy Air Force, the aviation branch of the Chinese Navy

RAAF: the Royal Australian Air Force

RAN: the Royal Australian Navy

RIB: rigid inflatable boat

STOL: short take-off and landing

USAF: the United States Air Force

VTOL: vertical take-off and landing

Warbird: an ex-military aircraft now in private hands, usually flown under a permit for historic aircraft

A confusing part of aviation-speak involves its system of measurement. The early aviation bureaucrats did themselves proud. Almost universally, distances in aviation are measured in nautical miles, which are equivalent to 1.151 statute miles, or 1.852 kilometres. On aviation maps, nautical miles have traditionally been used, but just to make it all a bit harder, kilometres are becoming more common.

Speed is usually measured in knots, where one knot is one nautical mile per hour. For high-performance aircraft, however, Mach numbers are often used. Mach 1 is equivalent to the speed of sound. If an aircraft is travelling at Mach 1, it could be reaching almost 700 knots or under 500 knots, depending on air density, which in turn depends on temperature and height. At average temperatures and at sea level, Mach 1 is 660 knots, 760 mph, or 1225 kph.

Height is normally measured in feet, but the Eastern Bloc countries use metres. Above 10,000 feet, Western civil aircraft use flight levels, where 10,000 feet is flight level 100, 20,000 feet is flight level 200, and so on. Often, the military uses the term angels; e.g., 10,000 feet is angels 10, and so on. Rate of climb is normally measured in feet per second, but again can be quoted in metres per second.

Fuel consumption can be quoted in imperial gallons, US gallons, litres, pounds, or kilograms per hour. This has led to a number of serious accidents due to fuel shortage, where a pilot orders fuel in one system and the fuel is delivered in another. For instance, a pilot might order 1000 kg, but receive 1000 lb.

You'll find a mixture of measurements used in this book, as it is beyond the author's ability to overcome this issue.

The concept that non-current pilots could manage to fly sophisticated aircraft like the F-15 Eagle isn't all that unrealistic. However, going to war in them is a totally different matter. In addition, doing so without substantial logistical backup is stretching things a bit. My Eagles were amazingly reliable.

CHAPTER 1

22 JUNE 2026

On the cold and rainy winter night, the four-lane highway leading past the village of Heatherbrae was deserted but for two old Toyota HiAce vans travelling close together. The three occupants of the leading vehicle were squeezed together on its sagging bench seat. For some time, the only sounds had been the swish of wet tyres, the drone of the tired engine, and the slap of worn-out windscreen wipers. Their faces were briefly picked out by street lighting as Weng Wei steered his once-white but now dirty grey van off the highway. The second nondescript van obediently followed.

The industrial businesses in Masonite Road were shut, but carpark lighting and LED advertising signs illuminated both sides of the road. Past this small commercial zone, the road narrowed, and the vehicles entered a thin forest. Soon, trees gave way to open pastures. All Weng could see were fences on each side, barely visible in the weak headlights. Now, the faces of his two passengers were lit only by the soft glow of an iPad held by the one seated in the middle. Tang Xin peered at the moving map on the tablet, which he held inches from his nose.

He jabbed a finger at the screen. 'Jimmy, it's just around the bend… slow down, slow down, here it is! Just as well we have this device, or we would've missed it altogether.' He lifted the tablet so Weng could see its screen.

'I've told you before, don't call me Jimmy.' Weng scowled as he braked for the turn. 'That's only for stupid Australians at the university who can't pronounce my real name.'

Tang laughed. 'You made such a poor student, *Jimmy* – it's surprising you weren't kicked out of the course weeks ago.'

'Cut out the jokes and concentrate on navigation, Tang. You seem to forget who's in charge of this operation,' Weng spat.

The two vans turned off the sealed road, cautiously nosing through a water-filled ditch and onto a muddy, unnamed track. Headlights off, they crawled along in the dim glow of their parking lights alone. Weng could only make out low scrub on either side and the occasional discarded drink can reflecting the sparse light. The rain had eased to a light shower, but that was enough to make him struggle to see past the defunct wipers that just smeared his windscreen.

The vehicles crept along the ruler-straight track for precisely six kilometres. Weng cursed as his van slid and lurched through several low spots, where the mud was thick and black. He could hear it spraying into the wheel wells, and constantly feared the vehicle might bog down.

'*Diu!* They give us an old van with old wipers and worn-out tyres, but it'll be us to blame if we break down or get stuck.'

'No, they'll blame just you, the leader,' Tang said with a giggle, drawing only a grunt from Weng.

Minutes later, both vans drew to a stop when Tang's electronic map showed that they had reached their destination. Engines and all lights were switched off. The occupants, four male and two female, exited quietly and congregated at the rear door of the lead van. They all wore tight-fitting black windcheaters, trousers, balaclavas and running shoes, so they were barely visible even to each other. Without uttering a word, Weng began hauling out six matt-black rucksacks from his van, one for each dark figure. When they had all awkwardly hoisted the heavy bags onto their backs, he passed each person a torch and a handheld GPS receiver.

'Remember,' he whispered, 'only use the torches if you must.'

'What are you worried about?' said Tang loudly. 'There's nobody around for at least a kilometre!'

'Whisper, idiot,' Weng hissed. 'We can't be too careful. Now follow me, and stay silent.'

The six melted into the darkness, heading due east. Fine raindrops coalesced on Weng's face and ran down his neck, and dew on the low foliage soon penetrated his boots to soak his socks. However, he was too anxious about the mission to register any discomfort.

After tramping 600 metres through thin, waist-high bushes, they bumped into an ordinary five-strand farm fence, which they slipped through with ease. The going was much easier on the other side of the fence, as the ground had been cleared of bushes, the grass cut to ankle-height. Within a minute, they were standing on the unlit western end of the runway shared by RAAF Williamtown and Newcastle's civil airport.

Weng wiped water droplets from his eyelashes and peered towards the distant eastern end of Runway 21. He could see no movement, and there was no sound other than his own heavy breathing. At the far end of the runway, on the right-hand side, he could see the bright glow of Newcastle Airport, though no more flights were scheduled for the night. On the left, he could just see the much dimmer lighting of the RAAF base.

The six black-clad figures trotted along the middle of the runway towards the lights, following barely visible centreline markings, before branching off onto a taxiway that led towards the RAAF side of the field, where two squadrons resided: 34 Squadron flew BAE Hawk trainers, and 76 Squadron flew the frontline F-35 fighters. Although it was ostensibly a simple job to place a small but powerful bomb into the tailpipe of each of the thirty-eight F-35 jets and twenty-four Hawks that sat in rows under the revetments, Weng's legs shook when he stopped for a breather. If his team was discovered, they would spend years in an Australian military prison. China would claim to have no knowledge of them or their mission. When eventually sent back to China, they would likely face swift execution, as failure was not acceptable in the clandestine operations of the PLA.

They found the dimly lit revetments just as aerial photos, courtesy of Google Earth, had predicted. There were seven of the open-sided buildings, the smallest of which could accommodate five aircraft, the largest ten. Electronic security appeared non-existent, just as they had been briefed to expect. All six saboteurs looked out for the lone watchman they knew should be patrolling somewhere.

They split up in the darkness, each seeking the individual targets marked on their GPS screen. One had been assigned aircraft in two separate revetments, but became confused when crossing from one row to another, and placed bombs in Hawk trainers that had already been attended to by a teammate, missing a row entirely.

Tang Xin was the youngest in the team, and the most cavalier. Not once had he shown any fear or hesitation. His colleagues considered him something of a loose cannon, and privately thought that if something was to go wrong, it would be Tang who caused it.

As he approached the first aircraft in his assigned row of F-35 fighters, he stopped briefly to admire the deadly machine. He'd never been this close to a real military jet before, as they'd used fibreglass mock-ups in training. He appreciated the purposeful look of the aircraft, with its matt dark grey paint, low-visibility national markings, and stubby underwing weapon pods. Vinyl covers plugged the twin air intakes, pitot tubes, and other vents. Tags on each cover twisted in the slight wind. He walked the length of the F-35, ducking under its wing, where he saw that the large tailpipe was also fitted with a plug. For a moment, he feared that his short stature would prevent him from placing the bomb as instructed. However, he found he could just reach just high enough to dislodge the cover and slide the small bomb into the exhaust.

In minutes, striding confidently between each fighter in the row, he had sabotaged ten F-35s, and with his remaining bombs could seek targets of opportunity. Smiling to himself, he calculated that those ten aircraft had cost the Australian taxpayers more than two billion dollars. They would not be so valuable for much longer.

Tang left the soft lighting of the shelters and crossed a wide, unlit expanse of concrete towards a row of five gigantic hangars. Each held aircraft undergoing maintenance, and at first sight, appeared to be closed and in total darkness. However, he noticed light spilling from one huge sliding door that was not completely shut. He stealthily approached the opening, then slipped through to hide behind a yellow-painted work platform that sat just inside. There were three F-35 fighters on his side of the cavernous hangar, and two Hawk trainers on the opposite side.

He froze at the sound of soft voices, but quickly realised it was coming from a portable radio on a shelf at that far side, just behind one of the jets. A blue-uniformed guard sat at a small table under the shelf, hunched over a take-away food carton and feeding scraps from it to a German shepherd that sat attentively at his feet.

Tang crouched motionless for a minute or two to allow his heartbeat to return to normal. He could hardly believe his ears: the radio was broadcasting the national news, and he clearly heard the announcer reading the lead story.

'The demands voiced by Chinese leader Zhang Wei to Prime Minister Roger Quick, regarding the independent operation of Chinese-owned farms and businesses in Australia, are heightening tensions between the two governments. Our PM has branded the demands as outrageous, and has asked the Chinese leader to withdraw them immediately. Concerns have been raised that China may force the issue by further restricting Australia's export of minerals and agricultural products.'

Little do they know those tensions are about to multiply! Tang thought, with a silent laugh.

With both patrolman and dog preoccupied, Tang thought it was safe to move. He crept from aircraft to aircraft on his side of the hangar, depositing a bomb in each F-35 tailpipe, three in all. He did not dare approach the two Hawks on the opposite side, as they were much too near the resting patrolman. Tang noiselessly exited the hangar the way he'd come in, melting into the darkness.

He still had four bombs left, and time was running short, so he put half under a large fuel truck parked near the hangar, and the last two in the engines of a small executive jet stationed nearby.

By 3 a.m., Tang had found his way back to the vans. He was the last to return, and he found his colleagues quietly but excitedly congratulating each other. He noticed that some were visibly shaking, and wondered if it was from the cold, the excitement, or a combination of both. As he dropped his empty rucksack by the lead van, he laughed out loud. 'That was just too easy! One stupid guard and one lazy dog to patrol a whole airbase. What a pity we can't stay to watch the fireworks.'

'Quiet, Tang, don't be a fool,' Weng hissed. 'Let's just pack up and get back on the highway. We don't want to be discovered now.'

In less than three hours, they were changing into fresh clothes in their rented flats near Sydney University, 200 km south of RAAF Williamtown. By 6 a.m., they had checked in at Sydney Airport for a 9 a.m. China Southern flight direct to Guangzhou. Their two vans had been abandoned in the public carpark.

* * *

At the two RAAF training bases in Pearce, Western Australia, and Sale, Victoria, other groups of Chinese 'students' placed bombs in Hawk trainers. In Katherine, Northern Territory, a team infiltrated the RAAF side of the airfield, where Australia's second F-35 squadron resided. The F/A-18 Super Hornets at Queensland's Amberley RAAF base were targeted by another group. Specialist divers from the PLA Navy hid limpet mines in the Australian Navy facilities in Sydney Harbour, Jarvis Bay, and Fremantle.

The only significant Australian Air Force or Navy base to not be successfully sabotaged was the maritime patrol squadron in Edinburgh, South Australia. A single van with three students on board attempted to evade a routine breathalyser roadblock near the base. After a short pursuit, the van was forced to stop. Suspecting a drug delivery due to the three rucksacks in the rear of the van, a police constable held it and its occupants while awaiting the drug squad.

At precisely 4 a.m. on 22 June 2026, a single phone call was made by Weng Wei. That call triggered the explosion of one hundred and ten small bombs and another forty limpet mines. Each bomb was powerful enough to destroy an aircraft, and each mine powerful enough to damage a ship. The last twenty bombs exploded in the van near Edinburgh, vaporising the three students, fatally injuring the police constable and destroying his patrol car.

At Williamtown Airfield, half of Australia's frontline fighter force and half of its jet training fleet exploded simultaneously. Tonnes of fuel from a ruptured tanker added to the conflagration that followed. Only two Hawks in the deep maintenance hangar and a row of them under a revetment were not destroyed. It was a similar story at Pearce, Sale, Katherine and Amberley.

In all, approximately twenty billion dollars' worth of defence assets had been destroyed or rendered inoperative by some forty young Chinese agents staying in Australia on student visas. Apart from the Boeing maritime patrol jets at Edinburgh, the country was left with no air defence and just one of its six ageing Collins Class submarines in seaworthy condition.

Australia didn't know it yet, but the battle for the nation had begun.

* * *

Nine thousand kilometres to the north, Commander Huang Bai of the People's Liberation Army Naval Air Force ran a finger between his perspiring skin and the stiff collar of his freshly pressed white shirt. Even in the air-conditioned back of the Hongqi LS8 limousine, it seemed hot and humid, and he feared he might stain the dark blue uniform perfectly tailored to his figure. He touched the knot of his tie and tugged at his shirt cuffs, ensuring that the correct amount of white sleeve showed below the twin yellow strips on his coat sleeves. He chided himself for being so nervous.

'I do have good reason, though,' he murmured to himself. 'It isn't every day that one is summoned to meet Admiral Shen Jun.'

For the hundredth time, he pondered why the summons had come, and what ramifications were in store for him. He knew they could be very good, or they could be very bad; anything in between was unlikely. Gloomily, he thought the latter scenario more probable.

Huang Bai, the son of a peasant farmer, had joined the PLANAF as a lowly cadet at the age of nineteen. It had soon become obvious that he was a natural pilot. He'd handled the training aircraft with confidence from day one, and won every mock battle during advanced training, even against his far more experienced instructors. Moreover, he had an innate ability to impart his new skills to less talented classmates. He'd progressed through the ranks with unprecedented speed, and was now, at twenty-eight, in charge of the Chinese equivalent to the USA's Top Gun fighter pilot school and the three elite squadrons it had so far produced. He had smooth and hairless skin, a small, firm mouth, high cheekbones, a narrow nose and thin eyebrows. His black hair was cut even shorter than the military demanded.

Huang Bai's forthright approach and analytical ability were his strengths, but perhaps also his greatest weaknesses: he stepped on too many toes. *Maybe*, he said to himself, *just one toe too many, and today I will find myself back at the bottom of a long list of aspiring squadron leaders.* He'd been outspokenly critical of the regular squadrons' training standards, and of the standing orders that kept them restricted to what he considered simple manoeuvres, which didn't stress either man or machine too far. He had a more aggressive approach in combat, utilising the full performance envelope of the fighters he flew. His elite pilots regularly practised twisting simulated dogfights and ultra-low-level bombing, but he'd pushed for increased training time to make them even better.

Intending to minimise costs, his superiors had restricted the number of hours that training pilots could fly each month. Huang Bai felt hamstrung by this, and regularly exceeded the allocation to his three squadrons. Because he got such good results, he'd escaped punishment for this flagrant disobedience. So far, anyway.

Huang Bai had also criticised the decision to equip the navy with locally built fighters, the J-15 and the newer FC-31, as he believed that the Russian-built Sukhoi Su-35 was a superior aircraft. Most recently, he'd derided the design of the navy's new carrier, its pride and joy.

Criticising the Mao Tse Tung *was probably my biggest mistake*, he thought. It was widely known that Admiral Shen, the commander of the South Sea Fleet, had been a strong backer of the carrier project, and now Huang Bai felt certain that Shen was going to haul him over the coals. Perhaps Huang Bai's negative comments had been taken as disloyal, or even seditious. The reward for the latter might be an appointment with a quiet courtyard and a bullet to the back of his head. He shivered at the thought.

Huang Bai continued to agonise over the possibilities as the limo crawled from intersection to intersection in the busy Beijing district of Xicheng. Bystanders gawked at the big car, trying to see which famous person was hidden behind the heavily tinted glass. At another time, Huang Bai might've enjoyed the looks of envy, but that was the last thing on his mind now.

The driver turned into the wide and relatively quiet Fuchengmen Street, then pulled over to the curb in front of Number 34. This address covered twin long but narrow two-storey buildings that stretched to the next street. A carpark, dotted with a few ornamental trees in large tubs, separated the two buildings. A lone uniformed naval rating in mottled grey and white camo stood at attention outside the left building's plain entry portico. The driver opened the limo's back door, and Huang Bai momentarily shrank back into the plush leather upholstery. Steeling himself, he climbed out of the car and stalked towards the entry. The driver ran to catch up to him, proffering the white peaked cap that he'd left behind. Embarrassed, he muttered his thanks and continued to the doorway, where the waiting sailor saluted and gestured for Huang Bai to follow him. A wide staircase took them to the second floor. The guard turned left and led Huang Bai past a number of open doorways, through which he could see uniformed secretaries busily working at computers. Halfway along the corridor, the guard stopped outside an unmarked door, told Huang Bai to wait there, and marched back the way he'd come. This end of the hallway was quiet and bare, and there was nowhere to sit.

Twenty minutes later, Huang Bai was finding it difficult to control the trembling in his left leg. He also had an urgent need to go to the bathroom, but dared not leave his post. His discomfort was becoming unbearable when he noticed that he'd somehow scuffed the toe of his polished left shoe. He was about to bend down and rub the offending patch when the door flew open without warning, and he was waved inside by an unsmiling middle-aged woman in a grey sailor's uniform without any marks of rank. Entering, he found himself in a large conference room, its cream walls bare but for one photo of the president. Five padded chairs sat behind a long table, with a single plain wooden kitchen chair in front of it. Huang Bai was acutely aware of the way his footsteps interrupted the silence. The woman pointed to the single chair, then left the room.

Occupying the five padded chairs were five senior PLANAF officers. Huang Bai immediately identified two-star Admiral Shen's craggy face and thin, receding hair, but was surprised by his diminutive size. He also looked considerably older than his widely used portrait, with his lined cheeks almost grey in colour. Huang Bai also recognised the ranks, but not the faces, of the four younger admirals. Two were two-star Vice Admirals, and two were one-star Rear Admirals. Nobody acknowledged him: all five watched him impassively. With this high-level committee, whatever was coming must be extremely serious.

Huang Bai caught himself before saluting, which would've been a breach of protocol, as none of the admirals wore their peaked caps, and sat awkwardly on the hard chair. He felt like melting in the silence, and his anxiety rose with every passing second. He didn't know which way to look. Feeling his face reddening, he forced himself to breathe deeply and slowly, focusing on a point just above Admiral Shen's head. Then Shen spoke in a surprisingly soft voice.

'Commander Huang, your fitness report by Captain Jian Zhi was highly complimentary. He said that you have excelled in training your three elite squadrons, which have achieved a higher standard than any other in the PLANAF. According to your own reports, with which Captain Jian concurred, your squadrons are ready to be assigned to a carrier. Our new supercarrier is also now fully operational. Therefore, this board must decide whether you will continue to command those three squadrons when they embark on the *Mao Tse Tung*.'

This favourable opening caught Huang Bai by surprise. 'It would be a great honour. Thank you, Admiral.' His voice sounded unnatural, even to himself.

Shen shuffled his papers. 'You are under consideration due to your and Captain Jian's reports. But I must emphasise that my colleagues and I must ourselves be convinced that you are the right person for an important assignment – an assignment that is critical not only to our navy, but to our entire nation. So, we have some questions for you. Admiral Wu, would you like to go first?'

Vice Admiral Wu leaned forward and stared at Huang Bai. His jowls and cheeks sagged, as did the corners of his mouth, but his face bore no clue to his attitude. Slowly, he shifted his gaze to the notes on the table in front of him. When he spoke, his tone was harsh and accusatory.

'Commander Huang. You are always agitating for more training funds. Why is that? Do you not think that your superior officers, who ran this navy years before you even left school, have a more intimate knowledge of what is necessary? What makes you think that you can continually ignore time and resource allocations that apply to everyone?'

Huang Bai swallowed. He would've liked to say that his students had only half the flying hours an equivalent American naval pilot would've had before being committed to a fighter squadron. But this was not the time to be blunt. He knew that his whole career hinged on the outcome of this meeting.

'Gentlemen, every graduate of our advanced combat flying course is incredibly capable. I merely wish to hone their skills further with more challenging regimes than the current course can include.'

He hesitated, but as there was no immediate response, he ploughed on.

'Our aircraft are superb, and are capable of more than our regular navy pilots are trained for, as I have shown with our elite course. An increase in flying hours would enable us to improve training in extreme combat manoeuvres and low-level flying for our elite pilots, and indeed for all navy pilots.'

Huang Bai again looked for some reaction, but all five officers stared back at him stonily. He was about to continue when the second vice admiral drummed his long fingers on the wooden table before breaking the uncomfortable silence.

'Commander Huang, I am Admiral Liu. You say that our aircraft are superb, yet you are on record criticising the aircraft in your squadrons. You have said that our Shenyang J-15 is inferior to the Russian Sukhoi Su-33 on which it is based. What's more, you have also claimed that the new Shenyang FC-31 stealth fighter is inferior to its contemporary, the American F-35.' Scowling, Liu shook a sheaf of papers at Huang Bai.

Perspiration ran down Huang Bai's face and neck, and his perfectly fitted jacket suddenly felt tight. How could he get out of this? Although he desperately hoped that his panic wasn't noticeable, he thought it probably was. He decided he had no choice but to express a moderate version of his real beliefs. He tried to make eye contact with Liu, who was fat-faced, dark-skinned and bald, but Liu's heavily tinted glasses made it difficult.

'Yes, Admiral, I have. Our J-15 fighters have had performance and reliability issues, which I have put together a tech team to work on. We hope that, in time, we'll bring them to a standard superior to any other fighters in the world.' Inwardly, Huang Bai cringed. There was little chance of achieving that target anytime soon. 'I have not had the opportunity to fully test the FC-31, but I know that its stealth technology is amazing. Unfortunately, the trade-off is that this technology is an impediment to outright performance, more than I would've expected. Again, I am working with the engineers to overcome this issue, along with some other teething problems.'

The five inquisitors exchanged glances, but no one spoke. After what seemed like hours, one of the rear admirals leaned forward, his bulbous nose reddening, and focused his prominent eyes on Huang Bai. Pointing a shaking finger, he almost shouted: 'Commander Huang, you have also recently criticised the design of our newest carrier, the *Mao Tse Tung*. Do you not realise that it is the culmination of fifty years of research and experimentation by the best naval architects in China? It is the largest aircraft carrier in the world, bigger even than the latest American warships!'

Huang Bai knew that the Chinese Navy had begun researching carrier design in the 1980s, with the purchase of the UK-built, Royal Australian Navy-operated carrier HMAS *Melbourne* for scrapping. To their amazement, when it had been towed to

Guangzhou, they'd discovered that the Australians had left the steam catapult, the mirror landing aid, and the arrester cable system fully intact. Those systems had been carefully studied by China's naval architects. That ship had been designed during World War Two, when the heaviest fighter aircraft weighed less than eight tonnes, and had take-off speeds of 80 to 90 knots. The Chinese Navy's modern jets had take-off weights of up to 30 tonnes and launch speeds of at least 125 knots, so much development work had been needed. Their first two carriers had been equipped with ski-jump decks, which aided the launching of STOL and VTOL aircraft, but no catapults. This new carrier was their first that would rely on steam catapults to launch its jets.

The Americans had perfected the steam catapult over the past seventy-five years, and had developed carrier aircraft handling into a fine art. Chinese engineers had utilised as much recent information as they'd been able to, but could hardly be expected to have the system perfected straight from the drawing-board.

Huang Bai was aware that he was on extremely dangerous ground, as speaking the truth was not necessarily the best defence. But there was no going back now.

'I do realise that, sir, but I have concerns about our new ship. Its parallel runways limit us to just one landing or take-off per deck at any one time, and landings cannot occur when other aircraft are hooked up to launch. We need time at sea with the new squadrons and supercarrier to work out the most efficient handling procedures.'

Expecting the attack to continue, Huang Bai was surprised when Admiral Shen held up both hands to cut off further discussion.

'Enough,' Shen said. 'We might not agree with Commander

Huang on these particulars, but I think that we can all now see that he does know his job, and is dedicated to improving both the navy's men and its machines.' He glanced sideways at his colleagues. 'Commander Huang has been tasked with producing elite squadrons of naval aviators, and he has done this well, though we can perhaps recommend that he exercises a little more circumspection before speaking on matters above his station in future.' A small smile creased the corner of Admiral Shen's mouth.

He then turned back to face Huang Bai, and instantly became serious again. 'This is top secret, and must not leave this room until further notice. Our illustrious president and his cabinet have decided that in 2027, the People's Republic will retake the land stolen by the Nationals in 1945. Taiwan will again be ours. Meanwhile, we – the South Sea Fleet and People's Liberation Army – are to do a practice run, so to speak, against a relative minnow. This operation will not require the air force or the other naval fleets that are at our disposal. It is ours alone. You will take charge of the air wing on the new carrier *Mao Tse Tung*, and as such will play a major role in the invasion of Australia.'

Huang Bai gasped and sat back. In one short meeting, he'd been put through the wringer by his superiors, then given a dream role in the modern navy's first real test.

'Your rank from today is captain,' Shen said. 'If you are completely successful during the Australian exercise, you will be a natural choice to head the air wings of both the navy and air force in the subjugation of Taiwan.'

Huang Bai could hardly believe what he was hearing. This was almost too good to be true.

'You will now return to your office and prepare to immediately embark on our new supercarrier, where you will work your three elite squadrons up to combat readiness as quickly as possible.' Admiral Shen raised a brow at his colleagues. 'Are we all agreed?'

The four junior admirals murmured to each other, then nodded in turn.

'Go now,' Shen said. 'Do not fail us, Captain Huang.'

Huang Bai rose, stood to attention, and walked stiffly to the door. Once outside, he sprinted to the bathroom at the end of the corridor, almost tripping as he pushed the door open with trembling hands.

* * *

Back in the limousine, Huang Bai allowed himself a grin. He fingered the black epaulets on his jacket, each featuring twin golden stars, and looked at the matching bands on its cuffs. Tomorrow, he would order a brand-new jacket with an extra star and stripe. There were such exciting opportunities ahead – invasion of Australia, and later Taiwan, with the chance to become China's top-scoring fighter ace of all time, while contributing to his country becoming the largest military, economic, and political power in the world!

Thoughts of the suffering that accompanied any military operation did not enter Huang Bai's head. China's forces would sweep all before them, and the enemy was just an obstacle in that path.

CHAPTER 2

1 SEPTEMBER 2025
(NINE MONTHS EARLIER)

The old warbird gleamed in the first rays of sunshine. She was eighty-three years old, but just as ready for action as the day she'd rolled off the production line on the other side of the globe, at a time when the world faced the twin perils of Nazi Germany and expansionist Japan.

Dave Pentreath hoisted himself onto the trailing edge of the wing, slid the front cockpit's glasshouse canopy open and climbed in. As he strapped into the firm canvas-covered seat, he breathed in the familiar smell of new paint, aviation fuel, engine oil, stale sweat and a trace of fear from the numerous fighter pilots who'd trained in this machine over many years. He felt at home as he slipped on the headset and scanned the khaki-painted internal framework. There was nothing delicate about this aircraft: she'd been built for war.

Dave heard the clang of a dropped seatbelt buckle from the rear seat.

'You alright back there, Ken?'

'Uh, yeah, Dave, I'm just figuring out how the buckle works.

I… I'm okay. I'm really looking forward to this.'

The North American SNJ was the US Navy's version of the well-known T-6 Harvard. This SNJ was built in 1944 and had served the navy until 1955, before being sold to a private owner. She came to Mayer Aviation direct from the west coast of the USA two years before, needing a full overhaul. As chief engineer at Mayer Aviation, Dave had supervised the rebuild, working on it whenever time permitted – his principal responsibility was keeping the company's fleet of corporate jets in the sky.

Every part of the SNJ's airframe and engine had been disassembled, repaired, and replaced where necessary. New instruments had been fitted, new radios and navigation gear installed. Repainted in her original yellow, with US Navy markings, she was now a real head-turner. She was ready for her fourth test flight, which was to be from Sydney's Bankstown Airport to Bathurst and back. For the first time, her proud owner, Ken Newstead, was coming along for the ride.

Ken had learned to fly years earlier, and had many hours in command of his Piper Twin Comanche four-seater. The SNJ had been a present to himself when he'd turned sixty, and he'd followed every milestone of the restoration. He and Dave had become firm friends during the long process.

Pre-start checks complete, throttle set, carburettor primed, Dave called 'Clear prop!' and pressed the inertia starter. The engine whirred through four revolutions before he switched on the twin magnetos. With a cough and a wisp of smoke, the engine caught, ran roughly for a few seconds, then settled into a steady throb. The slow-moving prop blades disappeared into a shimmering disc as the engine rose to 1000 RPM. It took several minutes for the cylinder heads to reach 100 degrees Celsius, then Dave released the brakes and began taxiing to the run-up bay.

He keyed the radio button on the throttle lever. 'Bankstown Ground, this is SNJ India Uniform Bravo on taxiway Lima for an upwind departure. Two on board, received information Charlie.'

The air-traffic controller replied: 'Roger, India Uniform Bravo. Cleared to holding point Alpha. Call 132.8 for departure.'

Dave steered the warbird to the holding point in a series of S-turns, as in the tail-down position, the big engine blocked his view directly ahead. He selected the departure frequency. 'Bankstown Tower, this is SNJ India Uniform Bravo, two on board, No SAR, for an upwind departure, two nine right, with information Charlie.'

'India Uniform Bravo, clear for take-off.'

'Are you strapped in, Ken?' Dave asked over the intercom.

'Sure am, Dave. All secure.'

Dave glanced again at the instruments and checked the windsock as he turned the SNJ onto the active runway. Slowly, he pushed the throttle lever forward, and the machine accelerated. His toes danced on the rudder pedals as engine torque, gyroscopic forces, and wind competed to swing the tail of the aircraft first one way then the other. When the airspeed indicator passed 75 knots, he gently eased the stick back and the mainwheels left the ground. After another quick scan of the panel, he took his left hand off the throttle long enough to lift the undercarriage lever. The climb rate increased with the drag of the extended undercarriage gone, and when the ASI passed 100 knots, he steepened the angle of climb.

The aircraft rose through the gin-clear air, leaving Sydney's controlled airspace just west of the Nepean River. At cruising level, Dave throttled back for a speed of 140 knots, and the engine settled into a loud but comforting throb. With the SNJ trimmed and stable, he handed the controls over to his passenger. Dave was curious to see how Ken, who'd only flown modern light aircraft, would handle the much heavier but nimbler WWII military aeroplane.

Immediately, the aircraft began to pitch and roll.

'Ken, relax, relax! Don't grip the stick so tight,' Dave said, with a chuckle. 'Just keep her straight and level.'

Although Dave had flown this route many times, he still enjoyed the scenery from the glasshouse canopy: that elegant wing with its military markings sliding over the rising forested hills, the sandstone cliffs near Katoomba golden in the morning sunshine. *Beautiful*, he thought, *but no place for an emergency landing.*

As if it had read his mind, minutes later, the engine went stone dead. There was no warning – no hiccup, no flashing instrument. The bellow of the big radial engine was instantly replaced by the roaring of the wind, and the prop blades flicked over only from the airflow.

'Dave, what's happening?' Ken shouted.

'I'm taking over,' Dave said. 'I'll handle it.'

He eased the stick back to slow the aircraft to its best gliding speed of 90 knots while he scanned the ground for somewhere to land. Three thousand feet below, there was nothing but natural and plantation forests, except for a small brown hilltop paddock about five miles to their left, just on the edge of what Dave estimated their maximum gliding range would be.

'Tighten your straps, Ken.'

Dave rolled left and aimed for the paddock. He changed the fuel feed from the left wing tank to the right, selected a full rich fuel mixture, and tried to restart the engine. It showed no inclination to cooperate, so he pulled the prop lever to feather the windmilling propellor, bringing it to a stop and minimising its drag.

He pressed the transmit button. 'Melbourne Centre, India Uniform Bravo, an SNJ, two on board, engine failure. We'll land in a paddock about fifteen miles east-sou-east of Bathurst.'

The reply was prompt. 'India Uniform Bravo, Melbourne Centre. Are you declaring a mayday?'

'Affirmative, Melbourne Centre.'

Dave felt the strange calm that all good pilots felt in an emergency, the type of emergency he'd trained for and practised many times. But this time it was real.

He'd judged the glide slope perfectly: holding 90 knots, the paddock neither slipped up nor down on the windshield, but just got bigger. At about a half-mile distance, Dave could see that it was probably no more than 300 metres long, nowhere near large enough for an SNJ. Twice that length would still be tight. It was surrounded by barbed-wire fencing, its surface was dry, dusty, and bare, and hundreds of sheep were eating from feed that had been dropped along its western boundary. Under or overshooting would mean going through a fence at best. Going into the gullies at either end would be catastrophic.

As soon as Dave was certain that the aircraft would clear the near fence, he selected the landing flap and urgently pumped the emergency hydraulic handle.

'Brace, brace!' he yelled. 'Get your head down, Ken. We'll land with wheels up. That'll stop us quicker.'

He eased the control stick further back as the SNJ cleared the first fence. With hardly a bump, the aircraft hit the loose surface. She skidded on her belly for about 150 metres, coming to a stop amidst a huge pall of dust and a wisp of smoke from the engine.

The nose of the aircraft was barely ten metres from the far fence. Just beyond it, the gully fell away steeply. Only three minutes had elapsed since the engine failed.

For a few seconds, the only sound was the ticking of cooling metal. With a cry of relief, Ken leapt out from the cockpit.

'Get out, Dave! Quick, get out!'

'It's okay – I'll just shut everything down, then try to contact Melbourne Centre on the radio.'

Ken was remarkably agile for a big man verging on overweight. Perhaps he'd seen too many movies where an aeroplane made a crash landing, skidded to a halt, then exploded in a ball of flame. Whatever the reason, he jumped back onto the wing, grabbed Dave by the collar of his flight suit and hauled him bodily out of his seat. Immediately, he overbalanced and fell backwards, taking Dave with him. The two men tumbled off the wing and landed heavily on the dusty ground.

'Shit, you bloody fool, what did you do that for? Dave spat, as he staggered to his feet and dusted himself off. 'You damn near killed me!'

A sharp, familiar pain stabbed into his lower back, and he found it difficult to remain standing. He knew then that Ken had antagonised an old injury – one that had cost him his career as a fighter pilot many years before.

* * *

Over the next few months, Dave supervised the repairs to the SNJ's engine and airframe in Mayer Aviation's hangar. A tiny manufacturing flaw had caused an invisible crack to develop in one exhaust valve. Eventually, it had broken, and the loose valve head had wedged between a rising piston and cylinder head, causing the latter's separation, taking a large piece of inlet manifold with it. Thanks to the efforts of Dave and his team, both engine and airframe were made as good as ever. With some hours of intensive training, Ken was eventually cleared to fly the SNJ solo, and he proudly displayed her at air shows for years after that.

Dave wished that his own body could be patched up as easily as the old warbird had been. Scans proved that he'd cracked a vertebra in his already-weakened spine when Ken had dragged him off the wing. He could have an operation to fix it, but the chances of success were less than fifty-fifty. If it failed, there was a small chance that his injury could be made far worse. The specialist recommended that Dave do appropriate exercises, rest frequently, avoid sitting or standing for long periods, and take it easy for the rest of his life.

Dave attempted to continue his normal work schedule, but the hour-long drive each way was hard for him, especially as the traffic seemed to worsen every day. He struggled to get out of the car at the end of every journey. At work, he was constantly restless. Standing or sitting still for more than a few minutes resulted in a persistent ache in his lower back.

On the third Friday of January 2026, after the Mayer Aviation staff had knocked off for the week, Dave entered the office of the company's managing director and major shareholder. Trevor Mayer looked up from his paperwork and smiled. 'Dave, come and have a drink to celebrate another good week. The usual?'

The two men had been friends for more than four decades and business partners for two. They were of the same age, and both had lean builds, but that was where their similarities ended. Trevor wore a freshly pressed white shirt with a stiff collar and epaulets, his navy trousers were sharply creased, and his black leather shoes were highly polished. Dave, on the other hand, wore the short-sleeved cotton shirt and work trousers of the engineers he supervised. His cheap trainers bore a few spots of oil.

Trevor and Dave's offices were side-by-side on the mezzanine level, but also couldn't have been more different. Trevor's floor was covered with a plush carpet in a fine blue and green check pattern, and custom mahogany cupboards and shelves lined two walls. His matching desk was decorated with a large gold pen holder and framed photos of his wife and family, and his chair was upholstered in dark green leather, as were the four lounge chairs that surrounded a glass-topped coffee table. Concealed lighting made the office feel like a classy gentleman's club.

Next door, Dave's office was all white. Metal shelving groaned with technical manuals, catalogues, and maintenance records for the company aircraft, plus those of outside customers. A few boxes of recently arrived parts sat in one corner. Fluorescent lights shone on a pile of work sheets on Dave's simple grey desk.

Dave eased into one of Trevor's lounge chairs and briefly closed his eyes as the cushioning eased his backache. He then took in the array of photos on the walls. They depicted Trevor's career, from RAAF basic training through to his time in the fighter squadrons, and then from the early days of Mayer Aviation to the present. Dave appeared in many of those photos, all the way back to when they'd both entered the RAAF at just nineteen years of age. A model of an F/A-18 Hornet fighter sat on the coffee table between the two men.

'Ah, that's good,' Trevor sighed, as he relaxed into the chair opposite, a crystal glass in hand. He wasn't a big man, but his deep voice and careful grooming added to his natural air of authority. 'There's nothing better than a G & T to finish off the working week.'

Dave raised his own glass. 'We've had a few of these over the years, Trev,' he said, swirling the ice cubes. 'Sometimes as very essential medication to calm the nerves.'

'Indeed. But that's not been necessary for some time, thankfully. We've had a smooth run this year, apart from your incident with the SNJ, and you got us out of that one with minimal drama.'

'More luck than good judgment,' Dave said, 'but yeah, the whole fleet's working well. The guys know what they're doing, and it seems they're all happy, which makes my job a lot easier.'

'And so are the customers.'

Dave put down his drink. He sat forward, his boyish grin disappearing as he steeled himself to continue. 'I have something important to tell you, Trev. I've been putting this off for months now, but I can't delay it any longer. My bad back's getting worse. The doc says the only way I'll get better is by taking a break from work for at least six months. I can't do my job without being here every day, so the only option I have left is to retire.'

Trevor's jaw dropped, accentuating the lines on his face. He stroked his trim moustache and took a sip of his drink before replying. 'Shit, Dave. That's not what I wanted to hear. Are you sure about this? Can't you just take a few months off, then come back to work when you're better?'

Trevor rarely swore, so Dave knew that the news had surprised him.

'I wish it were that simple,' Dave said, running a hand through his thatch of dark hair. 'I don't want to leave – it's a blow for me too. I thought I'd be here until I reached retirement age, but appointing a replacement to fill in for half a year wouldn't be fair on him. Besides, I reckon one of my engineers, Jake, is experienced enough to take my position permanently, so it won't be too disruptive for you.'

Trevor frowned. 'It's not just that, mate. When it comes down to it, I guess nobody is irreplaceable, and I'm sure Jake can take over the engineering side of the company. But you and I have run this place together for twenty years. I might be the MD, but we've shared all the ups and downs in that time, and I couldn't have handled it without you. At this stage in my life, I don't want to run the company all on my own.'

'Don't make it too hard on me,' Dave said quietly. 'I've been dreading this day for months.'

Mouth tightening, Trevor nodded. 'Look, I do understand. I've turned a blind eye to your problem, which was selfish of me, really. I should've foreseen this, and I should've been helping you reduce your workload. Dammit, I've felt guilty about your injury for bloody near forty years.'

'Geez, you know better than that, Trev.' Dave flicked a hand. 'But as they say in the classics, shit happens. It was just bad luck we hit the road at the same time that stupid P-plater chose to fiddle with her radio instead of watching where she was going.'

Trevor dropped his head into his hands, revealing to Dave that his grey hair had become quite thin over recent months. 'But I can't help thinking what that injury has cost you. If I'd seen her drifting across the centre line just a moment sooner... that accident changed your life. Don't you hold a grudge?'

For a moment, Dave reflected on this. The accident had been terrible, but the RAAF had taken care of him afterwards, putting him through an aeronautical engineering degree. He'd loved the following twenty years working on fighters. 'Nah. I think we both know you were the best jet jockey, and Wayne, Nick, and Alan were more skilled than me.'

'Dave, you've always sold yourself short as a pilot, and I know that just like me, you were hankering to fly the F/A-18 Hornet. After all, it was *the* hot new fighter of the time, and we were *the* hotshot jet jockeys.'

Dave shook his head, and said emphatically, 'Trev, I've been much better at engineering than I would've ever been at flying. I thought you were crazy when you decided to leave the RAAF, and even now I don't know how you persuaded me to join you here, but I'm really glad you did. No regrets, and life's been interesting.'

Trevor looked relieved when he laughed. 'It certainly has. Do you remember the three crates we started the company with? How you kept those old Navahos in the air, I'll never know.'

'How could I forget?' Dave asked, with a smile. 'But we did have some fun.' Standing, he winced and stiffened as he turned to the window that overlooked the hangar floor. Three gleaming modern corporate jets sat on the polished floor, one surrounded by work benches. 'It's a bit different now, thank heavens. Trev, I'm mighty grateful for all you've done for me. Chloe appreciates it too – you and Jenny are part of our family. But I guess all good things have to end, eventually.'

'Yes, I guess they do. But not our friendship, Dave.' Trevor stood up and stretched. 'Well, with what you've just told me, now I've got news for you,' he said. 'A week ago, I received an offer from a big road freight company. It wants to expand into air chartering, and it seems our little company is the ideal platform. I was intending to turn the offer down, but after what you've just told me, I might reconsider. You and I have been a team for such a long time… it just wouldn't be the same without you around.'

* * *

Two months later, Trevor handed over the reins of Mayer Aviation to the freight company and took away a very large cheque. Dave drove away from the premises on his last day with a smaller but still significant cheque, one that would allow him and his wife Chloe to completely remodel their house in Sydney's north-west Hills District, have a long holiday somewhere exotic, and enjoy a comfortable income for the rest of their lives.

Without the pressure of work and a daily commute, Dave's back improved a little each week. He and Chloe, who'd also recently retired from her work as a family court lawyer, busied themselves with gardening and supervising the house's remodelling, and he also tinkered with a couple of small projects in the well-equipped workshop in his shed. He filled his days so pleasantly that the pain of forced retirement soon faded. The only cloud on the horizon for him, Chloe, and every other thinking Australian was the ever-increasing belligerence of the Chinese administration.

'Bloody hell, our government is weak!' Dave exploded early one morning, when reading his electronic newspaper in their spacious eat-in kitchen. Cereal, coffee, and toast and marmalade were in front of him, and he was dressed in casual clothes and old but comfortable slippers. 'How much more land are we going to let the Chinese buy? They even control a couple of our ports, for God's sake! You'd think we would've learned after they made their fourteen demands back in 2021.'

Chloe opened the curtains that covered the floor-to-ceiling windows, revealing the view across a sparkling pool. Beyond was a wide expanse of lawn dotted with trees and edged by gardens.

A strip of natural bushland at the bottom of their paddock hid their boundary fence.

'What bothers me most is that they've often tried to influence our members of parliament,' she said. 'Free trips, cash, and goodness knows what else.'

'Yeah,' said Dave, shaking his head, 'and they push for ever more access to Australian assets. I wouldn't care if we could go over to China and buy *their* land or businesses, but we're not welcome. The real worry, though, is that they're making more and more demands of us. Just where do those demands end?'

Recently, Chinese leadership had called for the ability to deal directly with their enterprises in Australia, bypassing all normal controls and taxes, and to import unlimited workers from China. They'd also agitated for Australia to reduce its ties to the USA.

Dave set his tablet down. 'I fear this is going to end in war, sooner rather than later.'

Chloe looked around in horror. 'David, you can't be serious! Do you really think there'll be a war? Surely not in this day and age.'

'Probably not before they go for Taiwan. That's their main objective. Maybe after that, but who knows; look what happened with Russia invading Ukraine. No sense in that at all, but the president's ego demanded it.' Taking a sip of his coffee, Dave winced, finding it had gone cold. 'The Chinese are even more stubborn than the Russians – I can't see them backing down too readily, over Taiwan or Australia. They've got a pretty powerful military nowadays, and I'll bet there are a few generals over there just itching to exercise it.'

'But the Americans would back us, wouldn't they? Surely all these treaties we have would ensure that. Would the Chinese really risk going to war with the USA?'

'AUKUS should apply, but you've got to consider the Republican factor. Since their influence became so strong, I'm doubtful the Yanks will rush into a fight with anyone, treaty or no treaty. Remember how they hightailed it out of Afghanistan in 2021? Billions spent, thousands of lives lost, and for what?'

Chloe sighed. 'Well, thankfully, now you've turned sixty-two, and Adam's in his mid-thirties, both of you are too old for military service if it all blows up. You have to worry what sort of world we'll be leaving to our grandkids, though.'

Adam, their son, was an architect, and their two daughters, Kirsten and Georgie, were both health professionals. All three lived in Sydney with families of their own.

* * *

After breakfast, Dave relaxed in his favourite chair under an umbrella by the pool. He watched his wife as she roared past on a Kubota ride-on mower, her blond ponytail swaying to and fro, making short work of the lush green grass. Dave smiled at the sight. Mowing the lawn was a chore Chloe had insisted on taking over, but one that he looked forward to resuming before long.

To him, Chloe was just as beautiful as the day he first saw her in primary school, five and a half decades earlier, and just as beautiful as the day they met again by chance when Dave was flying with the RAAF and she was a trainee lawyer. It was a rare day that he didn't thank providence for that meeting.

His mobile phone began to chirp, so he put his fresh coffee down on the small table beside him. The caller ID made him smile again. 'Trev, how are things?'

'Hey, Dave. I'm fine. I've been asked to look at security at RAAF bases – we all know how weak it's been for decades. Not much has changed other than that. More importantly, how's your back?'

'Not too bad. Chloe won't let me do any serious work, so I read the paper cover to cover every morning. You've been volunteering as an advisor to our local federal MP, right? Wasn't he recently appointed as assistant to the defence minister? What do you think of China's latest demands?'

'I don't know much more than what you read in the papers, though I can say that at least a few MPs are panicking. And so they should. I'm not sure what the Chinese Government meant by saying recently that they must act to protect their interests, but it doesn't sound good.'

'Well, I can't see our pollies agreeing to their demands,' Dave said, grimacing. 'It would cripple our economy and send unemployment skyrocketing. All that in return for a token "facilitation fee" paid directly to the government? What a joke.'

Trevor grunted. 'I'm not a big fan of either of our major political parties, but at least they're talking about the problem, and the opposition supports the government's current stance. No way are they going to accede.' He paused, then added: 'Perhaps we're reading too much into the political huff and blow.'

'Let's hope so,' Dave said – though somehow, he didn't think they were.

* * *

One morning early in June, six weeks after Trevor's call, Dave woke to the sound of the bedside radio. He tried to roll into a comfortable position. Chloe was already dressed and busy with housework, making him reflect again on the effect his injury was having on him. Although his back was slowly improving, it still ached enough to wake him frequently during the night.

The news broadcast was headed by a statement from the Australian Prime Minister, Roger Quick, who said that Beijing hadn't yet responded to his refusal to meet their latest demands. The second report was on the Australian stock market, which was being deserted by investors, sending the ASX index to its lowest level since the Coronavirus outbreak. Five years of gain had been wiped out in the previous 48 hours.

'Great,' Dave muttered to himself. 'Just when I retire and we rely on our investments to live on!'

Later that morning, he opened his computer and checked his and Chloe's shares. All were down from the previous day, and they continued to fall as the hours passed.

Trevor rang in the afternoon. 'A lot has happened since we last spoke, Dave. Just between us, things are escalating rapidly. My minister and all the staff in his department are looking like they just lost their last penny. They really are fearing that the Chinese are prepared to act on their threats. Apparently, Roger Quick is to confirm tonight that the Australian Government won't capitulate to President Zhang's outrageous demands and naked aggression. He'll say that we have the backing of the free world, and he's banking that will convince the Chinese they have too much to lose by descending to military action.'

Stiff from sitting too long, Dave stood and stretched as he replied. 'We might have the moral backing of many countries, Trev, but will that help us? We both know that a large percentage of the American population thinks that isolating the USA will resurrect all the industry that went to China over the last thirty or forty years, and get them all their jobs back. Now that the bloody Republicans are back in, just as we feared, President Ainsworth seems to be distancing himself from our squabble with China.

He's said it has nothing to do with the USA.'

'Well,' Trevor said, 'to counter that, some US politicians and most of its military are very pro-Australia. After all, we fought side by side with them in World War Two from New Guinea all the way to Japan, and we've backed them in Korea, Vietnam, the Gulf Wars, Iraq, Afghanistan, Syria…'

'Yes, but the Republicans have convinced much of the country that their old Pacific and European allies are now expendable.'

Trevor hummed. 'Ainsworth does say that, and a lot of Americans are tired of getting into what are essentially civil wars that they can't win. On the other hand, if the balloon were to go up, he'd do himself enormous political damage if he didn't come to our aid. Most *thinking* Americans don't want to see the US losing any more influence around the world, and China's attempted dominance over Australia hasn't gone unnoticed by all counties in Asia and the Pacific. Don't forget the Yanks have bases here that are a key part of their military presence in the area.'

'I hope you're right and I'm wrong, mate,' Dave replied. 'Otherwise, you and I might find ourselves strapping into a couple of the old Hornets that are still sitting at Williamtown!'

Trevor groaned. 'Don't even joke about something like that.'

* * *

Over the following fortnight, Dave watched the news and read the paper every day. While he saw much speculation, there seemed to be no change in the verbal stand-off between the Australian and Chinese Governments. But as he sat sipping a cup of coffee, a crime novel in his lap, he could never have imagined that, after a successful but unspectacular career, never having so much as cheated on his taxes, and recently withdrawing to a well-earned retirement, he would soon be hailed as a hero by many, but considered an international criminal by the Government of the USA, and a murderer by the People's Republic of China.

CHAPTER 3

24 JUNE 2026

It was a cold morning when Dave reached out from under his woollen blanket to silence the alarm clock on his bedside table. He pressed the off button, but it kept chirping. He became aware that dawn wasn't far away at the same time that he realised his phone had awoken him, not the alarm. As he accepted the call, he noted that the time was only 5.15 a.m. He muttered, 'Trev, is something wrong?'

'I'm afraid so. It's serious. I can't tell you any details, but I need to see you as quickly as I can. Are you able to meet me in the hangar where I keep my warbirds? Say by 7 a.m.?'

Trevor's urgent tone drove Dave's drowsiness away. He sat up and shrugged off the covers. 'I can, but can't you give me a clue? Sounds bad.'

'Dave, it couldn't be worse. But I can't talk on the phone. Just get here, asap.'

If Trevor Mayer had a fault, it was that he did have a tendency to exaggerate possible outcomes, whether they were expected to be good or bad. Dave had learned over the forty years of their friendship that if Trevor was promoting an idea, one had to discount the likely benefit by ten percent; maybe even twenty percent. If he was forecasting some potential problem, Dave knew to discount the likelihood of it eventuating by a similar factor. But this time, Trevor's tone clearly showed that he was deeply worried about something, so Dave had no hesitation in shelving his plans for the day.

Two hours later, Dave met Trevor at the door of the hangar he rented in Bankstown for his two warbirds. He was dressed in casual clothes, but looked neat and trim, as usual. Dave did notice that his thin hair had greyed a little more in the couple of months since they'd last met, and the lines on his face were deeper.

'Come and sit in the lunchroom,' Trevor said. 'Before we start, I'll put on some coffee. I'll bet you need a cup.'

The small lunchroom was typical of an all-male workplace. Aside for a few calendars with aircraft photos on the wall, a sink, a refrigerator, a cheap formica-topped table, and half a dozen metal-framed chairs, it was entirely bare.

Trevor held up the coffee jar. 'White and two?'

'Yep. NATO standard. Haven't changed just because I've retired,' Dave said, with a chuckle.

Trevor smiled and busied himself at the sink. When the two coffees were ready, he sat down opposite Dave, all traces of his smile gone.

'You aren't going to believe this. It hasn't hit the airwaves yet, but last Sunday night, there were attacks by terrorist gangs at six RAAF bases and three RAN installations. Most of the aircraft were totally burned out. A few are repairable, but none will fly until September at the earliest. Four subs will also be out of action for months, and another is in deep maintenance that won't be finished anytime soon.'

Dave dropped his cup, spilling coffee across the table. 'Are you kidding? Bloody hell – you mean we have no combat aircraft left at all? Who were these terrorists? Why does nobody know about this? How have they kept it quiet?'

Trevor put up his hands to stop Dave's barrage of questions. 'I don't know anything for certain yet. Apparently, the raiders missed some Hawks in a revetment, and a couple more in deep maintenance, so the RAAF will be working twenty-four hours a day to get them operational. But that will take weeks, or even months. Nobody's claimed responsibility, though some CCTV footage indicates that the saboteurs were Asian. The educated guess is that they were Chinese. The federal government's banned all news outlets from reporting on it, but rumours are already flying. I'd say they're going to have to make an announcement today.'

Dave was so astounded that it took him some moments to respond. 'But what's the point?' he asked, still hardly able to believe what he was hearing. 'Why would the Chinese take such a risk?'

'We can make some guesses. Mine is that China's going to harden its demands while we're in a weakened position.'

Dave still had a shocked look. 'Bastards!' he muttered.

Trevor nodded in agreement, before continuing. 'I spent all day yesterday on a plan to salvage some air defence capability.' As he rubbed at his forehead, Dave noticed the deep shadows beneath his eyes. 'You know how when the new F-35s replaced our Hornets, the old aircraft were sold to an American company? That deal was made in 2019, and in 2021, most of the Hornets were shipped to the USA. But there were ten that stayed behind – they required work before they were fit to fly. The buyers got into financial difficulties, and those Hornets never left Williamtown.'

Trevor glanced out the window, momentarily distracted by the sound of a light aircraft taxiing past the hangar. He looked back at Dave. 'That's why I was contacted. Most of the RAAF's current fighter jocks converted from the Hawk to the F-35 without ever flying the Hornet, or if they did, it wasn't for long. They're whizzes with flying computers, but would need a lot of training to operate an old hands-on jet like the Hornet. The RAAF needs ex-Hornet pilots to help the new guys transition to the older aircraft, as well as engineers who know the Hornets and can get them operational as quickly as possible. So, to summarise, they need guys like you and me. Now.'

'Right, okay.' Dave nodded, though he was still grappling to digest the situation. 'I can be up in Williamtown this afternoon.'

Briefly, Trevor hesitated. 'There's another long shot. I haven't discussed this with anyone else, but I'm keen to hear what you think. Remember how in my RAAF time, I was seconded to the USAF for a few months, where I flew the F-15 Eagle?'

'Sure,' Dave said. The F-15 had been the American's premium frontline fighter, until they were replaced by the latest version of the F-22. Trevor had loved flying them, even preferring them to the Hornets.

'I've kept in touch with some of my friends over there, and one told me a few weeks ago that he'd just finished preparing some F-15s to be returned to the USA. As far as I know, those F-15s have been sitting idle in Guam for several years.'

Dave interrupted. 'But aren't they the F-15s that had suspect airframes?'

Trevor held up a finger. 'Yes, they are, but it's a long story. In a nutshell, one C-model F-15 had a structural failure in the fuselage. It must've had a fluid leak at some point, and corrosion got into the longerons. It was a once-only thing, but because of it, all F-15Cs have been grounded pending an inspection and modification. They have to go back to the factory for that. These ones in Guam have been waiting their turn. They've all had their whiz-bang weaponry removed for the ferry flight, but they still have their Vulcan cannons.'

'Right,' Dave said, 'but say we were able to get them here, who'd operate them?'

'The RAAF has plenty of F-35 pilots with nothing to fly now.'

Dave considered this, scratching at his chin. 'Flying an F-15 is one thing, but it's a generation behind the F-35. Going to war without that fifth-generation wizardry would be a big call for the current crop of RAAF pilots. And they'd be facing the Chinese versions of some formidable Russian aircraft, like the Su-35.'

Trevor nodded. 'The F-15 isn't the sharpest tool in the shed anymore, but it might be the only one we have.' He spoke more confidently now that he'd at least partially convinced his colleague. 'The US Government doesn't want to help us right now, so I've put in an urgent call to my old squadron boss to see if we can get them for the RAAF as a desperate interim.'

Dave raised his eyebrows. 'Good thinking,' he agreed, 'but how far will your mates go to help Australia if it means headbutting their own bureaucracy *and* the Chinese?'

Trevor shook his head, grimacing. 'Shit, I don't know. But we have to give it a try. I'm expecting a call back today, so hang around Sydney until tomorrow morning. I might need you to help me organise getting those F-15s to Australia.'

* * *

The first rumours of the raids hit the airwaves as Dave wended his way through the traffic towards home. Some civilians phoned the ABC National News radio station he tuned into, describing explosions and strange activity at Williamtown airbase, but were met with obvious scepticism by the host. Similar rumours began to spread from people living near the other infiltrated military installations.

Unable to keep a lid on the disaster, the government lifted its ban, and within minutes, news bulletins mentioned multiple accounts of sabotage at several RAAF and naval bases. Even the reporters sounded bewildered by the rapidly escalating scale of events. By the time Dave reached his house, news of explosions at military bases in all mainland states and the Northern Territory dominated the airwaves. The evening news began with an official announcement by Roger Quick, the prime minister, who gravely confirmed the rumours.

'No terrorist group has claimed responsibility as yet,' he continued, 'and the purpose of the attacks remains unknown.' He added that an attempt to attach limpet mines to the hulls of several RAN warships docked in Sydney's Garden Island naval base had been thwarted after routine patrols spotted divers in wetsuits near the ships.

Dave watched the news until midnight. Videos shot at long distance by civilians showed smoke and flame at the various bases, but no significant new facts emerged. At 6 a.m. the next morning, the opposition leader, Max Harris, deplored the actions of the unknown group and offered full bipartisan support to the government during the crisis. A sound clip from the PM followed.

'Military action against us, without declaration of war, is reminiscent of Japan's attack on the USA on 7 December 1941.

Like America at the time, we were unprepared for a brazen attack on our sovereignty. However, like America, we will stand by our principles and mobilise our forces to meet any future military action. Every effort is being made by the ASIO, and by federal, state, and military police, to identify the perpetrators. Already, some progress has been made. I expect that we will soon have more information.'

Dave tried to do something constructive and repair the disassembled chainsaw on his workbench, but found it hard to concentrate on anything but the radio. At noon, the PM came back on air with an announcement that confirmed his worst fears.

'The combined efforts of our intelligence and police forces have positively identified the terrorists that committed acts of war against our nation. All were Chinese citizens in Australia under student visas. Several have been apprehended, but it seems that most have already left the country.

'I have attempted to talk directly to the President of China, but he has so far declined to take my call. Our Minister for Foreign Affairs and Minister for Defence have likewise attempted to contact their counterparts in China without success. In light of recent demands by the Chinese Government, we can only assume that the recent sabotage is part of their aim to dominate our country.

'The Australian Government will not bow to this aggression. All Australian assets owned by the Chinese Government, either directly or indirectly, are hereby frozen pending a complete and unequivocal capitulation by the Chinese Government.'

Dave gave up on the chainsaw. He washed the oil from his hands, locked up his workshop, and returned to the house. Turning on the TV, he caught the beginning of an interview with the US President, Stuart Ainsworth.

'The Australian Prime Minister has been in contact with me,' Ainsworth said, 'with claims that the Chinese Government is behind last week's attacks on Australian military bases, and has asked for support in resisting their aggression. I have explained to him that while we deplore both terrorism and military violence anywhere in the world, the ANZUS Treaty has been effectively dead for a decade, and the AUKUS treaty proposed by my predecessor has never been ratified by my administration. The US has no intention of involving itself in a regional spat.'

When asked if the US would offer to replace the jets that had been destroyed in the guerrilla attacks, President Ainsworth stated that any additional aircraft would only be supplied via a commercial contract, as per normal, which would require Defence Department and congressional approval.

Dave swore. 'Bloody isolationism rising again. If only the Democrats had been able to win the 2024 election.'

* * *

For years, Huang Bai had luxuriated in his dream of becoming China's leading air ace, and now it had every chance of coming to fruition, with two wars to look forward to within twelve months. The famous pilot Zhao Baotong was China's all-time top air ace, and he'd shot down nine enemy aircraft in 1952 during the Korean War, while flying a MiG-15. Huang Bai desperately wanted to beat Zhao Baotong. He knew he could do it. He would become China's most famous pilot while leading his three elite squadrons in combat.

His state of euphoria lasted just four days. The sealed orders arrived as promised, and the first item was a major disappointment.

All three of his squadrons were to leave behind their beloved mixed fleet of Sukhoi Su-35s and locally built J-15 clones. In exchange, they would fly the newer FC-31, which had been shaped by careful research to optimise stealth. It was theoretically almost invisible to radar, and it was equipped with the latest fire-and-forget missile operating system designed to automatically track and destroy up to five enemy aircraft simultaneously at ranges up to 150 km. But optimising stealth meant compromising performance and manoeuvrability, and in Huang Bai's opinion, the latest whiz-bang technologies often failed at the critical moment. If he ever had to go toe-to toe with a jet like the American F-22, he'd rather be strapped to the older and simpler J-15, with its bags of power and extreme manoeuvrability. It was a true pilot's aeroplane.

The second item in the orders instructed him to embark with his squadrons aboard the new carrier the very next day. He was shocked. He would've asked for six months to transition his squadrons from one fighter type to the next, not half a day! This confirmed his private belief that the aging admirals had little idea of what it really took to operate a fleet of modern combat aircraft. He also knew that every problem they would inevitably confront would be his to solve, not the admirals'.

Within hours, he received some relief: the embarkation had been set back one week. That at least allowed for a rapid conversion to the new fighter, but Huang Bai knew he was trading one problem for another, as each day of extra training at the home airfield was one less for training aboard the carrier. Two hours later, the embarkation was delayed another three days.

His first action was to cancel all leave for his pilots and ground crew. The coming week would be packed full of theoretical and practical training, as his team adapted to the new jet's features, systems, and stealth capability, and the combat manoeuvres that would best utilise them.

Huang Bai knew that the much-hyped FC-31 was actually the result of intense espionage and infiltration of the US Department of Defence and the McDonnell Douglas Corporation, the manufacturer of the F-35. The Shenyang FC-31 was basically a slightly enlarged version of the F-35. In theory, it could outperform the original, but in reality, there were rumours that it was something of a disappointment. Neither the F-35 nor the FC-31were pretty aircraft, unlike the older J-15, or its contemporary, the American F-15 Eagle. These new designs appeared stubby, almost fat in the fuselage, with canopies that seemed too big for a single pilot. The Chinese version looked a little better: it was longer than the F-35, and had the advantage of twin engines instead of a single one. Huang Bai believed that sticking to the older J-15 would've made more sense for this first operation. At least his pilots were familiar with it.

The intensive conversion training quickly revealed some startling shortcomings in his students. Nine days in, Huang Bai stared at the window of the classroom in the PLANAF training base in Yantai, Shandong Province, but he did not take in the expansive view of the airfield and the low hills beyond it. His usually fresh and unlined face was red, and his mouth was twisted in anger. Whirling away from the window, he spat: 'Does anyone know the answer? You are the cream of China's naval aviators. You have spent four years at this university. You have cost the Chinese people your weight in gold. Tomorrow, you will embark on our new supercarrier, and yet none of you can answer this simple question?'

Forty young pilots remained silent, each avoiding eye contact with their chief instructor. Huang Bai focused on a student in the middle of the first row. 'Chen. You must know. If your Shenyang FC-31 fighter has full main fuel tanks, what is the maximum weight of weaponry it can hold?'

Chen cleared his throat, but was interrupted by Huang Bai. 'Stand up, Chen. You tell these worthless classmates of yours. Don't be afraid to speak out. There are no party representatives in this room, so you can speak the truth!'

'Yes, sir. With full internal tanks, the manual says that the FC-31 can carry eight thousand kilograms payload–'

'Yes, yes,' Huang Bai cut in again, 'we can all parrot from the flight manual, but that won't help you when your arse is in the cockpit and you're about to be hurled from an aircraft carrier by a catapult. Now, I'll ask you again: what is the maximum payload you would feel safe to launch with?'

Chen coughed, looked down, then spoke quietly. 'In fact, sir, with the engines not quite meeting the target thrust, the real figure could be twenty-five percent less.'

Huang Bai nodded. He was once again on dangerous ground, as questioning the new jet's published performance figures was akin to treason. But he'd worked with these men for two years, during which time he'd prodded and pushed them to be the best they could be. He doubted any would squeal to the resident political advisor because he didn't always adhere to the authorised manual of operations.

'And what if the catapults on the new carrier do not perform as expected?'

'Then, sir, further reductions in payload or fuel will have to be made.'

Huang Bai nodded and was about to speak when his phone

chirped. He turned his back on the class and listened to the caller for a minute in silence. The forty pilots saw his neck redden even more, and heard him shout into the receiver: 'Yet another delay! I had orders direct from Admiral Shen to embark on the *Mao Tse Tung* ten days ago. The delay has been beneficial for extra training, but we are all ready to go. Now you tell me that reactor problems are still keeping the ship in port? Hadn't you sorted this out during your extensive sea trials?'

Huang Bai listened in silence for another minute, then threw the phone onto the lectern. He paced back and forth, with eighty eyes following his every move. He stopped, looked at his audience, and with an obvious effort to compose himself, said evenly: 'The new supercarrier has experienced some teething troubles, so your first experience of real naval aviation has been delayed yet again. The *Mao Tse Tung* is anticipated to leave port the day after tomorrow. When we're on board, your real training will begin. No longer will your "carrier deck" remain stationary. You will be operating from an airfield that is in constant motion, including up and down. You will each have to do eight take-offs and landings during daylight, then another eight at night to be fully operational. I am relying on you to bring honour to your squadrons, to the navy, and to your people.' Studying the faces of his students, he gave a single sharp nod. 'I will see you here at 7 a.m. two days from now. Rest up tomorrow, as it'll be your last break for some time. Do not fail me!'

CHAPTER 4

6 JULY 2026

The elite squadrons' sequential departure from the training base went smoothly, despite their lack of familiarity with their new mounts, with four additional pilots following in the carrier supply aircraft. However, Huang Bai had no time to reflect on the favourable start, as the transit to the carrier was in solid cloud from just after lift-off. Single-pilot IFR flying required his full attention.

He shifted his gaze from the instruments of his FC-31 fighter to the outside world as he slipped below the cloud base, into clear air. The *Mao Tse Tung* materialised out of the last wisps of vapour exactly where he'd expected it to be: 2000 feet below and three nautical miles away in his ten o'clock position, steaming towards him on a parallel path. A magnificent sight! The largest carrier in the world, and he was about to make the first landing on it.

He stabilised his descent at 250 knots airspeed before levelling at 1800 feet altitude, then altered heading slightly to pass the carrier down its port beam. Although he'd made hundreds of simulated carrier landings at his home base, his stomach lurched. The carrier might've been the world's biggest, but the landing area still looked awfully small. Like his student pilots, he'd only ever made a few arrested landings under perfect, calm conditions with a J-15 fighter. This time, they were out on the ocean, where the warship was heaving through a moderate sea.

When Huang Bai judged that he was almost half a mile past the carrier, he pulled the jet into a steep 4G turn, washing off both speed and altitude. He began levelling the wings as he neared the ship's broad white wake, and completed the turn with the nose pointing directly at its afterdeck. Now with full flaps, and undercarriage and hook down, he juggled the stick and throttles to maintain a steady 130 knots. His aiming point was about 100 metres past the rear end of the deck, and to his relief, the landing system lights showed that he was right in the centre of the desired glidepath.

The ship grew quickly in the wide view from the bubble canopy. His instincts shouted that he was still going too fast. But intensive training told him to trust his instruments, and he resisted the urge to ease the stick back for a flare and soft touchdown. There was no room on a carrier for that luxury, not even on this one.

His descent rate increased as he hit the turbulent air just above the deck, and the jet thumped down so hard he winced. He shoved the twin throttles fully forward in case the FC-31 hadn't caught an arrester wire, but thankfully, it had, and his body strained against the harness as he fought to keep his head up. The thick steel cable dragged the jet to a shuddering halt against the thrust of the two screaming engines.

He pulled the throttles back to idle thrust. As he did so, he became aware that a crewman in helmet and earmuffs was alongside the nose of his aircraft, signalling that he was now unhooked from the arrester cable, and was clear to taxi forward.

He flexed his fingers on the control stick and slowed his breathing in an effort to ease the tension that had gripped him. Relief flooded his senses. History would record that on this day, Captain Huang Bai had made the first landing on the world's largest aircraft carrier.

* * *

Dave had a lot on his mind. He hadn't slept until well after midnight, and woke instantly when his phone chirped at 5 a.m. He glanced at the screen before answering.

'Trev, what's happening?'

'Not good news about the F-15s. My contacts in the USAF would gladly hand over everything they have – they'd give us F-35s from their active squadrons, if they could – but it seems that a very firm decree has come from the White House all the way down to squadron level. America doesn't want to get involved in another war. Of course, supplying aircraft to a foreign power, no matter how closely aligned, has to be a political decision. We have no chance at all.'

'Then the US Government obviously believes that China's behind all this, to be so frightened of getting involved.'

'I'd say so, but who really knows?' Trevor replied. 'I think all you and I can do is help the RAAF get those derelict Hornets up and running.'

'It's a tough ask. They've been sitting outside for years, and apparently most avionics were removed and sent to the US with the first batch sold. It could take months to obtain and reinstall that gear, even if the Yanks cooperate with making parts available.' Dave hit his thigh in disgust. 'Dammit! We should just go and steal those bloody F-15s.'

The phone went silent. After a few seconds, Dave asked: 'You still there?'

'Call you back,' Trevor said at last, and the line went dead.

Dave kept his phone at hand all day, expecting Trevor's return call. The radio stations were alive with details of the terrorist raids. Every commentator had an opinion, but all they could do was rehash the limited information available. The electronic newspaper he read was the same.

At 6 p.m., he turned on the TV. The news opened with another broadcast by Roger Quick, who stood at a lectern on the steps of Parliament House, with a line of sombre-looking cabinet colleagues behind him.

'I have very grave news. The Chinese Ambassador called me at 4 p.m. this afternoon with a list of final demands from his government, which included those previously specified – unlimited Chinese investment in and immigration to Australia, in addition to uncontrolled importation to and exportation from Chinese-owned enterprises in Australia, which would also be exempt from the Australian taxation system – all in return for what they called a facilitation fee.

'In every way possible, these demands are unacceptable. It is particularly galling that, like most of the Western world, we have encouraged China to join the global economy over the last five decades. We have welcomed Chinese investment. We have allowed Chinese imports to compete with our own industries to the point of near decimation of our industrial sector. We have encouraged immigration from China. In return, the Chinese Government has blocked imports from Australia, only accepting our goods when it suits them. They have sponsored cyber attacks on our government and industry. They have encouraged theft of our intellectual property. And now, they threaten us, unless we lie down for them to walk all over us.

'At 5 p.m., I formally replied to the Ambassador. I said, in essence, that the Australian Government confirms its previous statement: we reject these outrageous demands. While we welcome investment from overseas generally, and from China in particular, we expect – in fact, we *demand* – that all foreign-owned businesses operate within our legal and economic systems.

'It is with a heavy heart that, considering the timing of the terrorist attacks on our defence facilities, we conclude they are linked to the demands. We fear that the Chinese Government intends to flout international law by taking military action. If they do, they will send the entire world spinning back to the dark days of territorial ambition that led to World War Two.'

* * *

Huang Bai leaned into the 30-knot wind generated by the passage of the great grey warship. It lanced through his light woollen pullover to chill him, even on this mild evening. Flying spray stung his face, as the catwalk just below the flight deck offered no protection. The curling bow-wave reminded him of how his father's plough split the earth at the family farm, and he had a rare moment of homesickness.

Through his feet, he could sense the slight vibration of the two enormous screws that pushed the 200,000-tonne ship up to 35 knots, regardless of the sea conditions. The horizon ahead moved rhythmically up and down, but he took little notice. His head felt like a railway crossing, trains of thought thundering through it from various directions, without order.

The weather for the four days and nights since their arrival aboard the supercarrier had been calm, if overcast. He was proud that, so far, his pilots had suffered only two disasters. It could've been much worse, given their lack of real carrier experience.

Huang Bai's face creased in a grimace as he relived some of the poorer landings. The tenth touchdown had gone well, but after pulling to a stop, the pilot must've looked down to his left cockpit panel to find the switches for flap and hook retraction in the still-unfamiliar aircraft. He hadn't noticed that he'd relaxed pressure on the tow-brakes, so the FC-31 had begun to roll forward at walking speed. Even a warning radio call from the controller on the bridge had failed to alert him to the imminent danger, and the controller and deck crew had watched in horror as the nose wheel dropped over the leading edge of the deck and the jet tumbled over the bow.

Nobody aboard the carrier had even felt a bump. The only sign of the aircraft the escort destroyers had found was a slick of fuel from a ruptured tank.

The very next day, on the first round of practice launches, the fourth aircraft had failed to reach flying speed after being catapulted. Fortunately, the pilot had reacted quickly and ejected as the FC-31 hit the water. His chute had opened seconds before he landed back on deck, just as the carrier ran over his fighter.

So, two aircraft lost, but just one pilot.

In those four days, Huang Bai had used up almost all of the fuel allocated to familiarisation practice, and while there had been no more serious incidents, few of his pilots had reached the high standard he'd expected. If he'd had his way, the trainees would've had more than twice the number of flying hours before this first cruise. But it hadn't been his decision to make. He worried what accidents there might've been if the sea had been rough, or the visibility poor.

Not only were his pilots new to real carrier operations, but the ship's launch and recovery systems needed fine-tuning, and their operators needed far more practice. The ideal steam pressure for each launch depended on the type of aircraft, its take-off weight, the ambient temperature, and the wind speed over the deck. It was taking time to tabulate all the combinations. As a consequence, that one fighter had been lost, and there had been other close calls when heavy aircraft were launched at dangerously low speeds.

An aircraft carrier deck was probably the busiest and most dangerous workplace in the world, and none of the crewmen had even seen a steam catapult in operation before joining this new ship. Neither did they have much experience with the cable-arresting gear. The handlers had to load and fuel dozens of aircraft of different types – the fighters, tankers, AWACS, and helicopters – tow them to their launch positions, hook them to the catapults, adjust steam pressure, and synchronise the pilot's powering-up prior to each launch, all in an area just a fraction of the size of the airfield they'd trained on. They had to do this while dodging moving tow vehicles, cables, and fuel hoses, as well as white-hot jet exhausts. Although there had been a few dangerous incidents, miraculously, no aircraft had been damaged and no crewmen had been run over, blown overboard, sucked into a jet's air intake, or burned to a crisp by exhaust.

As Huang Bai had feared, the engines of the Shenyang FC-31 had proven inferior to the Russian originals, and the ship's catapults weren't capable of launching a fully laden FC-31 safely. That meant every sortie was compromised by a less-than-ideal fuel load, reduced ordnance, or both.

Although it wasn't his responsibility, he fumed as sailors grappled with the procedures. Because of the straight-deck layout of the catamaran hull, there was little parking space on the flight deck. Aircraft were stored in vast hangars below, and it took time to work the giant lifts that brought up aircraft to be launched, and to take down the ones that had landed. Huang knew that the pilots and crewmen would need months of training to reach an efficient standard, probably as much as a year. He'd originally been allocated weeks, but the delayed launch had cut this down to days. He was expected to have his three squadrons combat ready by tomorrow. It was useless to point out to his superiors that the Americans had had almost a century to develop supercarrier operations, and would spend a year perfecting procedures on any new ship. His navy was trying to match or even surpass them in a little over a week.

At least now he knew why there was such a rush. The Australian operation mentioned by Admiral Shen had already begun. In its very first cruise, the *Mao Tse Tung* was to be the flagship of the invasion force. Another set of sealed orders had been awaiting his arrival on board, which outlined the details of the strategy. The carrier was to join up with armed escorts and dozens of specialised troop-carrying ships to form a powerful but somewhat unwieldy task force. It was already weeks behind an optimistic schedule. The admirals had originally planned the invasion to take place within three days of sabotaging certain Australian military bases, before the Australians had time to mount any sort of alternative defence. It seemed that nobody had thought to delay the sabotage when the task force's launch had been set back.

Huang Bai had conflicting emotions about the saboteurs' apparent success. On one hand, it made the task of achieving air superiority simple for his pilots – which was a relief, given their less-than-ideal experience level. On the other, he wouldn't become an air ace if there were no enemies left to shoot down.

'Damnation to the gods,' he said to the wind. He'd dreamed of fighting the American-built F-35s and proving that his people were superior. Now, he would be limited to suppressing whatever pitiful opposition the Australians might be able to cobble together.

Huang Bai turned away and headed for the entry hatch. He had to arrange a pair of replacement FC-31s to be flown aboard. As he did so, an image of an Australian beach appeared in his brain. He'd seen the video on TV. The Australians seemed a harmless lot, and their only crime was resisting his country's dominance.

Why are we going to war with them, and why am I so keen to kill them?

Huang Bai quickly banished the thought from his crowded mind.

* * *

Parliament House, Canberra, was in turmoil. Roger Quick was constantly bombarded with requests for information from parliamentarians, foreign diplomats, and representatives from every newspaper, TV channel and radio station.

'Just get them off me!' he yelled at his press officer. 'I can't personally deal with every Tom, Dick, and Harry. Do your job, for shit's sake!'

He returned to his large office, where Defence Minister Andrew Adamson and his assistant minister, Rick Salmon, were waiting impatiently. Stripping off his dark blue tie, he slammed the solid Tasmanian oak door behind him. 'Just get to the gist of it, Andrew. I don't have time for chit-chat.'

Andrew Adamson, short and overweight but immaculately

dressed in a grey Italian-made suit, leaned forward and spoke earnestly. 'Roger, we have to face facts. We're in deep shit. The US didn't renew the ANZUS treaty because of the Republicans' old "America First" campaign. The Democrats' AUKUS pact was promising, but hasn't been ratified, since they lost the recent election. This new president is sticking to his party's old mantra, which is supported by some US media, if not the military. The general population over there is trying to return to normality after the Covid recession. Getting into a war on the other side of the world is the last thing they want, even if it means breaking promises to old allies. You have to admit that it would be political suicide for Ainsworth if he jumped in to support us.'

Pausing, Adamson smoothed his bright-red tie. 'On the plus side, our military commanders have close relationships with their counterparts in the US, so we're at least getting a lot of intel. We know that the Chinese have assembled a fleet, and it looks horribly like one set up for an invasion.'

Quick rolled up his sleeves and glanced at the air conditioning vent above his desk. The room was getting stuffy. 'Yeah, I know all that, and I know we've just lost all of our fighter jets and most of our subs are out of action for months. But you said you had an idea that might get us some breathing space. Spit it out!'

'I was coming to that,' Adamson said. 'Our big problem is that without air support, our Army and our surface ships can't operate against a Chinese force that's well equipped with fighter jets. Right now, all of our F-35s and Super Hornets are out of action. We can't get replacements for months, maybe even years.'

'I want solutions, not problems,' Quick replied testily. 'Get on with it, for God's sake.'

'Okay, here it is. There are thirty-six US Air Force fighters sitting in Guam. They're due to return any day to the US, as they've been replaced with new aircraft. We've approached the US Government already to immediately buy or lease them, but it simply isn't going to happen. My assistant minister here has come up with the idea that we simply steal those aircraft.'

Quick exploded. 'Steal aircraft from the USA? Are you *crazy?* No way. We'd destroy that relationship once and for all!' He sank into his oversized chair and slumped forward. Adamson couldn't help noticing that the top of his balding head reflected glare from the downlights above his desk.

'I don't think so,' Adamson said. 'Sure, they'll be mad. But these aircraft are to be returned to the US by a private contractor, and are probably destined for scrapping, so it isn't like we're stealing from the USAF's active squadrons. I also believe that if China really does invade us, the American public's opinion will swing rapidly in our favour, despite what the politicians say.'

Quick sighed. 'The whole idea sounds absurd, but okay, you have five minutes. Tell me how you could steal thirty-six aeroplanes from the USAF.'

'Well, I'll hand over to my assistant minister. It was his idea, so I'll let him explain it.'

Assistant Minister Rick Salmon leaned forward as he spoke. He was tall and wiry, and also wore a tailored grey suit. 'Firstly, let me explain that it wasn't my idea either. The suggestion came to me from a long-time friend I've been using as a consultant on defence matters. His name is Trevor Mayer, ex-RAAF wing commander. It was his best mate, a retired RAAF engineer named Pentreath–'

'Who cares who thought of what? Get to the point,' Quick growled, thumping his fist on the desk.

Salmon hesitated for a moment. 'Mayer discovered that a team of contract civil pilots, made up of retired US fighter jocks, is due to fly those surplus F-15 Eagle jets from the USAF base in Guam back to the US in a matter of days. He proposes we slot in a few hours before the US team is due to arrive, masquerade as them, take the jets and fly south instead of west.'

Quick tilted his chair all the way back, looked at the ceiling and shook his head. 'We can't have RAAF pilots stealing from one of our closest allies. If that's the best you can do, get out of here and stop wasting my time.'

'We thought you'd say that,' Salmon replied, then continued, undeterred. 'So, Mayer proposes that he put together a team of *retired* RAAF fighter pilots. Most would still be flying for airlines, but none would be in the RAAF Reserve. Call them mercenaries if you like. He'd need a plane to carry them to Guam, but it could be a privately owned jet on charter. Of course, once back in Australia, the F-15s would be handed over to RAAF pilots.'

Quick rested his chin on his steepled fingers. He rotated 360 degrees in his chair. Despite the absurdity of the proposal, he found himself asking, 'Are they any good, these F-15 Eagles?'

Both men nodded. Salmon spoke first. 'According to Mayer, the F-15 was the world's premium fighter from the time it was introduced in 1976 until the advent of the fifth-generation fighters thirty-odd years later. The F-15 can still go toe-to-toe with them in most aspects, though it doesn't have the stealth capabilities of the latest jets.'

Adamson broke in. 'We must point out that the F-15s have had their missile operating systems removed. They normally carry both heat-seeking and radar-guided missiles, and electronics that enable them to destroy enemy aircraft at long distances, but these had to be removed before the aircraft could be flown by civil contractors. They still have guns, and they can carry "dumb" bombs. Compromised as they may be, they'd give us some chance of putting up an air defence against an invasion fleet.'

'Okay, time's up,' Quick said. 'It sounds like bullshit, but put together a plan and come back to me asap. I have to say that I think you're insane. I'll be amazed if you can come up with a feasible plan, and if you do, I'll still have to take it to the cabinet. If by some miracle it gets the nod, then we'd support where we can – however, political considerations are as important as military ones. Now get out of here before I have you thrown out. I've got serious work to do.'

* * *

A day later, Quick, Adamson, and Salmon strode down the corridors of Parliament House, heading towards the party room for an urgent meeting of the inner cabinet. Before they entered, Quick turned to his two colleagues. 'You might've sold this ridiculous idea to me, but geez, how are we ever going to convince this lot? The arseholes from the National Party are so far behind the times they still deny climate change and think China's our new best friend!'

Salmon frowned. 'Surely, under the circumstances – I mean, the Chinese Government *has* just started a war with us–'

'Those Neanderthals won't believe we're at war with China until they have to eat with chopsticks. They're so committed to looking after their mining mates that they're blind to everything else.' Quick tugged at his blazer, then put a hand on the door. 'Let's face the music. Good luck, but don't blame me if they boot you out so hard you'll be standing up for a week.'

Seventeen MPs and senators crowded the room: five from

the National Party, the junior partner in Quick's coalition government, and the rest from the Liberal Party. Quick didn't delay in getting down to business. 'Gentlemen and ladies, in our urgent meeting yesterday, we discussed the attacks on our military bases that have left us with no air defence and a crippled naval force. This morning, I received a proposal, via the Assistant Defence Minister, to acquire some thirty-six fighter aircraft as an urgent and temporary defence force. I'll let Rick outline that proposal now. I'll just say that it initially sounded preposterous to me, but our current options are so limited that I've had to reconsider my attitude. Once you've heard the proposal, we'll adjourn for one hour for you to consider it, then reconvene for a vote. Over to you, Rick.'

Thirty minutes later, the inner cabinet members boiled out of the door and rushed to separate Liberal and National Party meeting rooms. After another hour, Quick called for quiet as they noisily reassembled.

John Dunstan, the Deputy Prime Minister and leader of the National Party, jumped to his feet. 'Prime Minister, this proposal is ridiculous. You can't be serious!'

'John,' Quick replied wearily, 'I agree it would be ridiculous under any normal circumstances–'

Dunstan, often called 'the Dunce' behind his back, shouted over Quick. 'Who's to say the Chinese intend to invade? So a group of terrorists bombed some aeroplanes. Do you know for certain that the Chinese Government had anything to do with it? Leaping to that conclusion risks our relationship with China. Even after the unfortunate trade barriers that they imposed in 2021, our export trade with them is worth billions each year. Now you openly accuse them of terrorism! That might trigger even more restrictions on our exports.'

Red-faced with anger, Dunstan thumped the table in front of him, and continued hoarsely. 'Stealing from the Yanks will destroy our relationship with them too. Think of how that will affect our export of beef to America, and our existing defence agreements with them. Are you guys mad?'

Adamson broke in. 'John, we've just been subjected to a series of terrorist bombings almost certainly sponsored by China. This is equivalent to the Japanese attack on Pearl Harbour in 1941. As of right now, we have no air defence at all, and neither our Navy nor our Army can operate when an enemy has total aerial superiority. We are desperate. The Americans have already said they won't help us, defence agreement or no. We have nowhere else to turn.'

The National Party Minister for Home Affairs stood to join Dunstan. 'Why do we have to steal aircraft from a major trading party? Why do you believe we're at war? Throwing these accusations at the Chinese will crucify our remaining export of iron ore and coal.'

Quick was clearly losing patience. 'You two don't seem able to put together three rather obvious hints. Firstly, China's demands to bypass this government in operating Chinese-owned Australian assets; secondly, the bombing of RAAF and Navy bases; and thirdly, the fact that intelligence from both our people *and* the US tells us that the Chinese Navy has assembled a large task force that is right this minute heading south.'

Dunstan barked, 'And what have you and your Liberal colleagues done to mitigate the situation, eh? Your predecessor stuffed up our relationship with China back in 2020, when he called for an independent enquiry into the source of the Covid virus. Our trade has suffered terribly since. You should be working *with* the Chinese Government, not going head-to-head against them.'

The Liberal Minster for Foreign Affairs leapt up and shouted: 'You bloody Nationals may just be mouthpieces for the mining industry, but right now, we have a situation that demands action. Can you stop worrying about how many millions your mining barons might lose for five minutes?'

Dunstan hit the table once again. 'The National Party will not support any covert military action involving US aircraft, or against the Chinese! We call for an urgent motion of no confidence against the government.'

Quick held up his hand to stop the babble of voices. 'That's outrageous. You want to play politics *now*?'

'What good are thirty-six clapped-out old planes anyway?' Dunstan scoffed.

'If this invasion isn't a figment of your imagination, the Chinese will use their modern navy that outnumbers ours probably fifty to one. Their biggest ship makes ours look like a bath toy. And you want to steal some ancient fighters destined for the scrapyard to defeat them? You're having us on. I say we open talks with the Chinese and appease their concerns. So what if we have to eat a little humble pie? So what if we have to give them direct control of their assets here? That has to be better than going to war against our biggest trade customer!'

Another Liberal stood up and pointed his finger at Dunstan. 'You Nats are so far up the arses of the export lobbies that you just can't see daylight, can you? We think an *invasion* force is on its way, for God's sake! We have to grab any opportunity that arises. Even a handful of rusty Sopwith Camels would be better than nothing at all!'

Several of the Liberal members agreed, with a chorus of 'Hear, hears'. The five National Party members marched out of the room, grumbling as they went.

Quick sighed. 'I don't know how much longer I'll be prime minister, and this may be my last decision, but I'm going to give these guys the green light for their proposal, with one major proviso. We won't send active RAAF personnel outside Australia to help in any way. They'll have to get those old jets here all by themselves. We'll give them unlimited access to RAAF fuel and munitions stores, but otherwise, they're on their own.'

* * *

A few hours later, Rick Salmon and Trevor Mayer sat in the minister's spacious office in Parliament House. Salmon had rolled up his sleeves and his tie hung loose. Even Trevor had undone the top buttons of his shirt, and his short, greying hair was untidy. Over several cups of instant coffee, they'd gone over every detail of the plan. Trevor would have to find thirty-six civilian pilots who had F/A-18 or F-15 flying experience, still practised some sort of flying, and were willing to drop everything to join a very risky and illegal venture that might see them thrown into a US military prison for decades.

Salmon had to find a suitable civil jet to take the hypothetical team to Guam. Several big companies in Australia had jets capable of the job, but the first call he made was to an old friend in Perth – the majority owner of a mining company that rarely made the headlines, but was one of the most efficient in the state. Their early-model Boeing 737 was used to fly workers in and out of remote mines. It was quite old, but it was in excellent condition.

It was also plain white, with its only markings the mandatory Australian VH registration letters. Salmon's friend agreed to provide the 737, no questions asked.

Meanwhile, Trevor started at the top of his very long list of aviation contacts. Each person he spoke to wanted to know much more information than he was willing to give, so after twenty or thirty calls, he'd refined his spiel to a single question: 'Australia is in imminent danger of being invaded by the Chinese military, and our air defences have been eliminated – are you prepared to drop everything right now and fly to a foreign country where you will risk being thrown into jail for years, but if successful, may give Australia some means of air defence?'

He got some immediate knockbacks, and a few maybes, but after spending hours on the phone that left his ear sore and mouth dry, he had thirty-five positive responses. That left two very large holes in the plan: supplies and support. He knew the ideal man to fill them. With his last reserves of energy, he called his old mate Dave Pentreath.

'Dave, remember how you suggested we just steal those F-15s? With the assistant minister's help, I put a plan to the PM, and we've just received the go-ahead.'

'*What?*' Dave spluttered, almost dropping his evening cup of coffee. 'Are you serious? That was a throw-away line!'

'Well, I've acted upon it, and now I need your help to finalise the plan.'

Dave was silent for a few moments, then spoke slowly, picking his words with care.

'Trev, the idea is crazy. You think someone can just waltz in and take them? You can't possibly expect to get away with it. I'll bet the Yanks have much better security than we do, and who's going to fly the F-15s anyway? You'll never find thirty-six guys stupid enough to risk it!'

Trevor hadn't expected such a negative response, but refrained from reacting. 'We have a small window of opportunity. Because the USAF has declared them unfit to fly by military personnel, it seems that a civilian operator, using retired USAF pilots, has been contracted to fly them home. We'll just slip in and grab them first.'

Dave laughed. 'I know that you're a ballsy guy, Trev, but that's a hairy undertaking, even for you. Okay, let's say you can pull it off. What then?'

'I've found the pilots, stupid or not, so I want you to figure out the logistics of getting those aircraft here without aerial refuelling. We have access to any RAAF base in Australia, but if we have to resupply en route, we'll need permission to land and access to fuel.'

Dave was staggered that the proposal was making any progress at all. He took a moment to get past a feeling of unreality. Sighing, he shook his head. 'You'd have to refuel halfway, so Honiara is ideal. I'd suggest you ask your minister mate to get clearance to land there. But thirty-six Eagles would need a lot of fuel… they'd carry Jet A-1 at Honiara, of course, but probably not near enough.' Dave did some quick calculations in his head. 'With ferry tanks, each aircraft would take about twelve thousand litres, so altogether that's about three hundred and sixty tonnes of fuel.'

He hesitated, then continued. 'I've had a thought, though. Do you remember Rob Wood? He trained under me at our company, then went on to be chief engineer at a place in Papua New Guinea. They have three Hercules based in Port Moresby that they use for mining support. You know, lifting of heavy drilling gear, that sort of thing.'

Trevor hesitated. 'Oh, yeah, I do remember him. Great idea.

Which model Hercs do they have?'

'I think they're fairly old – J models, probably – but if Rob has anything to do with it, they'll be well-maintained. As I recall, a Herc can carry about nineteen thousand kilograms. The flight from RAAF Amberley to Honiara would take them a bit under four hours, so in two or three days, they could ferry the fuel we need there, even without relying on local supply. They'd also have loadmasters and crew used to handling heavy gear, so they'd be our best bet. I'll give them a call.' Dave sighed, rubbing at his forehead. 'I still think your thirty-six pilots are going to risk spending the rest of their days in Leavenworth. I hope you're not including yourself in that number.'

Trevor didn't answer that last question. 'I'm counting on you to organise that fuel lift,' he said, after a short silence. 'Today's Wednesday, so we'll need it ready by the early hours of Saturday. You'll need to be at Sydney Airport at 5 a.m. on Friday. Bring a light suitcase only, one you can carry on board and put in an overhead locker. Include enough clothing to be away a few days. And bring your flight suit and helmet.'

Dave's voice rose an octave. 'Shit, Trev, what do you want me there for?'

'I've got thirty-six pilots, including myself. The F-15s will be fuelled and waiting, but in case of any last-second technical hitch, I need you there.'

'And how will I get back? Or will I be staying as a guest of the US Government?'

'No, no. As soon as we're strapped in, you can fly out in the 737. Or, if one of the F-15s is a two-seat model, you can ride in it.'

There was silence on the line for a few seconds, then Dave responded, his voice heavy with sarcasm. 'Wonderful! Now I have to go tell Chloe that I'm off to Guam to steal some aeroplanes, and if I don't come back, to send letters care of the United States Government Leavenworth Prison. If it was anybody else, Trev, I'd be telling you to fuck off… but okay, where exactly do I meet you?'

'I'll be in the carpark in front of the executive jet terminal,' Trevor said, with a grim smile. 'Don't be late.'

CHAPTER 5

10 JULY 2026

When Dave pulled into the executive jet carpark at 4.45 a.m., there were already about twenty other men standing around in the darkness. He recognised three of them immediately. Wayne Swanson, Alan Taylor, and Nick Corbett had been on the same course as he and Trevor way back in 1984, and the five of them had become tight friends. They'd worked, played sport, holidayed, and partied together as young men. As they'd married and had families one by one, these new members had been added to the intimate circle. Like Trevor, who'd often led their group activities, they'd gone on to work in airlines after their RAAF careers. Dave greeted them, and they shook hands warmly.

Wayne stood out amongst any group of fighter pilots, as he was quite tall, easily four centimetres over Dave's height. The ideal fighter pilot was actually slightly below average height, and solidly built, as that body shape better withstood high g-forces. However, Wayne had overcome that inherent disadvantage to become a brilliant fighter pilot during his time. Both Alan and Nick were about the ideal build, being stocky and just short of 180 cm.

'It looks like we're in for one last big adventure, boys,' Wayne said cheerfully, as he looked over a couple of new arrivals. 'I wonder what Trev has cooked up for us this time?'

Over the following fifteen minutes, more men arrived, all wearing casual clothes and bearing small carry-on bags. Most Dave knew by sight, if not by name, despite the passage of two decades since he'd served with them. He counted forty men altogether.

At exactly 5 a.m., Trevor appeared at a side gate and swung it open.

'Okay, gentlemen, this is it. Please don't ask questions now. Just follow me.'

On the airside of the closed terminal, there was a white Boeing 737 with lights on in the cockpit. An air-stair led to its open side door. As they trooped across the tarmac towards the aircraft, Dave noted the lack of markings – even the VH identity had been hastily painted over. When he climbed the front steps, he saw that four rows of seats at the front of the cabin had been removed.

The atmosphere was taut with apprehension as everyone filed aboard. Once they were seated, the air-stair's motor started, and without any sort of announcement, a crew member closed the cabin door. First one engine then the other began winding up, and almost immediately, the aircraft was taxiing to the runway. Minutes later, it was climbing out on a northerly heading.

At cruising level, the lights in the cabin brightened, and Trevor stood and faced the passengers. Using a handheld microphone, he introduced a man who looked vaguely familiar to Dave. After a moment, he realised he'd seen him interviewed on TV.

'Gentlemen, thank you all for responding so quickly in our

nation's hour of need. I want to introduce you to Rick Salmon, who, as many of you might already know, is assistant minister to our Minister of Defence. Now, we all hear lots of jokes about politicians, but I can assure you that Rick is not your average pollie. He's been a mate of mine for a long time, and he knows his stuff. He'll now update you on the situation we find ourselves confronted with.'

Rick Salmon, like everyone else aboard, was dressed casually. He surveyed the sea of intent expressions and cleared his throat. 'At midnight last night, the Australian Government received a statement from the Chinese administration. It said, in essence, that unless we agreed to all of their demands, our two countries would enter a state of war. This evening, our PM will conclusively reject their demands. We must expect, therefore, that China will declare war on Australia.

'Most worryingly, US agents have informed us that their spy satellites have picked up a large flotilla of Chinese ships, which has left the Zhanjiang naval base. The Chinese Navy had previously announced that they intended to conduct exercises in the Philippine Sea, but instead, this fleet has turned south. If their destination is in fact Australia, they could reach our east coast in as little as four days from now.

'As you may be aware, the Chinese Navy recently commissioned a new aircraft carrier. It is the biggest carrier in the world, and can, we believe, carry up to one hundred of the latest Shenyang FC-31 fighters, plus a few AWACS and helicopters. Along with this carrier, there are a number of destroyers, troop ships, and fleet supply ships in the approaching flotilla. In all likelihood, there will also be nuclear subs that cannot be detected by the Americans' satellites.

'Against that armada, we have just one Collins Class sub, fourteen Boeing P-8A Poseidon anti-submarine patrol jets, and a few frigates. The sub sailed from Perth yesterday, but will not be in position to intercept the Chinese fleet before that worst-case ETA. The Poseidons carry Harpoon anti-ship missiles, but they can't be successful without fighter top cover. We have three missile frigates in Sydney now, and they are preparing to sail. However, sending them out against that Chinese fleet without air cover would be suicidal.

'We currently have no air defence force. The US will not sell, lease, or lend us replacement fighters without going through the congressional approval process. That could take months, or even years. We have days.

'That is our situation. Without any other options, we are planning to steal USAF jets from Guam to plug the enormous gap in our defences. Our original intention was for you to fly those F-15s from Guam all the way to Australia. We now know we don't have time for that. A few hours ago, the PM decided that RAAF pilots will take over at Honiara, and attempt to halt the fleet before it reaches Australian waters. A couple of C-17s will take munitions from Richmond RAAF base to Honiara. Your job is to get those F-15s from Guam to Honiara.'

Salmon paused to allow his words to sink in. He saw some shocked expressions, but nobody made a sound. 'Obviously, you must be anxious to know how we're going to pull this off. Since you all know Trevor, I'll hand over to him to present the plan. Please note that it is *not* officially approved. All of us are here as private citizens. Let me conclude by saying that what we're doing here today may well decide the future of our country.'

Trevor took back the microphone. 'Firstly, this whole idea

didn't originate with me. It came from my long-time colleague and very good friend Dave Pentreath, who's sitting down the back. Many of you will remember him from his RAAF days. Give us a wave, Dave.'

Dave did, and everyone craned their necks to look back at him.

'Now, to our plan. We're on our way to the island of Guam, which, as you'd know, hosts one of the US Air Force's largest bases outside America. We aim to abscond with the thirty-six F-15 Eagle fighters that are currently stationed at the Andersen Airfield. A team of US civilian pilots, all ex-USAF, are due to arrive in Guam in twelve hours. We will arrive around three hours before them. If all goes well, you'll stand in for those pilots. You will fly to Honiara, where the aircraft will be refuelled, then handed over to RAAF pilots. We will return home on a C-17 or 737 from the RAAF.

'The US Government knows nothing of this, nor does USAF Command at the Pentagon. All we have is the *unofficial* cooperation of a couple of USAF generals and a few of their loyal staff. If the operation turns to worms, they'll deny any knowledge of us. A couple of officers in Guam do know about us, and they'll make sure that the aircraft are fuelled and ready for departure when we get there. They've also managed to submit altered flight plans to Guam's air traffic control, so our early arrival won't ring any alarm bells. They can do nothing else for us. Apart from those few insiders, nobody in Guam will have any inkling that we're not the authorised pilots from the US.

'Once we land in Guam, we cannot afford delay. We expect that this 737 will be directed to park on the north side of the parallel runways, where heavy aircraft normally operate from. A military bus will take us to a hardstand on the south side, where the F-15s have been sitting for some time. This aircraft will then refuel, ready to head back home immediately before us. If you have a technical problem, get Dave. Do *not* interact with the USAF staff any more than you have to. Try not to use Dave if at all possible, because the 737 is his only way out of Guam.'

The thirty-five pilots all looked stunned. That was understandable; they'd already been told that they were stealing USAF aircraft, but had been allowed to assume that the USAF were complicit. They hadn't realised it was to be under the very noses of US base security.

Trevor continued to explain that the F-15s had been stripped of some weaponry, principally their air-to-air missile systems. They still had guns, but would carry no ammunition, because they needed as much fuel as possible for the long ferry flight.

'Now, gentlemen, you know the basics. I must remind you that if you cooperate in this mission, the US Government will probably forever regard you as a criminal. You will never be able to travel to the US or anywhere that might have an extradition treaty with the US. That means your international airline careers will be over. There is also an outside chance that if our little deception is discovered before we're a safe distance from Guam, resident F-22 Raptors might be sent after us. Our friends in the USAF will try to prevent that, but they can't give us any guarantees. If you're unprepared to accept all this, say so now.'

Looks were exchanged. Some faces were ashen, others red with anger. Several of the pilots huddled together. There were a few raised voices, then silence but for the roar of the slipstream outside. All heads swivelled as one man stood up in the aisle.

'Trevor, I can't. I'm divorced, with two kids in private school, plus a new wife with two youngsters. Both my families will be destroyed if I lose my job. I was prepared to take a risk for my country, but you hadn't made it clear just how big that risk actually was.'

Several pilots spoke at once. More than a few heads were nodding. For a few moments, Dave thought that the mission was going to be over before it really began, but quite frankly, he couldn't blame them. He, Trevor, Wayne, Alan and Nick were in their sixties. The others ranged in age from about forty to fifty, and were in the peaks of their airline careers.

The hubbub subsided, and Alan Taylor called out. 'Hey, Trev, I had twenty years flying fighters in the RAAF. In Qantas, we're not allowed to bank more than twenty degrees in case we spill the drinks in first class. Going back to zooming around in a fighter will be as good as a second childhood.'

There were a few laughs, which eased the tension a little. Then one man asked why civilians were to fly the F-15s back to the US, rather than USAF pilots. Trevor looked embarrassed, so Dave quickly stood up.

'There was a one-in-a-thousand structural failure in an F-15, so in a typical overreaction, the USAF declared all F-15C models unairworthy pending modification. They'd allow civilian contractors to fly them, but not frontline pilots, most of whom have moved on to the F-22 and F-35 anyway. Don't worry, the F-15s are good.'

There were a few uneasy glances, but no more questions. Trevor announced that they would take a break, then he would brief them on the differences between the F-15 and the F/A-18, which all but Dave had flown in the RAAF. The time for more questions would follow.

Thirty minutes later, Trevor lowered himself into the empty seat beside Dave. He looked tired and drawn, and he closed his eyes for a few moments before speaking. 'Well, we have only one in the thirty-six who won't fly. Every aircraft counts, so I'm going to ask a big one of you, Dave. Can you fill that last seat?'

Dave was thunderstruck. 'Trev, the closest I ever came to operating a Hornet was in the simulator at Williamtown, and that was decades ago. I've never done any combat training. I can't fly an F-15, for God's sake!'

'You can. You've got a fair number of hours in my L-39, and as you well know, the Russians still use the L-39 to train their fighter pilots. It's not that big a step to fly an F-15. Besides, it's not like you're going into combat – you just have to get it to Honiara for us. You know what's required. We need you; it's as simple as that.

You know I wouldn't ask if the situation wasn't so desperate.'

At that precise moment, Salmon stood up and called for attention. In sombre tones, he announced that he'd just received a message from Canberra. China had declared war on Australia.

* * *

For some time, Dave's mind refused to grasp what he'd just agreed to. He felt that his brain and body had disconnected. By the time the briefing about the F-15 was over, and questions were answered, the 737 was well past midway through its eight-hour flight. Lights were dimmed, and Trevor recommended that they try to sleep for the couple of remaining hours. Dave doubted that anyone would succeed, but later found himself waking as the seatbelt warning beeped.

They were on descent into Andersen Air Force Base, their path taking them over thickly wooded country. The base was on the north-east coast of the island, the ocean visible beyond the airstrip. Minutes later, the 737 touched down and taxied past a row of sombre dark grey B-52 bombers. Two buses awaited them.

Few spoke as they exited the 737 and filed into the buses. Dave assumed that most, like him, were struggling to cope with the reality of their task. The buses skirted the eastern end of the field, passing a row of open-sided shelters. Each shelter housed several F-22 Raptors, the US's top interceptor, and arguably the best interceptor ever built.

They halted on a vast concrete hardstand, where the two rows of F-15 Eagles sat in the bright sunshine. Although the Eagle had been designed in the early 1970s, it was still impressive – and still effective – some five decades later. Up until a couple of years ago, its electronics had been continually upgraded to keep it competitive with the newest fifth-generation fighters. Only in stealth technology were the latest fighters clearly superior.

A wave of excitement rushed through Dave, almost immediately followed by a tsunami of dread. He'd thought he'd lost the opportunity to fly a frontline fighter forty years previously, and now it was about to happen. He figured he could get an F-15 off the ground okay, but wasn't nearly as sure about getting it back in one piece.

'We have fifteen minutes,' Trevor told them, shading his eyes against the glare, while the buses rolled away from them. 'Get your flight suits on, and help each other fit the harnesses for the ejector seats. Assemble right here at precisely 3.30 p.m. If you didn't bring your own helmet and oxygen mask, we have spares. Pick one that fits you. Do *not* dally.'

Suitably kitted, the pilots assembled on time. As they did, Dave saw their 737 taxiing for departure. That was their last lifeline. Thirty-six Australians would now be leaving Guam piloting the F-15s, or in shackles under US military guard. He expected an alarm to go off at any moment. Nobody could stand still: some walked in small circles, others stepped from one foot to the other.

Dave still couldn't quite comprehend that he was about to fly a frontline fighter that he'd never even sat in previously. Just twenty-four hours ago, his most exciting prospect had been to mow the lawn. A feeling of unreality enveloped him. When the call to go to their assigned aircraft came, he had to will his legs to move.

The thirty-six pilots hurried to the row of parked aircraft. As they passed each jet, one pilot peeled off to climb into it. Awaiting them were members of the resident USAF ground crew, there to assist in buckling in.

Dave's allotted F-15 Eagle was the last in line. As overwhelmed as he was by this whole situation, he couldn't help but admire the magnificent machine. It was big for a fighter, over 19 metres long with a wingspan of 13 metres. Dave could walk beneath its wings without needing to duck his head. It had been sitting unused for a couple of years, and its matt grey paint had faded in the tropical sun, taking on a slightly bluish tinge. Dave noted that the USAF 'stars-and-bars' insignia had been hastily sprayed over for the civilian-operated ferry flight. Only the tail numbers remained: his was 056. He thought that few aircraft looked as purposeful and lethal as an F-15, even when a tad dishevelled.

Dave's crewman stood at attention by the portable ladder. He saluted, and Dave was momentarily uncertain whether to salute back, unsure of the USAF protocol. After throwing a hasty salute, he dropped his bag at the foot of the ladder. He then busied himself with the customary walk-round any pilot did when about to fly, to look for anything out of place – fluid leaks, bungs left in intakes, pitot covers left on. He kept glancing across at his colleagues, and when they began mounting their aircraft, so did he. The crewman gave him time to settle in, then climbed the ladder and leaned over to strap and plug Dave in.

Glancing at the small Australian flag on the shoulder of Dave's flight suit, he said, 'Aussie are you, sir? You're a long way from home. How well do you know the F-15?'

Dave grinned. 'I did a tour in the States years ago with F-15s, and I work as a contractor for the company doing this ferry job,' he lied. 'It's been a while since I flew one of these. In Australia, we use the F/A-18, so give me a quick refresher.' Dave could never admit that he'd never really flown either F-15 or F/A-18.

The crewman's rundown on the cockpit layout was quick and

comprehensive. Fortunately, most fighters had a similar basic layout, though individual controls could vary considerably.

'You're fitted with the conformal tanks and two drop tanks,' the crewman said. 'That'll give you enough range to get to the air-to-air refuelling point. Then you'll be ready to enjoy Honolulu's nightlife by 8 p.m. tonight. Have a good flight, sir!' He climbed down, unhooked the portable ladder, and carried it away.

While Dave awaited the signal to start the two huge Pratt & Whitney engines, he scanned the panels. There was a curious mix of knobs, buttons, and gauges that were chipped and worn from forty-odd years of use, plus much more modern 'glass cockpit' electronic touch-screen menus for the latest weaponry. He began with the panel on his left, checking that the switches were set and the throttles were closed. The twin throttle levers also had switches for the microphone, target designation, chaff and flare release, and for air-brake deployment. The panel directly in front housed the back-up primary flight instruments, head-up display controls, radios, and three glass screens. The screens were blank now, but once alive, they'd give him his digital primary flight information, a radar display, moving map, information on other aircraft in rage, and a weapons list. On the right-hand panel were controls for the engines, air-conditioning, lights, pressurisation, and hydraulic systems. He waggled the control stick, noting the position of its thumb switch for the trim and weapon release. The gun firing trigger was on the front of the stick.

Dave thumbed the master switch on. Inverters began to hum, cooling fans whirred, instrument needles moved, and the glass panels flickered into life. He glanced out. With a jolt, he realised that the crewman was making a circle with his upraised finger. Time to start engines!

Dave breathed in deeply, then began the start sequence. As he settled in to do what he had to, his dread faded away. The jet fuel starter hummed, the right engine began winding up, and at eighteen percent RPM, he slid the throttle to idle. With a dull thud, the fuel ignited, and the RPM counter rapidly spiralled up.

Dave repeated the process for the left engine, and the airframe quivered. Even at idle thrust, the jet wanted to begin rolling. He pressed the switch to close the canopy, and with a whir, clunk, and hiss, it closed over him and sealed, instantly cutting out all sound from the outside world.

At the far end of the line, the lead aircraft, Trevor's, was already taxiing, its image distorted by the intense heat of its own exhaust. Adrenaline surged through Dave's body. In no time, the F-15 next to him moved to turn onto the taxiway. He glanced at the crewman outside, who immediately came to attention and saluted. He gave a hasty salute in return, pushed the throttles up, and released the brakes. The aircraft lurched forward. After pressing the top of the rudder pedals to test that the brakes were working, he allowed the jet to move forward again. Eagle 056 entered the taxiway, last in the line of thirty-six jets.

Dave reflected on the fact that he was now a criminal. He only half-listened to the tower instructions, though he did note the wind measurements – 130 degrees and 15 knots. Trevor answered the tower on behalf of all thirty-six aircraft. About a kilometre ahead, Dave saw the lead F-15 emerge from the haze of seventy-two whining jet engines as Trevor turned onto the short taxiway that led to the active runway, then onto the threshold of Runway 08 Left itself. The second F-15 followed close behind, as the plan was to take off in pairs at one-minute intervals. The take-off path would bring the jets back past Dave.

The metallic drawl of the controller echoed through Dave's helmet. 'Ferry One and Two, Runway Zero Eight Left, clear for take-off.'

Trevor's voice responded matter-of-factly. 'Clear for take-off, Runway Zero Eight Left, Ferry One and Two.'

Colourless plumes of super-heated exhaust billowed from both F-15s as they accelerated rapidly towards Dave. They lifted their noses simultaneously, passing his position with a thunderous roar that he could barely hear inside the sealed cockpit, but could feel in his chest. They were airborne seconds later. By the time they passed the far end of the runway, their undercarriages were folding away and their climb rate was steadily increasing.

This process was repeated sixteen more times. With each successful take-off, Dave's confidence grew. *We're going to pull this off*, he thought. Then it was the turn of ferry numbers thirty-five and thirty-six. Ferry Thirty-Five turned onto the runway, and Dave began to follow. But instead of moving to the left-hand side of the strip, thus allowing Dave to hold position just behind his right wingtip, Ferry Thirty-Five lined up close to the centreline. There wasn't quite enough runway width for another F-15, so Dave stopped mid-turn to avoid turning into the exhaust blast.

'Ferry Thirty-Five and Thirty-Six, clear for take-off.'

Ferry Thirty-Five responded and advanced his throttles, staying on the centreline of the runway. Twin rivers of heat and cones of orange flame sprang from the jet's tail, blasting Dave's aircraft so intensely that it rocked. Fine grit hammered the canopy. He had no choice but to wait an agonising ten seconds to avoid turning directly into the fierce jet-blast.

The radio crackled. The tower was calling, and not in a controller's usual laconic tone.

'All ferry aircraft, your clearances are cancelled. Return to Guam. Ferry Thirty-Six, return to the parking bay immediately.'

'Oh, shit!' Nerves forgotten, Dave pressed the transmit button. 'Ferry Thirty-Six rolling,' he said, and advanced the throttles smoothly to full military power, then to full afterburner. Even with the F-15 fully loaded, the push was much greater than Dave had ever experienced. For a few seconds, he was just a passenger in the big fighter: she was going flying all by herself, whether Dave liked it or not. He consciously forced himself to relax his death-grip on the stick and take control over the hurtling jet.

The aircraft had accelerated to 100 knots before he mentally caught up. It was drifting to the left of the centreline, so he put in a touch of rudder with his right foot, easing the weight off the nosewheel with a touch of backwards stick. He could see vehicles with flashing lights on the taxiway ahead, and with horror he realised they were turning onto the runway itself, directly in his path.

The tower was calling stridently. He didn't listen. He had enough to deal with as it was. The oncoming vehicles and his increasing speed ate the gap at a frightening rate. He snatched the stick back when the airspeed indicator went past 150 knots, and the F-15 hauled itself off the ground, passing over the oncoming vehicles by at least fifty feet. The nose bobbled up and down as he groped for the unfamiliar levers, fumbling to put the gear and flaps up. Once aerodynamically clean, the F-15 settled into a rapid climb over the bright blue sea. Dave could see a line of swells with a few whitecaps advancing from the east, but as the land fell rapidly behind, the ocean became a uniform dark blue. The sky was clear, the horizon sharp, the air smooth. He began a climbing turn onto the heading for Honiara.

With the ASI showing 350 knots, he took a breath, lowered the nose a little, and eased the thrust lever back to reduce the prodigious fuel burn rate. Even then, the F-15 was still accelerating and climbing at 10,000 feet per minute. When steady on a heading of 165 degrees, Dave began looking for Ferry Thirty-Five. He couldn't see it. The controller was still going berserk over the radio, shouting that F-22s were launching and the departing F-15s would be shot down if they didn't immediately return to Guam. Dave didn't want to hear that, so he switched to the chatter frequency they'd been briefed to use. It was silent. The thirty-five pilots ahead of him were probably too absorbed in learning their jets to talk to each other. He checked the gauges: all were correct. He'd dialled Honiara Airport's code on the GPS while taxiing, and the pink course line showed that he was two nautical miles left of track. He altered his heading, and soon after, the pink line straightened.

The cruise altitude was to be 45,000 feet. Dave reached that in minutes, so throttled back to maintain a true airspeed of 500 knots – slow for an F-15, but that was necessary to conserve fuel for the three-and-a-half-hour flight. The air was so smooth and clear that there was no sensation of speed.

Dave sat high in the prominent bubble canopy, its clear plexiglass extending down to his elbows. Initially, he felt naked and exposed, but soon came to appreciate the stupendous view in all directions. For the first time in the last thirty-six hours, he began to relax.

A shadow entered his peripheral vision. He glanced right. Just off his wingtip was the menacing matt black nose of an F-22 Raptor. There was no point in trying to flee; the F-15 was loaded to the gunwales with fuel for the long flight, whereas the

Raptor was travelling light for a fast intercept. It carried lethal air-to-air missiles, while Dave's F-15 was unarmed. He switched to the international area frequency and caught the F-22 pilot mid-sentence.

'…return to Guam via heading three hundred and sixty degrees and descend to flight level two zero zero. If you fail to comply, you will be fired upon.'

Being shot to pieces while 14 kilometres above a wide and empty ocean wasn't how Dave had ever imagined his life might end. In seconds, he weighed his options. He could refuse and risk imminent death, or he could return as instructed and spend the rest of his life in a military prison on the other side of the world from home, giving up on any chance of contributing to his nation's defence. After a moment, he keyed the mike and huskily replied: 'Sorry, mate. No can do. This is life and death for us Aussies.'

Background static was his only reply, the F-22 keeping perfect station in the still air as both aircraft hurtled south. Then there was a click on the radio. Dave almost missed the transmission.

'Good luck, buddy.'

Dave glanced directly at the Raptor pilot as he gave a quick salute, rolled 120 degrees and pulled into a descending turn. Briefly, Dave also rolled right, watching the stealth fighter disappear on a heading that would take it back to Guam. He breathed a huge sigh of relief as he returned to his southerly course.

His nerves remained taut for an hour, as he repeatedly checked every gauge and monitored his fuel consumption. He found himself gripping the control stick tightly again and had to consciously relax his fingers. With almost 500 nautical miles behind him, he began to feel at home in the partially reclined seat, designed to reduce the effect of high g-forces in combat manoeuvres. As he traversed the wide Pacific at almost 1000 kilometres per hour, the wings out of view way behind, he felt like he was sitting in a rocket-propelled glass bubble. He was at the point of a spear, one that responded to his slightest touch.

After another hour, he felt the heat of the late afternoon sun searing his face. Sweat ran down from inside his helmet and into his T-shirt, despite the air conditioning being set at 20 degrees Celsius. He was hungry and thirsty, but there was no cabin service on this flight. He slaked his parched throat with a swig of lukewarm liquid from his water bottle. The firm seat began to feel more like it was made of concrete every minute. A real fighter jock would've been accustomed to the unyielding seat of a fighter jet, but he wasn't. His bad back also began to make itself felt.

To distract himself, Dave began planning his landing, the stage of any flight where an accident is most likely. Heavy landings could bend or even destroy aircraft. The F-15 wasn't meant to be particularly difficult to land, but any aeroplane weighing over 15 tonnes and travelling at 180 knots over the boundary fence needed to be handled properly. A good landing started at the beginning of descent. It required the pilot to make turns at the right places, at the right speeds, with gear and flaps and throttles all handled correctly. Honiara's airport, better known as Henderson Field, was relatively short for an international airport, so it was critical that he got his wheels on the ground without floating too far along the strip. He rehearsed the numbers in his head.

The sun was dipping below the horizon as he began his descent, twenty minutes and 120 nautical miles out. He could see a build-up of clouds above the ocean ahead, a sure sign that land lay underneath. The tops of the grey clouds were tinged with pink. Gently, he lowered the nose and reduced thrust, switching to Honiara Control Tower's recorded information frequency and noting the current weather and active runway. Changing to approach frequency, he heard the first of the F-15s call to the tower. Soon enough, it was his turn to enter the pattern. He contacted the traffic controller, and as instructed, slowed to 350 knots, then 250, then 200. At 8000 feet, he entered cloud, instantly plunging into an amorphous grey world. At 3000, he popped out into light rain, still over the ocean, but with visibility just good enough to see the beach ahead and the lights of Runway 24 stretching out towards the hills behind Honiara.

Dave powered up to hold 200 knots and lined up with the runway centreline. A few miles out, he let the F-15 gradually slow to 180 knots, selected full flaps, and juggled the throttles and stick to maintain that speed and rate of descent to the threshold. The boundary fence swept beneath the jet's nose. Once over the piano keys, he closed the throttle and brought the stick back. If he got this right, there'd be a solid bump, but no bounce.

He did get it right. He then held the nose up to maintain drag, as there wasn't a lot of runway left. The brakes shuddered, so Dave eased off them a tad. He let the nose drop. As he turned off the active runway onto a taxiway, it was getting so dark that the taxiway lights were quite bright.

Dave's was the thirty-sixth jet to land. They'd all made it! He saw a Hercules cargo plane parked near the international terminal, the airport's only modern building, which left almost no room for other aircraft on that hardstand. The F-15s filled the larger domestic hardstand, and some were being directed onto the grass. *That's going to be fun if the ground is soft, but it least it won't be my problem,* Dave thought.

Using hand signals, a crewman in dark blue overalls guided him into a parking spot. Others were already refuelling the first F-15s to land. He pulled the twin throttles to idle cut-off, waited for the engines to spool down, then switched off the various systems. The cockpit was silent. He'd done it. He could breathe again. The enormous weight was off his shoulders; he could hand over to someone who really knew how to fly a combat jet. With luck, he'd be home in Sydney with Chloe in less than twenty-four hours.

Dave pressed the canopy opening switch, and the glass bubble rose above him with a whine. The heat and humidity of the Solomon Island evening fell on him like a cloak. Quickly, he unbuckled his chinstrap and eased his helmet off. His hair was matted and soaked with sweat.

For a couple of minutes, he sat flexing his stiff fingers. The F-15's portable ladders were back in Guam, but a small strut had automatically extended from the belly of the aircraft when the canopy opened. He had to gingerly climb down the side of the fuselage, using the recessed handholds below the cockpit sill. The last step on the extended strut was almost a metre above the ground, so he hesitated before letting go. When his feet hit the ground, he stumbled and fell backwards. He lay on his back as Wayne Swanson rushed over.

'Dave, are you okay?' he asked, as he helped Dave to stand.

'Yeah, all good,' Dave said. 'It's just my back. I'm not used to being strapped into a hard seat for so long.'

Darkness fell as thirty-six exhausted but relieved pilots gathered at the terminal building to congratulate one another, then two battered white buses driven by cheerful, dark-skinned locals arrived to take them to their hotel. Eighteen men squeezed into each fourteen-seat bus, and with no functioning air conditioning, they were all hot and clammy in their flight suits. Some were silent, others boisterous. As they passed along the foreshore and into town, Dave could see that Honiara had grown since he'd been there on a contract some years before. Many modern buildings had replaced dilapidated storefronts. The three-storey Mendana Hotel they were heading for was quite old, Dave knew, but it had always been clean and well-maintained when he'd stayed there. He was impatient to get out of the crowded bus.

The Mendana's entrance portico was surrounded by leafy vines and huge tropical flowers, and the reception area was airy and cool. The pilots were quickly allocated rooms by a pair of smiling young Islander girls, each sporting a flower in her dense black beehive hairdo. Everyone then headed straight to the bar, which was styled like a large village hut, with mahogany rafters, a thatched ceiling, and lots of driftwood and seashell decoration. Previously strained faces were now jolly. They all talked too loudly and allowed alcohol to lower their reserves. Men who hadn't met in decades until that morning, not much more than fifteen hours ago, were now mates again. Dave relaxed his normal self-imposed limit and had two gin and tonics. But fatigue quickly set in, and one by one, they drifted off to shower and change out of their sweat-stained flight suits. They were to meet for dinner and a briefing at 8 p.m.

Dave finished his shower with a burst of cold water. After dressing, he stretched out on the double bed and shut his eyes for a short rest. *Flying the F-15 was an experience I'll never forget*, he thought, *but I'm glad the adventure is all but over.* Fighter jets were for young hotshots, not old guys like him.

* * *

Trevor tapped a knife against his glass, and someone called for quiet. 'Gentlemen, you've done it,' he said. 'I heartily congratulate each and every one of you. It was a close-run thing, but thankfully, we've delivered thirty-six beautiful, undamaged F-15s for our RAAF boys to take over. Your country will be proud. You can all go home in a few hours with the knowledge that you've given Australia the means to fight back.'

They cheered and drank. Trevor took a sip of his own whisky, then continued.

'You've seen the Hercules. It's one of three that has shuttled between Amberley and Honiara, bringing in fuel and other supplies. A RAAF C-17 is on its way with other supplies, and a 737 will be departing Amberley shortly, bringing the flight crews to take over the F-15s. It should be here by midnight. You'll return home on that aircraft, leaving about 4.30 a.m. But before I forget, I'd like you to know that the Solomon Island Government, under the able leadership of Prime Minister Harry Wickham, has bent over backwards to help our cause. Not only have they allowed us to use Henderson Field, but they've put a total clampdown on all telephone and internet communications in and out of the Solomon Islands for twelve hours. That means that Chinese personnel or their sympathisers here cannot alert anyone in China of our presence until tomorrow at 5 a.m. By then, we'll be gone.'

There were a couple of soft cheers, and someone clapped, before Trevor continued. 'It also means that you cannot call your families. However, Assistant Minister Rick Salmon has arranged for his people in Canberra to contact your nominated family members and advise them that all is well. Once again, well done today. Be here at reception, ready to board the bus, by 3.15 a.m. That gives you time for a few hours' sleep. Go now. You've done enough for today!'

* * *

Roger Quick took a gulp of the Chivas Regal that his private secretary had poured for him. As he put the glass down, his hand shook so much that he spilled a few drops, and he quickly mopped up the liquid with his handkerchief before his polished mahogany desk was stained. A call he'd been dreading all afternoon was being transferred to his office. It was now 6 p.m. He jumped when the handset buzzed.

'The US Ambassador is on line one, sir,' said his secretary.

'Thank you.' He sighed as he lifted the phone. 'Hello, Henry.'

'Prime Minister, I'm sure you're very busy, so I won't beat about the bush. My government is mortified that you have, apparently, authorised the blatant theft of USAF property, namely thirty-six F-15 Eagle fighters. I understand that those aircraft are en route to Australia now. The president has expressed outrage that a close ally would commit such an act, and has asked me to inform you that this would be considered an act of war but for the long friendship between our two nations. We will shortly deliver a written demand that those aircraft be returned forthwith.'

Quick closed his eyes before replying. 'I understand completely, but let me just correct you on a significant point. I did not authorise the theft of your aircraft. A proposal was put to me a couple of days ago that we buy, beg, borrow or steal these aircraft. It was rejected by the cabinet out of hand. The theft was carried out, I believe, by Australian civilians, with no assistance of any kind by my government.'

The silence on the line stretched for so long that Quick momentarily thought the line had dropped out.

'Roger, it's stretching credibility that civilians could've

conducted this crime without any government help. However, in view of our past relationship, our president is prepared to accept your word. Should we discover your claim to be false, or if those aircraft come to be operated by your Air Force personnel, then you can expect the full wrath of our administration. You can also kiss goodbye to the idea of any future cooperation.'

Quick grimaced. His head felt like it was being squeezed in the jaws of a vice. 'Okay, I've got the message. As I said, I understand that President Ainsworth is angry... nevertheless, you might remind him that your government has refused to consider helping us, which is actually a breach of our AUKUS arrangement. We didn't think that borrowing aircraft due for the scrapheap was too much to ask. In fact, we're very disappointed that despite all the recent rhetoric about a unified Western world, when it's come to the crunch, we've got no support at all.'

That comment might strike a nerve, he thought, which was confirmed by the immediate change in the tone of the Ambassador's response.

'Prime Minister, off the record, we're on your side. You know that. But as with so many international conflicts, it's not just black and white. This whole thing has blown up at a bad time for our president, and he's had to take a hard line over this issue.'

'Henry, I'll make you a promise. No RAAF pilot will touch those aircraft. If they do get to Australia, we won't stop the thieves from flying them, but it'll happen without government support.'

As Quick put the phone down, his Minister for Defence, sitting opposite him, said quietly: 'Well, you've fucked that up properly, Roger. You've just made a promise to the president of the USA, a promise you've broken already.'

'Eh? What do you mean?'

'You've forgotten the RAAF C-17. It landed in Honiara a short while ago, and bombs are being loaded aboard the F-15s right now.'

* * *

Admiral Ming Ze scowled as he paced his roomy teak-panelled day cabin aboard the flagship. His task force had been more than a week behind schedule in leaving port, due to the reactor problems with the new ship. He'd been scathing with the engineers responsible, but had admitted to himself that any new vessel was bound to have teething troubles, let alone one so unconventional as the *Mao Tse Tung*. To plan a major operational cruise without extensive working-up exercises was plain stupidity, and he knew that the blame lay with China's president and war cabinet, who'd set the unrealistic schedule. But he also knew that they would never admit to making an error of judgment. They would pass on the blame for the delay – and any that followed – to Admiral Shen Jun and his committee of senior admirals. They, in turn, would pass it down to him, and he would try to shift it to his underlings.

After the task force had departed port late, their sailing speed had been impeded by the slowness of some of the troop-carrying vessels and the need to coordinate the training requirements of the carrier's aircraft. The war cabinet's original plan had been for the invasion landing to take place within a few days of the commando raids, while the Australian Government was reeling from the attack. Too many days had passed, and the Australians, stupid and complacent as they were, had to know that the force was bound for their waters, even if they didn't know its intent. The only consolation was that the Australians had so few military resources left it was unlikely they could put up much resistance, if any at all.

Ming Ze stopped pacing and held his hands up. He couldn't stop the tremor that had developed in the last few days, nor could he rid himself of the stomach pain that accompanied it.

'Ah, won't something go right?' he said.

To add to his irritation, that brash young captain, Huang Bai, had requested an audience and was due at any moment. The ship's captain had tired of dealing with Huang Bai's constant complaints that his pilots needed more practice and had fobbed him off to Ming Ze. Now it was time to put Huang Bai in his place, once and for all. Ming Ze wondered if he realised that the carrier was the centre of a large task force, and its speed was limited to that of the slowest ship, which was one of the troop carriers. When the pilots wanted to launch, the carrier had to increase speed and swing out of formation into the wind, with all escorts trying to stay in formation. The warship captains were mostly good at that sort of manoeuvre, and had the speed to comply, but the troopship captains were little better than merchant sailors, so they kept on the original course. Once the launch or recovery was over, the flotilla had to return to formation. Crossing paths at night with blacked-out ships would've been dangerous and confusing. Therefore, Ming Ze had refused permission for night take-off and landing operations.

The expected knock on the door came, precisely at the appointed time. 'Enter,' Ming Ze called, as he glanced in a mirror and straightened his blue jacket. Huang Bai hesitantly stepped into the luxuriously appointed cabin. 'What is it, Captain Huang? More of the same complaints that you've badgered Captain Leung with?'

'Yes. Er... no, Admiral,' Huang Bai replied. 'I'm a little concerned about our readiness now that we're so far from our home waters. I've tried to discuss it with Captain Leung, but he suggested I talk to you.'

'Readiness? We're in international waters, and our only enemy has no ability to project a defence beyond its coastline.'

'Yes, sir. But, ah, I understand that the commando raid on the Australian Air Force base at Edinburgh actually failed, so the P-8A Poseidon maritime patrol aircraft are still operational. As I'm sure you know, they can operate out to around two thousand nautical miles, and they have Harpoon anti-ship missiles. We'll be within that range late tomorrow.'

'Of course I know that, but so what? If they approached us, our spy satellites would warn us. Failing that, our own radars would pick them out with enough time to launch our fighters.'

Huang Bai didn't point out that satellites couldn't see in the dark or through cloud, and that surface radars didn't have the range to give the required warning. He was already on bad terms with the ship's captain, and he didn't want to upset the admiral as well. He chose his words carefully. 'Sir, cloud cover has protected us from observation by American spy satellites for the last couple of days, but in a few hours, it will begin to dissipate. I fear that the Americans will quickly find us and will send out AWACS aircraft from Guam to shadow our progress. The information they gather will likely be passed on to the Australian Government. I think we should begin a standing combat air patrol to intercept and deter any such aircraft before they come into range of the task force.'

Ming Ze snorted. 'Those USAF AWACS can probably detect us at twice the range that our much smaller ship-borne systems can detect them. However, I take your point. As of first light, you are authorised to have a single AWACS airborne at all times. We'll be within three hundred miles of the Solomon Islands then. You will also launch a CAP of just two fighters and have two more on the catapults ready for launch. We'll maintain this state of readiness until we reach Australia – not that it's necessary. The Australians probably don't have a single fighter, and certainly none capable of operating as far north as the Solomon Islands. Sending out their P-8A patrol aircraft without fighter cover would be suicidal. Does that meet your expectations?'

Huang Bai knew that a fighter CAP should be initiated right now, but instead he said, 'Most certainly, Admiral. I'll draw up a roster of pilots immediately. If nothing else, it will allow us to further refine our procedures for launching and retrieving aircraft. We've had very little opportunity to do so, and both pilots and crewmen need to consolidate their training in actual sea conditions.'

'You do realise, Huang Bai, that it isn't easy to accommodate everybody's wishes? To launch your CAP at, say, two-hourly intervals, this ship will have to accelerate out of formation. The destroyer escorts are going to have a fine old time scurrying to and fro to maintain a screen against an enemy attack, unlikely as it is, while we're out in front and the troopships are lagging behind.'

'Yes, sir, I fully appreciate the difficulties. However, with an AWACS plus two FC-31s aloft at all times, I will personally guarantee no enemy aircraft will get within a hundred nautical miles of this illustrious force.'

Ming Ze laughed. 'That is an easy promise to make, given the circumstances!'

As Huang Bai returned to the aviation control room, he pondered the admiral's edict that the CAP was to last two hours. His fighters would have to carry external tanks to stay aloft that long, while maintaining a safe margin of endurance, and that would limit their armament to perhaps two heat-seeking missiles each and their internal guns. Still, there really was no possible threat, so what did it matter? The most important point was that his pilots and all the launching crews would be obtaining practice at round-the-clock combat readiness.

* * *

The discordant tones of the hotel bedside phone penetrated Dave's deep and dreamless sleep. His first thought was that it had to be the alarm he'd set for 2.25 a.m., but the digital time display showed that it was just 11 p.m. He'd been asleep only minutes. He picked up the handset, listened in silence, then gasped.

'Trev, what more can they ask of us, for Chrissake? The guys are going to rebel at this! That weak bastard Roger Quick has left us right out on a limb.'

'You can imagine how I feel, Dave. I've dragged everyone into this on the promise that all we had to do was get the F-15s to Honiara, and you all trusted me. Now I've got to go back on my word and convince a bunch of civilians to go to war against a far superior enemy. I feel like shit already, and now I have another big ask of you.'

Dave listened for a couple of minutes, then he said: 'Seriously? Mate, that'll never work.'

Neither man spoke as Dave shook himself properly awake.

'Okay, Trev. I'll do it. But remember, it's about five years since I did that contract here in the Solomons. Harry Wickham was a junior MP then. He might not remember me. Even if he does, now that he's prime minister, he probably won't talk to me. Especially when it's not far short of midnight!'

Dave rang the number Trevor had provided. When it

connected, he said: 'My name is David Pentreath. I'm one of the Australian pilots who landed here this evening. I know this is an outlandish request, but I must speak to your prime minister. It's a critical matter. Please give him my name, and my apologies for disturbing him.'

'I will call you back, sir.'

Dave sat back. Would Harry even remember him?

Fifteen minutes later, the bedside phone rang. Dave listened, then said, 'I'll hold.'

After a few clicks, a deep voice came on the line. 'Dave, how nice to hear from you. How have you been?'

'Prime Minister, it's so good of you to take my call at this time of night.'

'Nonsense, old friend. And it's Harry, of course, we needn't be formal. I thought you were an engineer, not a fighter pilot. What are you doing here?'

'I was asked to come as support crew, but one pilot dropped out. I got drafted to take his place. Harry, I have a very big request to make, but before I do, please tell me, how is your father?'

'Ah, well, he's getting very old, you know. He doesn't do much more than sit in his home on Ghizo, talk to old friends, and look at the view. His legs are weak, and he can barely climb the stairs anymore.'

'Oh, what a shame. I remember him so well – such a fine, upstanding gentleman. And I remember his house on the top of the hill. Three-hundred-and-sixty-degree views, and a sea breeze to cool you no matter the wind direction! But he must be very proud that you've become PM so soon after entering politics.'

'Indeed, he is. But lovely as it is, I doubt you rang me at this time of night just for a chat about old times. I'm intrigued.

What's this request you have of me?'

Dave quickly explained the situation Trevor had just briefed him on. For political reasons, the RAAF pilots wouldn't be coming to take over the F-15s. But with the Chinese fleet only a few hundred miles from the Solomons, on its way to presumably land an invasion force in Australia, Dave asked for permission to mount a strike from Henderson Field.

Harry sighed. 'Our relationship with the Chinese is touchy. As you would be well aware, my predecessor signed a deal with the Chinese Government that allowed them to build a base here. It wasn't a popular decision with my people, and no doubt contributed to my election last year, but the agreement still stands. Besides that, the Chinese buy a lot of timber and seafood from us. Without them, our economy would be in ruins. On the other hand, Australia was a benevolent friend to our nation long before the Chinese took an interest in us, so we owe you a debt of gratitude. We're also horrified by China's recent belligerence. It's clear that they want to be the dominant power in the region, and perhaps not always a benevolent one. But let me talk to some colleagues. I will be back to you within two hours.'

'Thank you, Harry. And when you talk to your dad next, please pass on my fondest regards.'

'He'll like that. I'll talk to you soon.'

Dave paced the room for ninety minutes, all chance of sleep gone, until the phone rang.

'All of tomorrow's inward and outbound flights are being cancelled,' Harry said. 'Our airport staff will not attend Henderson Field. You have it to yourselves. Do what you have to do, but only for tomorrow. Is that clear?'

'Of course, Harry. You have my word. And thanks.'

'Goodbye, and the very best of luck, old friend.'

Dave phoned Trevor. He answered on the first ring.

'It's on,' Dave said.

CHAPTER 6

11 JULY 2026

The phones in every room occupied by the thirty-five pilots rang at 3.15 a.m. The same message was relayed on each call: 'Sir, you are required downstairs for an urgent briefing. You have ten minutes. Bring all your belongings.'

Trevor stood near the door of the conference room as they all shuffled in. Most looked bleary-eyed from lack of sleep.

Once they were all present, he carefully locked the door before addressing them. 'Gentlemen, I have dire news on two fronts,' he said. 'Firstly, by dawn this morning, the Chinese invasion force will be just three hundred nautical miles north-east of us here. In under four days, they will be within striking distance of the east coast of Australia.'

Trevor looked pained as he continued. 'Even more importantly, the RAAF 737 that was due to bring the replacement pilots will not be arriving. I can't go into details, as I don't have the full story yet, but in a nutshell, I gather that the US Government is livid about our "acquisition" of their F-15s. The US President has taken it as a personal affront, and has given our prime minister an ultimatum: if RAAF service pilots operate the stolen fighters, all cooperation with the US military will immediately cease. All US forces currently based in Australia will be withdrawn, and any discussion of future cooperation will be terminated indefinitely.'

SOLOMON ISLANDS

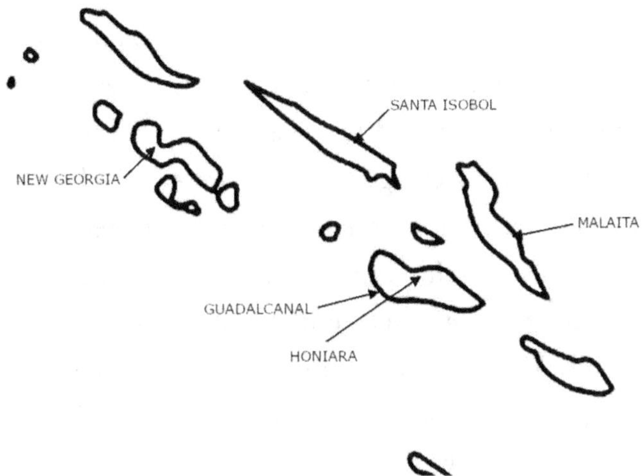

Trevor paused, and took a couple of deep breaths. 'That leaves me in a very unpleasant position. I have made promises to you that I must now break. I have no alternative but to ask you to once again put your lives on the line – to go to war against the Chinese armada in the F-15s. We are Australia's only hope of stopping it. Before the PM decided that he couldn't risk allowing serving RAAF pilots to man the F-15s, three C-17 Globemasters with full loads of Mark 84 bombs and 20mm ammunition for the cannons took off from RAAF Richmond. Those aircraft arrived before midnight, so the F-15s will be armed and ready to fly by 4 a.m.'

Dave felt like a man who'd been given the death sentence. Going by the gasps and expletives he heard, most of his compatriots probably felt the same, and when he glanced around, he saw a few white faces. Despite the shock, within minutes, the prevailing mood became one of stoic acceptance.

If Dave had felt unprepared to fly an F-15 from Guam to the Solomons, that was nothing to his emotions about going to war in it. However, he had to quickly put those thoughts aside as Trevor continued the briefing. 'You are no doubt aware that the F-15 was originally designed as an air-superiority interceptor, not as a strike aircraft. However, these C-model F-15s do have eight weapons pylons under their wings and fuselage, which can carry a variety of weapons from heat-seeking missiles to laser-guided bombs. You also know that much of the standard weapons targeting systems in these thirty-six aircraft was removed for the ferry flight. Each pylon can still carry a single nine-hundred-and-fifty-kilogram "dumb" bomb. Without the electronic weapons systems, we'll be dropping them by guesswork, like pilots did in World War One.'

Dave's stomach lurched. Unlike the thirty-five others in the room, he had never fired a gun or dropped a bomb from an aeroplane, not even in a simulator, as his RAAF pilot training had been curtailed before reaching that stage.

The briefing went on. Using a blackboard that had been set up in the function room, Trevor outlined the situation. The Chinese fleet was steaming south towards Australia, and would be at its closest point to Honiara in just a few hours. He nominated nine flight leaders, and three wingmen for each. Dave was tail-end Charlie in the in the ninth group.

Trevor continued. 'The Chinese fleet's first line of defence will obviously be their fighters. In this case, we understand they're equipped with FC-31s. Under the guidance of AWACS, they'd use air-to-air radar-guided missiles to target any incoming threat at one hundred and fifty to two hundred nautical miles. Any strike aircraft that penetrated that screen would then be targeted by the FC-31's close-range heat-seeking missiles, then short-range ship-to-air missiles, and finally rapid-fire radar-guided guns.'

Every man in the room was so intent on Trevor's briefing that there was not a sound or movement from the thirty-five there. 'Usually,' Trevor said, 'our strike aircraft would be armed with stand-off missiles, and we wouldn't attempt to get close to the enemy fleet. Aircraft armed only with dumb bombs would normally have little chance of penetrating the enemy's defences. Our one and only asset in the present situation is that the Chinese are, we think, totally oblivious to our existence. Even if they do have AWACS aircraft aloft, they'll be mystified by any signal they pick up from our approach. They may or may not have a standing CAP. It's highly unlikely that their ships will be on alert status. Given that their carrier is brand new, and they haven't had time to get its offensive or defensive capabilities into shape, we have a once-in-a-lifetime opportunity. We have to make the most of it.'

As Dave slowly made his way to the door, he was intercepted by his old friends, Trevor, Wayne, Alan, and Nick. Trevor spoke first. 'Dave, you don't have to be part of this. You never trained for ground attack, and you'd be risking your life for nothing.'

Nick said, 'Yeah, you've done your bit, so leave the rest to us, okay?' Alan and Wayne nodded.

Dave looked at his mates, and with false bravado, replied, 'You don't think I'm gonna let you guys have all the fun, do you? No way, I'm coming too.'

As they slowly walked away from the room, Dave felt a stab of guilt. He'd probably just consigned Chloe to becoming a widow.

* * *

They exited the buses at Henderson Field in total darkness. It was 4 a.m., and the night was black, still, and heavy with humidity. Only the closest F-15s could be seen in the glow of the few weak terminal lights. The aircraft now looked even more lethal, with eight bombs under the wings of each.

Before the pilots dispersed to their individual aircraft, Trevor called, 'Good luck, gentlemen. See you all back here afterwards.'

What are the chances of that? Dave wondered. Grimly, he remembered that in the WWII battle of Midway, the first strike had been by US Douglas Devastator torpedo bombers against Japanese carriers. The whole squadron had been shot down without landing a single blow on the Japanese ships.

At 5 a.m., they began launching into the still pitch-black sky, one at a time and at thirty-second intervals. Honiara's Lungha district reverberated with what sounded like continuous rolling thunder for eighteen minutes, but from the ground, each departing F-15 was visible only as a pair of glowing cones of fire. At 2000 feet, Trevor throttled back to a 500-knot cruise speed, allowing all thirty-five fighters to bunch up behind him. At this low level, so close to land, they were safe from detection by any Chinese AWACS that might be shadowing the fleet. For a while, anyway.

As they streaked past Savo Island, Dave briefly reflected that almost exactly eighty-four years ago, US, Australian, and Japanese forces had fought vicious air, sea, and land battles for Henderson Field. The rusted hulks of many ships still lay in the waters below. The looming battle would take place not far from where the Battle of the Coral Sea had unfolded in 1942, which had been a major turning point in WWII. Both sides had suffered heavy losses, but the balance had ultimately been in the Allies' favour.

But Dave was too fully occupied with flying the big fighter to ponder this for long. His night vision had never been perfect, and with age, it had deteriorated further. He peered nervously at the barely visible formation lights of Number Thirty-Five and juggled the stick and throttles to maintain station.

The first 200 nautical miles went quickly, even at their economical cruise speed. Using their nose-mounted radars, they formed a spread of approximately five miles between each element of four aircraft. At 60 nautical miles from the anticipated enemy position, they switched off their radars and accelerated to Mach 1.5. That was as fast as they dared go without ripping the underwing bombs from their pylons. Each element moved into a wider battle formation as they began a gradual descent, keeping their speed at 900 knots.

The indigo sky had lightened perceptibly and was now broken on the horizon ahead by a pale orange glow. They could discern whitecaps on the waves just 300 feet below. At any moment now, Trevor and his three wingmen in the lead element would be making their attack. Dave felt totally ill-equipped for the situation he found himself in, and wished that he were anywhere but inside that cockpit!

* * *

Between the twin hulls of the *Mao Tse Tung* was the nerve centre of the supercarrier. In the radar room, data was linked between spy satellites, AWACS aircraft, the fighter CAP, and the ship's own radars. In the communications room, radios were in constant contact with the PLANAF headquarters and the other ships of the convoy. In the combat plotting room, the positions of all aircraft and ships were displayed on large screens.

As a lowly junior ensign, slightly built and just nineteen years of age, Chui Ying was frequently left with the mind-numbing shift from midnight to dawn. He was on his first cruise, and wasn't yet able to fully interpret all of the information on the glowing screens in the darkened radar room. He'd listened many times to his supervisor, Lieutenant Zhong Xin, as he bragged of the radar system's capabilities – of how any threat to the task force would be detected initially by satellite, then by AWACS, then the CAP, then the shipboard radar. A few minutes ago, their first AWACS and standing CAP had been launched, so those two levels of radar coverage would soon be feeding into the computers. Not that there would be any threat, he'd been assured.

When the satellites had indicated some aerial activity at Honiara's Henderson Field, some 300 nautical miles to the sou-sou-west, Zhong Xin had dismissed the signals as local inter-island flights by small aircraft. 'Either that or ground clutter,' Zhong Xin had said, then promptly racked back his comfortable chair and nodded off to sleep. Chui Ying wasn't so sure, but he was reluctant to wake his aggressive superior, in fear of another chastising.

Chui Ying watched as the satellite signals faded away, but he kept an eye on that part of the screen. He noted periodic momentary 'paints' from the satellites. After twenty minutes or so, the still-climbing AWACS picked up a similar paint, one that was much closer to the ships. *Could this be inter-island small aircraft?* he asked himself. *Surely not before dawn.*

With mounting misgivings, he saw that the momentary paints were now appearing along a direct line from Honiara to the task force, but the sophisticated system hadn't linked the paints as a single target, and therefore hadn't given an approach speed. A quick mental calculation, however, indicated a speed much greater than any prop-driven inter-island aircraft would achieve. He sat bolt upright. 'Lieutenant Zhong, please come and look at this!'

Zhong Xin groggily opened one eye, and coughed. 'What is it this time, Ensign Chui? A flight of seagulls?'

'No, sir. It's something moving very fast and low.'

Scratching at his sagging belly, Zhong Xin ponderously dragged himself up from his comfortable chair to look over Chui Ying's shoulder. The screen was momentarily blank. He was about to deliver a verbal lashing when it lit up with multiple clear, bright paints. The computer system immediately identified the threat as multiple aircraft accelerating from 500 to 900 knots, barely 50 nautical miles away and closing at 15 miles a minute.

'*Shit!*' Zhong Xin shrieked, as he hit the transmit button to the combat centre.

* * *

From the carrier's centre island, Captain Huang Bai had watched the launch of the AWACS aircraft, a strange-looking twin turboprop, with quad tail fins and a large radome above its fuselage. The catapult gave the heavy aircraft barely enough speed to fly, and after it went over the bow, it dipped below deck level, wings waggling as the pilot fought to keep it aloft. Huang froze when it went out of sight, and only began breathing again when he saw it climbing away into the night. Soon, he knew, it would be above 30,000 feet in altitude and able to detect any threat out to 200 miles. That was the theory, anyway.

He began to relax after his long-awaited CAP of two FC-31s successfully launched. Shifting his gaze to the east, he saw the greyhound shapes of escorting destroyers just becoming visible in the first glow of dawn. The worrying gap in their defences would be filled as soon as these aircraft reached altitude, so it was time for him to rest.

He'd barely turned to go below when the klaxon above his head began to wail, and a loudspeaker shouted, 'Action stations, action stations!'

* * *

Without any warning, the dawn sky erupted with flashes of brilliant white light, allowing Dave to make out ahead the sleek shapes of destroyers silhouetted against the glare. Plumes of white smoke marked the launch of ship-to-air missiles, and the destroyers' main guns flashed. Twinkling lights decorated the dark shapes as every enemy vessel opened fire. Within seconds, the smoke created a pale fog over the entire fleet. Glowing red balls drifted through the air. Dave saw one grow in intensity then change to an orange blur. He realised that a missile had just passed between Number Thirty-Five and himself, its proximity fuse igniting a half-second too late.

They flew on into the maelstrom. *No time for fear now,* he thought. *Just fly the aeroplane. Do the job.*

Vivid flashes, fireballs overhead, an explosion. An F-15 down, or was it a bomb hit on a ship? He couldn't see. Where was that carrier? There! It was huge, but between it and his flight of four F-15s were plumes of smoke from missiles, black puffs from the exploding shells of the destroyers' big guns, and streaks of tracer fire from smaller guns. A red flash, then debris rained down ahead: it was an F-15 from the flight ahead of his. *Fuck, this is scary beyond belief!*

A smoke trail arced overhead – a missile, high, but curving down towards him. He jinked hard right. It followed. He shoved the stick forward, and it swept by so close that he instinctively ducked. Rolling left, he fell back into formation with Number Thirty-Five. A red ball of fire ahead had been an F-15 a second ago. He dodged the fiery debris, large pieces leaving trails of smoke before they plunged into the sea. *Am I next?*

Orange tracer rounds arced over his head like a stream from a fire hose. The gunner lowered their aim, and he pushed forward again. Well ahead were two F-15s, maybe Numbers Thirty-Three and Thirty-Four. Missiles and tracer fire criss-crossed in front of them. Number Thirty-Three veered out of control, rolled, and plunged down. His wingman panicked and released his bombs far too early. They exploded as they hit the sea, creating a huge column of water that towered hundreds of feet above Dave as he passed it.

Stuff this, Dave thought. He had to get it right the first time – he didn't want to do a second run. His right hand had a death grip on the stick, and he forced himself to relax, flexing his fingers. The carrier was getting closer by about half a kilometre every second. Another missile streaked towards him. He rolled hard left towards it and pushed the stick, and it zipped overhead. The carrier was dead ahead, but he was far too low, just metres above the sea. Even if his bombs hit the ship, they might not have time to arm after release.

He wouldn't survive another attempt. It was all or nothing. The carrier's deck loomed above him, and he eased the stick back a touch, just enough to take him over the deck. The ship filled his vision. He pressed the bomb release. If his bombs did detonate, he was so close he might be destroyed with the ship.

Over the deck, all eight bombs gone, he pulled hard and slammed both throttles to full afterburner. He realised his mistake a moment too late. Climbing at 45 degrees, he'd made himself a perfect target, presenting the belly of his F-15 to a destroyer just beyond the carrier.

Red-hot balls hurtled past. He rolled inverted, diving towards the ocean, then rolled back upright, almost too late. Waves reached for the F-15's underside. The destroyer was directly ahead, his nose pointing at its bridge. He felt for the armament switch, and flicked from bomb release to the cannon. His right forefinger tightened on the joystick's firing button.

With the sound of a giant zipper, the fearsome M61 Vulcan cannon's six barrels spun, vomiting a hundred explosive shells every second. He was staggered by the destruction it wreaked on the hapless destroyer. In a burst of three seconds, the bridge, main mast, funnel, and fire control centre disintegrated in a cauldron of flying debris. The destroyer's guns stopped firing.

That felt good. 'Gotcha, you bastard!' Dave yelled into his oxygen mask. He rolled left, yanked on the stick, and g-forces pulled at every part of his body. Vision greying, he tensed his stomach and breathed in short grunts.

I'm still alive, he thought. He didn't know if he'd hit the carrier or not. He wasn't going back to look, but he did risk a glance over his shoulder. Although he was already miles past the carrier, he thought he could see a red glow where it should've been.

There was a troop ship behind and to the left. He rolled into an attack position. He was too fast – he'd overshoot – so he came out of afterburner and lowered the nose, pressing the gun button. The Vulcan howled again, and the ship disappeared in a cloud of spray as his shells punched into the sea around it. He saw an explosion, so he knew some had hit. He pulled out at about 100 feet.

The F-15's fuel level had plummeted with all that use of afterburner. He was done; he was going home. He stayed low until he figured he was well past the danger area. Just as he began to relax, a stream of glowing red balls sailed just over his head. *Shit!*

Realisation hit like a hammer blow. There was a fighter directly on his tail.

He rolled left, then right, then pulled hard into a 45-degree climb. The stick trembled as the F-15's wings clawed at the air. It was hard to hold his head up, but when he managed to glance into the curved mirror inside the canopy bow, he saw that the enemy aircraft was glued to his six. He had a split second to save his own life.

He hauled back the thrust lever and popped the big dorsal airbrake, washing off speed so quickly the harness dug into his waist and shoulders. A dark shape slid past his right wingtip. The Chinese pilot hadn't reacted quickly enough and overtook Dave, putting himself in a vulnerable position. Dave slammed the thrust levers forward and closed the airbrake. His F-15 leapt forward as the Chinese pilot realised his mistake and pulled hard straight up, his afterburners creating twin cones of fire.

They were both going vertically upwards, Dave's F-15 climbing a little faster. He blipped the firing button but missed. The enemy aircraft veered into a half-loop and he missed again. He didn't have the ammunition to waste. Glancing at the head-up display, he saw that the target designator, a small green square, was below the enemy aircraft.

Dave pulled back even harder, his G-suit squeezing his body. His face felt like it was being dragged down off his head. The designator square crept towards the target, then covered it. He fired. A flash, then a wisp of grey smoke, the sign of a definite hit. His thumb stayed on the firing button, but the cannon whirred down. Out of ammunition.

The enemy fighter maintained its speed and high-G turn for a few more seconds, and Dave feared that he was now stuck in an aerial brawl with no ammunition and rapidly diminishing fuel. The smoke trail intensified, and the FC-31 broke out of the turn, raised its nose, and slowed. An orange glow appeared at the wing root. Simultaneously, the aircraft exploded and its pilot ejected, a split second too late. The seat and pilot separated, but both were on fire. Dave lost sight of both as they tumbled towards the sea. He searched for a parachute, but there was none.

Horrified that he'd just watched a man die, Dave circled what remained of the jet as it plunged into the sea. He jolted back into awareness of his perilous situation when a yellow warning light reminded him of his depleted fuel status. He turned onto the heading for Henderson field.

* * *

Lieutenant Chang Li was the officer responsible for all aircraft movements in the starboard hangar of the *Mao Tse Tung*. When the action stations call came, he'd just supervised the pushing of two fighters required for the next CAP onto the lift. As specified, they were heavy on fuel, but light on armament. With the alarm ringing through his skull, he then had a panic call on his personal earphone. It was from the flight control room deep in the base of the superstructure.

'Lieutenant Chang, urgent launch required. We are under attack. This is not a drill.'

After freezing momentarily, Chang Li yelled at the closest

handlers. 'Get that lift going. *Hurry!*'

The lift started to ascend. Then an ear-splitting boom rocked the hangar, knocking him off his feet and slamming his head against a railing. He picked himself up and tried to make sense of what was happening. Several men had disappeared. The only traces of them were bloody smears and unrecognisable lumps. Lights flashed through a number of jagged holes in the hull. Seawater cascaded in. Fire roared. He knew instantly that the carrier was doomed, but no call had yet come to abandon ship. Even as he yelled for his surviving handlers to get the next pair of fighters ready, he saw a battery cart begin to roll across the floor. The deck was tilting!

The fighters being hooked up by tugs also began to roll backwards. His shouts didn't prevent two handlers from being crushed by the colliding aircraft. Within seconds, the tilt was so pronounced that he had to grab hold of the handrail that ran along the wall. Crewmen who tried to move fell and rolled into the oil-contaminated water swirling through the hangar. The screeching of aluminium wings and fuselages tearing at each other was drowned out only by the roaring of fire and water. The incoming flood went from a cascade to eight liquid columns that cut swathes across the hangar. Li found himself dangling almost vertically from the handrail, until one of the columns reached for him. His hands slipped, and he fell 30 metres to his death.

* * *

Immobilised by the events unfolding before him, Huang Bai watched helplessly from the carrier's central island as each wave of four aircraft attacked. He recognised the twin upright tails of F-15 fighters, but how could that be? Only the USA, Japan,

Saudi Arabia, South Korea and Israel flew the type, and China wasn't at war with them.

He yelled in triumph and relief whenever an attacker was destroyed before reaching the carrier, or whenever one missed the ship with its bombs. But more kept coming. Four bore down on him, and he could see but not hear them, as they left their sound behind. Missiles and gunfire streaked all around them. Two were hit and became fireballs plunging into the sea. Another dropped its bombs too early, and they exploded well off the beam. The F-15 climbed away untouched. But the last still came on, twisting left and right, diving so low Huang Bai thought it would hit the sea. But it didn't: it kept coming on. When it was only a few hundred metres from the ship, its nose lifted, and Huang Bai watched eight bombs detach from the wings. They appeared to lose height slowly as they fell. The aircraft crossed the twin flight decks, just in front of the island structure, so close that Huang Bai clearly saw its pilot in profile. It had no national insignia, but its tail designation was clear. The number 056 was instantly seared into Huang Bai's brain.

For a second that seemed much longer, nothing happened. Then the deck heaved upwards. Flame jetted from the lift well and roared out of every hatchway. A fountain of burning fuel gushed into the space between the two hulls. Fire crews dashed to and fro, but despite their efforts, the entire ship was covered by thick and toxic smoke within minutes. Burning figures leapt into the sea 20 metres below, their screams drowned by the roar of the flames.

Huang Bai shook in anger as the scale of destruction engulfed him. 'You bastards!' he yelled. 'How dare you do this to me?'

The *Mao Tse Tung* began to lose its way and make a slow turn.

Soon, there was a detectable heeling. Huang Bai knew that his duty was to his pilots, and that he should go belowdecks to find a phone and order his men to assemble near the bow. Instead, fear overtook his sense of duty. Terrified that he might be trapped there, he scrambled to the nearest lifeboat station and leapt aboard the dangling boat. An ordinary seaman stood by the davit. 'Launch!' Huang Bai screamed, but the young man shook his head.

'We must wait for the order to abandon ship, sir.'

Huang Bai went to draw his service pistol. He would shoot the man if necessary and operate the controls himself. His hand grasped at empty air – he'd left his side-arm safely locked in his cabin early that morning.

The call to abandon ship rang out from the bridge. Quickly, the lifeboat filled with severely burned crewmen. Huang Bai did not attempt to help them. He sat near the stern, tears streaming from his eyes, as he watched his ship, his fighters, his pilots, and his dreams of victory burn to ashes.

* * *

Dave's exit from the F-15 was no more graceful than it had been when he'd first arrived in Honiara. He collapsed onto the tarmac, his legs like jelly. Two crewmen rushed to help him stand, and he saw Trevor behind them, face ashen.

'Are you alright, Dave?'

Dave nodded, but anxiously peered around the parking area. 'Where is everybody? Are they still out there?'

Trevor slowly shook his head. 'No... I think you'll be the last one home. It's bad. We've lost twenty-four aircraft, and I don't know how much damage we've done.'

Dave was stunned. Twenty-four gone of thirty-six F-15s!

Were all their efforts for nothing? 'Are there any survivors out there?' He peered at the other F-15s' tail numbers. 'I can see that Alan and Nick are okay, but where's Wayne?'

'Wayne's gone down. I think he may have ditched on the way back,' Trevor replied. 'We have no way of knowing any more at the moment.'

Dave's shoulders drooped, and he swung away from Trevor to hide his face. 'Ah… shit,' was all he could say.

Trevor stood, looking at the empty sky, and spoke so quietly that Dave barely heard him. 'And it's all been for nothing.'

Dave turned back and hesitated before speaking. 'Trev, I can't be sure, but I think I may have hit the carrier.'

Trevor didn't reply immediately. He stared, stricken, at the sadly depleted row of F-15s. Then he shook himself, and Dave could see him recover some of his organisational ability. 'We must make another strike. It's all or nothing, now.'

* * *

Their second strike consisted of three flights of four F-15s. Trevor hadn't registered Dave's claim that he'd damaged the carrier, so fully expected to run into a wall of defending Chinese interceptors. There were none. Instead, from 50 miles out, they saw a vast column of black smoke. It rose 10,000 feet, before creating its own white cumulus cloud, which topped at well over 15,000 feet.

Minutes later individual burning pyres materialised out of the smoke haze. The carrier was no longer recognisable. The lack of fighter interceptors and the disarray of the flotilla told Trevor that their first strike had succeeded in its main aim. The carrier was no longer a threat.

In the fear, the excitement, the horror, and the bitterness of losing colleagues, the details of the second strike subsequently became confused in Dave's mind. He did recall that there were a couple of destroyers and several troop ships in various degrees of distress, and that other destroyers seemed to be without leadership as they dashed around the scene of carnage. He dropped bombs over a troop ship, but in the smoke haze, he couldn't tell whether he hit it or not.

Although the defensive fire had fallen dramatically, with only a few anti-aircraft missiles and some gunfire still coming from the circling destroyers, one Eagle went down. Dave saw a missile from a destroyer hit the F-15, which immediately spun into the sea. A red rage overtook him, so he lined up with the destroyer and rammed the thrust levers forward. His first pass inflicted fearful damage from his Vulcan cannon. The destroyer lost its way, and smoke rose from it in a mushroom cloud. Dave passed over it, reversed course, and strafed it again.

No gun or missile fired back that time, and when he departed the battle area, the ship was dead in the water.

CHAPTER 7

12 JULY 2026

At 8 a.m. on the dot, Prime Minister Roger Quick strode into the packed conference room, only to be immediately bombarded with questions shouted by the gathered media. Imperiously, he held up his hand for quiet, and refused to speak until the room was silent.

'Ladies and gentlemen, I have news of critical importance to all. A flight of privately piloted fighter jets operating out of Honiara Airport, with the support of this government and the permission of the Solomon Islands Government, has intercepted the Chinese invasion fleet that was bound for Australia. We don't have all details as yet, but satellite images indicate that several Chinese ships were sunk, including their flagship, the aircraft carrier *Mao Tse Tung*. We also know that the surviving ships have reversed course, and we believe that they are right now sailing for home.'

The room erupted. Every media representative wanted to ask a question. Quick tried to shout above the noise, without much success. After three minutes of pandemonium, five questions seemed to be foremost. How did the Australian Government organise this so rapidly? Who were the pilots? Were there any casualties in the friendly force? Where did the jets come from?

Quick avoided answering any of them, while giving the impression that he was not only fully on top of the situation, but that he'd instigated the repulse of the Chinese force himself. Some of the reporters actually believed him.

* * *

As his F-15 swept down towards Williamtown Base that afternoon, Dave could see people and private cars crowding the beach and the highway. News of the battle the day before had obviously broken. After taxiing in and parking, he and the other ten surviving pilots were hastily whisked away to a briefing room via a small RAAF bus. The room dated back to the 1950s, with cream-painted walls, slow-turning ceiling fans, small windows, and hard seats. Dave sighed as he collapsed into one.

Senator Rick Salmon greeted them. 'Yesterday was a momentous day. We saw great victory, but also the tragic loss of so many friends and colleagues. I can only say that Winston Churchill's famous words to the Battle of Britain pilots must equally apply to the thirty-six of you: "Never in the field of human conflict was so much owed by so many to so few." Highly appropriate, gentlemen, and you deserve to be honoured accordingly.

'However, I am sad to say that politics has reared its ugly head. Some US politicians are furious that you stole their aeroplanes from under their noses. They'd love your heads on a platter. Countering that, there has been a groundswell of opinion within the civil service, the opposition, and the military that the US should be supporting us. It looks as if the media is taking up that cry too, so we wait and hope.'

A few smiles broke out with that news. Salmon continued.

'Here in Australia, our PM is trying to balance on top of a barbed-wire fence. In a press conference this morning, he implied that he was responsible for everything from acquiring the F-15s to supplying your ammunition and fuel. But at the same time, he is placating the US President by saying that his government had nothing to do with the theft of the F-15s. He must also be aware that, sooner or later, the press is going to ask why civilians had to step in to take the initiative after the RAAF fighter force was knocked out cold. That does not look good for our government.

'So, you will find some mixed sentiments out there. The public story is that an Australian group, using USAF aircraft, has stopped the Chinese invasion force in what the press is calling the Second Battle of the Coral Sea. Their geography is a little out, but it makes a good headline. Nevertheless, the public knows that we are still at war, so tensions are high.'

Salmon paused for a few moments to let this situation sink in. 'The Chinese Government is also seething. They have denied responsibility for the terrorist attacks on our air and naval bases, and the president has personally denied that their fleet was intending to land an invasion force in Australia. Their military leaders have figured out that a civilian group, *not* a part of the RAAF, was responsible for the acquisition of the F-15s and the subsequent attacks on their fleet. They have branded you as mercenaries and murderers. For that reason, we have not given any details on your identities. There are almost certainly Chinese operatives in Australia that would act if they were able to identify you.'

That was a revelation. The surviving pilots now knew that they were still in danger.

'We have qualified pilots in the RAAF who are ready and willing to take over the eleven aircraft you have brought home,' Salmon said, 'but the PM is unwilling to exacerbate the tensions between himself and the US President by letting them do so just yet. We think that could change quite rapidly if public sentiment in the US follows the line their media is taking. Meanwhile, we would like you to remain on standby pending further developments. It is by no means impossible that the Chinese might try again – and next time, they might take us seriously.'

A few hours later, Dave returned to his home in Sydney's north-west Hills District, courtesy of a government car and driver. He eased his body into his favourite chair as Chloe fussed about him and he described what had occurred in the Solomons, along with what he'd been told since.

Horrified by the possibility that Dave and Trevor might have to go back into action, she shook her head. 'Darling, you and Trevor are no longer young men. What were you thinking? You should've flatly refused. You have to leave this to the Air Force people now!' She sighed. 'Thank goodness you two are okay, but I feel terrible for Wayne and the families of all those who didn't return. So many lost, and in the prime of their lives.'

'But we really didn't have an option, and we still don't, Chlo. You've seen the news. The Americans are cranky, and our government can't risk agitating them further by having the RAAF take over the F-15s. What do you expect us to do? Sit around while the Chinese invade us?'

Chloe leaned down, squeezed his shoulders, and kissed the top of his head. 'Dave, I was so frightened you wouldn't come back. I could never go through that again. I am so, so glad to have you home.' She sniffed back tears, then laughed. 'Even with your dodgy old back.'

Later that night, as he and Chloe lay in bed, their bodies

pressed tightly together, Dave whispered a promise to himself that once this war was over, he would never be apart from his wife, not ever again.

* * *

Captain Huang Bai looked forward to his second meeting with Admiral Shen with even more foreboding than he had the first. This time, there was no possibility of a good outcome. The only question was exactly how bad it was going to be.

Huang Bai stood in that same bare room, before the same silent panel of senior and junior admirals. Admiral Shen looked to have aged years in the weeks since Huang Bai's last audience. The four others peered at him with obvious distaste.

'Captain Huang,' the old admiral began, picking up a report with the tips of his nicotine-stained fingers as if the paper itself were toxic, 'you have failed totally in the mission we entrusted you with. Your fighters, far from achieving an easy victory over pitiful resistance, are now lying at the bottom of the sea, as are many of your elite pilots. Do you have anything to say before we pass judgment on your disgraceful performance?'

Huang Bai was tempted to say that Admiral Shen himself had promised an easy victory without having to face any air defence, that he, Huang Bai, had pleaded with Admiral Ming to have more effective early warning and combat patrols, and that Admiral Ming had refused to allow enough practice flights from the carrier to bring pilots and ground crew up to the desirable standard. But stating the obvious was more likely to increase the wrath of this board than decrease it, so he held his tongue.

'No, sir. I have failed, and I have brought dishonour to myself, my family, and the navy.'

'Indeed you have, Captain Huang. You are, as of now, reduced to the rank of Commander. You're actually no longer in command of anything, so consider yourself lucky to retain that rank. If we weren't so short on pilots, you would've been dismissed altogether. You will hand over your command to your replacement as soon as he is appointed. Now go!'

Huang Bai left the conference room, head bowed. He knew that his career was all but over. He would never command a squadron again, let alone the elite naval fighter force. His entire adult life had been devoted to becoming China's best fighter pilot. He had no wife or children. His love life had been restricted to one brief affair and occasional visits to a red-light district. He had no home other than the naval barracks or a tiny cabin on a ship. All for what?

He had to forget the old dreams and focus on the matter that had been occupying his mind since that terrible day in the sea off the Solomon Islands: taking retribution on the pilot who'd flown the F-15 with the tail number 056. He hoped fervently that the admirals were planning another attack against Australia, that he would still be a fighter pilot in the force, and that 056 would survive until the day Huang Bai destroyed it and its pilot.

A replacement for his position was likely to be announced within twenty-four hours, so Huang Bai instructed the taxi driver to take him directly to the office he'd soon vacate at the training base. Once there, he immediately phoned the chief intelligence officer for the carrier squadrons.

'Lui Jingnuo, what can you tell me of these Australian F-15 pilots? Do you have individual names?'

'We have some. Those who were killed in the cowardly attack on our flotilla have been named by the Australian Government.

The others have not. However, we're now scanning our databases to identify them. Our government has been collecting data for years, some of it stolen, from social media platforms, customer lists, medical records, etcetera. We'll find them sooner or later.'

'When you have, could you please give me the list? I'm particularly interested in the pilot of tail number zero five six. If you can assist, I will be forever grateful.'

The following day, Huang Bai handed his responsibilities over to Cheng Hou, the newly appointed captain of the naval fighter squadrons. Just before he left his old office, Lui Jingnuo sent him a note and the list of surviving F-15 pilots. Huang Bai's eyes widened as he read:

This man was hard to identify, as he had no social media profile. Anyway, we found him eventually.

Pentreath, David. Tail number 056. Age sixty-one years, married with three adult children. A retired RAAF engineer and private pilot. No recorded background of military flying.

Huang Bai snarled. He had been ruined by an amateur pilot. If he could achieve anything at all in the rest of his life, it must be to take his revenge. He would make David Pentreath pay.

CHAPTER 8

21 AUGUST 2026

Trevor and Dave had been home for a few weeks when they received tremendous news. Their mate Wayne Swanson was alive, and as well as could be expected after a harrowing ordeal. He was recovering in Honiara Hospital, and from there had sent a report to them both. It related what had happened to him over the past fortnight:

During Wayne's attack run on the carrier, a missile exploded directly in front of his jet. The cloud of shrapnel sounded briefly like hail on his canopy as he flew through it. One engine began to wind down immediately, and the other began vibrating so badly he had to reduce its thrust. He pulled away from his three wingmen, jettisoned his bombs into the ocean, and set a course to return to Henderson Field.

Quickly, it became apparent that the aircraft was dying, so he changed course for Malaita Island. If he had to eject, he had more chance of surviving over land than over open ocean. The vibration worsened. As he approached the highest point of the island, the remaining engine died without warning. He tried to turn back towards the coast, but his airspeed was decaying rapidly, and he'd lost a lot of height.

Suddenly, his options were reduced to one. He had to eject immediately.

The ejection was successful, but scary as hell. Even worse was looking down on thick jungle as far as the eye could see. Not a clearing anywhere. As he drifted closer to the enormous trees, he tried to steer between them, but the foliage was so dense that he couldn't pick any bare ground to aim for. He hit branches halfway between two monsters over 30 metres high, and his chute snagged right near the top of the tallest one. He hung in his harness, stuck at least 20 metres above the ground, on the side of a gully that was thick with undergrowth.

It was still early morning, quite cool, and there were birds everywhere. Brightly coloured parrots were busy in a flowering tree nearby; Kokomos flew overhead regularly. He could hear their slow wingbeats from a long way off.

Other than the noises of the birds, there wasn't a sound. Wayne hung there for hours, wriggling and swinging, trying fruitlessly to dislodge the chute or reach a branch that he could climb onto. As the day got hotter, he became more desperate. The harness was biting into his crotch, and no amount of twisting could relieve the pain. It was clear by then that nobody had seen him eject, or if they had, they couldn't come to rescue him.

He'd have to cut the chute cords. The knife on the inside leg of his flying suit was there for just that purpose. With each cord he severed, he dropped lower. However, by the time he got to the last, he was still at least seven or eight metres above the base of the tree.

He cut it. As he fell, he adopted the correct posture, but he landed on a slope. He rolled backwards, crashing through undergrowth as he went. That slowed his descent. Eventually, he came to a halt, crossways on a fallen log. The pain was so intense that he thought his back was broken.

When he plucked up the courage to roll off the log, he found his back was likely only strained at worst, but he'd hurt his ankle too. Using the light plastic poncho in his emergency kit as a groundsheet, he stretched out under the log for the night. This proved to be a bad idea. The creepy crawlies found him when darkness fell – the jungle floor was alive with them, and the mozzies were nearly as big as his F-15.

Wayne thought he'd probably die on that mountain, but after a few days of scrambling downhill through thick jungle, he was so covered in mosquito, leech, and sandfly bites that he ceased to care. His emergency rations lasted only a couple of days, and his canteen was almost empty when he found a small stream at the base of the mountain. There were tiny fish in it that were impossible to catch, but some freshwater snails that weren't. The jungle had become thinner and drier, so he was able to light a fire and cook the snails in the tin cup from the survival kit.

By the seventh day, Wayne had reached flat land. Here, the creek widened from a trickle to an expanse of deep, still water. The trees on each side met over the middle, creating a tunnel through which it flowed, and the thick bush on both banks made keeping close to it a struggle. He considered trying to swim, but then he saw a muddy slide on the bank. He didn't fancy being croc bait.

Wayne lost count of the days he stumbled along. While his back and ankle improved, he was getting weaker every day from lack of food. Luckily, one day he found an abandoned, overgrown native garden where a few wild edible roots and some sweet potatoes grew.

Two weeks from the day he was shot down, he heard voices. Moments later, around a bend in the creek came a dugout canoe, with two Malaitan kids paddling and jabbering excitedly. He would never forget the sight: they must've been only about seven or eight years old, just wearing shorts, fuzzy heads of hair, and big grins. He stumbled through the undergrowth to the water's edge just in front of them and waved. They froze, eyes as wide as saucers, then turned and paddled furiously away, wailing in fear as they went. Perhaps they'd never seen a white man, Wayne mused. Or perhaps they hadn't been able to tell he was white, as by that time, his flight suit had turned from khaki to black with dirt, and he guessed his face wasn't much cleaner!

Wayne hoped the children would've alerted some adults, but it was twenty-four hours before he again heard voices. This time, they came from a larger dugout canoe, with two Malaitan men and the same two boys in it. The men wore shorts and ragged T-shirts, and their skin was so black it looked bluish. They called out when they saw him. With big smiles and handshakes, they helped him aboard, and handed him some delicious fruit. Oh, man, was he glad to see them!

They put him in the canoe and started downstream. There were no seats: the Malaitans rested on their knees as they paddled. Nor was there room for Wayne to stretch out, and no matter how he tried, he couldn't find a position that wasn't agony for his back.

They reached the ocean after less than an hour. By then, Wayne was in so much pain he begged them to stop – they understood his English quite well, although he couldn't follow more than a few words of theirs. They pulled into a beach fringing a quiet bay.

Dense trees overhung it, so Wayne could lie on the soft, white sand, out of the tropical sun. They left him with some fruit and water, and he understood they were going for help.

Late in the afternoon of the following day, he heard an outboard motor, and into the bay came a long, narrow fibreglass boat. This time, the two Malaitan men were accompanied by a third, who was dressed in neat, casual Western clothes and a baseball cap. He spoke good English, and explained to Wayne that he was the head of a mission some miles further around the coast. He'd brought more food: sandwiches, fruit, and best of all, a thermos of hot coffee. Wayne thought he was in heaven!

It was almost dark when they arrived at the mission, where they looked after him for the night. The next morning, they took him to Afutara, and he was airlifted to Honiara within hours.

CHAPTER 9

14 SEPTEMBER 2026

After calling Wayne and ensuring that he'd be alright, Dave's priority was to service the remaining eleven F-15 Eagles and secure a cache of spares. From his comfortable chair at home, he contacted the maintenance sections of four air forces: those of Saudi Arabia, Israel, Korea, and Japan. All four countries had operated the F-15 Eagle for many years, initially as an air-superiority interceptor, and later as a ground-attack fighter bomber. Dave wanted spares like tyres, hydraulic seals, and fuel and oil filters, as well as a detailed maintenance manual. The Saudis wouldn't respond, the Koreans said that it might upset the Americans if they helped, and the Israelis wanted outrageous prices, but the Japanese were anxious to assist. At no charge, they shipped everything Dave asked for aboard regular Japan Airlines flights into Mascot. From there, the parts were trucked to Williamtown, where maintenance staff waited. Dave drove to Williamtown and spent a few days making sure that every aircraft was thoroughly checked.

* * *

Dave was an avid reader of the *Sydney Morning Herald*, and most mornings, he had time to read the electronic version of the paper on his laptop. He saw how quickly the war disappeared from mention on the front pages of the newspaper, but a rising succession of small articles on the inside pages gave him hope that Australia might not forever be alone in its stand against China. While the governments of Vietnam, Thailand, Malaysia, Singapore, Philippines, Indonesia, and several small Pacific Island states all enjoyed the benefits of trade with and investment from China, statements from these countries showed that they had concerns about China's aggression against Australia and growing dominance in the region. Via official press releases and deliberate leaks, they let the Chinese Government know of these concerns.

Dave called out to Chloe as she busied herself in the kitchen. 'Listen to this, Chlo. There's an English MP calling for the UK Government to back us against China. His name is Jeremy Fortescue, and he's put a question to their prime minister. I'll read the quote here in the Herald: *Sir, it cannot have escaped the notice of this House that the People's Republic of China has attempted an invasion of Australia. The attempt was preceded by covert action, without any declaration of war, by Chinese citizens in Australia on student or tourist visas. By employing some innovative action aided by great good luck, the invasion was foiled. However, it is widely expected that the Chinese will try again.*

'I do not think that I would have to remind the members of this House that in Britain's times of greatest need, Australia has been there to support us. During World Wars One and Two, the cream of Australia's young men came to our aid, and suffered appalling casualties in doing so. Any student of military history can tell you that the Australians fought above their weight, whether it was in the

Somme, North Africa, Britain, Asia, or everywhere else we fought.

Now, surely, it is Britain's turn to support our former colony. Can you advise the House what aid, if any, is being planned? Philpott, the UK PM, has put the question on notice, but that'll put the cat amongst the pigeons, hey Chlo?'

* * *

Trevor's call to Dave one Monday morning was brief. 'We need to talk. Can you meet me at the hangar?'

Ninety minutes later, as Dave settled into the familiar chair in the Bankstown hangar's lunchroom, he found it hard to believe that just a month earlier, he'd sat in the very same chair discussing how he and Trevor could help their nation. So much had happened in those weeks.

Trevor looked solemn. 'Dave, I've been contacted again by Rick Salmon. He says that US spy satellites have been carefully watching Chinese ports, particularly the Zhanjiang base where their two remaining carriers are based, and there's been a lot of activity. Could be that the carriers are preparing to sail, maybe as early as tonight.'

Dave paled, a mental picture of going to war again in the F-15 immediately appearing in his mind.

'Apparently,' Trevor said, 'the US Navy has positioned one of its nuclear subs just outside Chinese territorial waters, despite the presidential decree that the US military stay clear of the conflict. If the Chinese do sail south, the sub will be in position to shadow them, and the Americans will alert us immediately. If they do, it looks like we'll be called upon once more.'

'What about the RAAF pilots?' Dave asked incredulously. 'Is the PM still too scared to give them the F-15s? Trev, you and I are too old for this sort of shit. Haven't we already done our bit?'

'Of course we have, Dave, but we both know that the pollies make the rules, not us. At least the eleven of us are pretty familiar with the F-15s now.'

Dave tapped his fingers on the table. 'What would our move be? Would we meet them up north, or defend from bases in Australia?'

'I think we'd go straight back to Honiara. Obviously, the earlier we stop the Chinese, the better – and the Solomon Islanders have been supportive, no little thanks to your personal contact with their PM. They've given us permission to use Henderson Field again. It could be that allowing us to do so last time burned their bridges with the Chinese, so they're throwing their lot one hundred percent behind us. One thing in our favour is that the two carriers the Chinese have left are the smaller ski-jump type, without catapults. They'll use the Shenyang J-15 fighters, but with restricted payload, so they're limited in both range and firepower.'

'Shit, Trev,' Dave said, grimacing, 'the J-15 is based on the Sukhoi Su-33, and you know the original can go toe-to-toe with an F-15 anytime. They'd have the latest in long-range air-to-air missiles, too. Eleven against probably thirty or forty of them, us without the element of surprise, and with only guns.'

Trevor sighed. 'Yeah, not the best odds. But what else can we do?'

Dave shook his head. 'How am I going to tell Chloe?'

* * *

When Dave's alarm woke him at 6.30 the next morning, he was relieved that there'd been no call from Trevor. Maybe, he hoped, no news was good news. Maybe they were off the hook; maybe the Chinese hadn't mustered another invasion fleet after all.

Still, he didn't eat much for breakfast, as his stomach was knotted with tension. At his age and stage in life, he certainly didn't want to go back to war.

He jumped when his phone rang at 10 a.m., and his arm felt leaden as he reached for it. Trevor's name was on the screen.

'Not good news, I'm afraid, old mate,' Trevor said, false cheer doing little to hide the exhaustion in his voice. 'I'm organising all the others to get to Williamtown early tomorrow. If you want to come with me, I'll pick you up at 5.30 a.m.'

The next morning, as they wound their way onto the M2 motorway tunnel in Trevor's Mercedes, both men were in a sombre mood. Trevor talked as he drove.

'It seems that heavy cloud is covering the east coast of China at the moment, so the satellites can't see much. However, the US sub reported that after a slow exit from Zhanjiang, the carriers have been joined by multiple destroyers and smaller vessels, and the combined fleet has turned south.' He looked across at Dave, who had his head back against the headrest, his eyes closed. After a pause, Trevor continued. 'The RAAF strategic planning guys will brief us this morning, and together, we'll figure out a plan of action. I hate to say it, but it's going to be tougher than last time. They'll be expecting us, and they're bound to have much stronger CAPs, with AWACS out front and on both sides of the fleet.'

Dave nodded. 'Their J-15s may be limited in what fuel and weapons they can carry, but they're still pretty hot fighters. With AWACS up and ahead of the fleet, they can probably track and engage us at least a hundred nautical miles out, and if their air-to-air missiles are any good, we'll have no chance unless we go in at wave-top height again. Bloody hell, Trev, I thought we were done with this bullshit!'

The briefing at Williamtown didn't offer much to offset their fears. About the only comfort they had was that they'd be back in the air in one of the best fighters ever built. Outwardly, all pilots professed confidence that their Eagles would carry them through, but Dave suspected that he was about to face his greatest challenge ever, and he wasn't at all sure he could handle it.

* * *

Huang Bai had considerable difficulty coming to terms with being just another fighter pilot in a squadron, one with no authority above any of the others. Worse was the fact that as most of his special pilots had gone down with the *Mao Tse Tung*, and the operations of his elite training school had been suspended during the war against Australia, none of his colleagues had been subjected to the rigorous training he believed was essential. Nevertheless, he knew that he was lucky to be aboard at all. The new air-wing captain hadn't wanted him, but the shortage of experienced pilots after the debacle in the Solomons had forced Captain Cheng Hou to accept him.

Huang Bai had to share a tiny cabin in this smaller carrier, the *Liaoning*. It was a windowless cubicle, just big enough for two bunks and a tiny table with one upright chair. Air that was either too hot or too cold came from a rattly vent in the ceiling. The room was lit by a single naked bulb also in the ceiling, so if one occupant was reading, the others had to put up with a bright light directly overhead.

The single consolation was that Huang Bai would not be flying the FC-31, but the older J-15, which he much preferred. It was sleeker than the FC-31, and its long nose drooped slightly, giving it the appearance of a raptor looking for prey. With a J-15, a good pilot could confidently go head-to-head with an F-15. He looked forward to finally having that opportunity.

The *Liaoning* would normally carry up to twenty-four fighters, plus two AWACS aircraft, and a few helicopters. For this voyage, however, they were carrying a number of helicopter gunships that were to support the landing of troops, so the fighter complement was down to twelve. The sister ship, the *Shandong*, had the same capacity. The two carriers had been in service for more than eight years, and that time had been used to hone their crews and equipment into highly efficient fighting units. Every seaman aboard was expert at his job.

This time, the fleet sailed under a different admiral, one who'd already decreed that at least one AWACS and a CAP of four fighters would be aloft at all times. The Chinese Navy South Sea Fleet would not be caught napping again. Left behind to follow later were the slow troopships that had hampered operations before. This time, the armada comprised the two carriers, six powerful cruisers, and ten destroyers. Huang Bai was certain that the criminal group flying stolen F-15 Eagles would be first humiliated, then finally destroyed.

★ ★ ★

At midafternoon, Dave, Trevor, and their nine colleagues crossed the dense jungles of Guadalcanal on descent into Henderson Field. White cumulus clouds dotted an azure sky, dark green mountains spread out below, and crescent-shaped offshore reefs enclosed turquoise lagoons. It was a very beautiful sight from altitude, but Dave knew that both the jungle and the water held dark secrets, from the days of head-hunting to the bloody battles in 1942.

Dave's spine had begun to ache after an hour in the fighter's unyielding seat, and by the time they landed, he felt like his lower back and hips would never move freely again. He longed to just stretch out on a soft bed. They knew the Chinese fleet was still far distant, so they stayed at the Mendana. At least there, the air conditioning was reliable and effective, and the pool clean. They had nothing to do but wait. Tension rose by the hour. They hid their fears by bantering about all sorts of things, from politics to sports.

At 4 p.m. the following day, the latest satellite photos and sub reports confirmed the position of the Chinese fleet. At its present course and speed, it would be just 200 miles north-east of Honiara by dawn the next morning.

Trevor pulled Alan, Nick, and Dave from sitting by the pool, and asked them to come to his room. As soon as the door was closed, he said, 'Something's up. The Chinese aren't stupid. They *must* know we're here this time, yet they're sailing even closer to us. What do you think they're playing at?'

Bracing his hands on the table, Dave studied the map laid out before them. 'Maybe they're confident that by being prepared, they can take us on and kill us before we do any damage.'

'It's too obvious,' Nick said. 'Perhaps they're trying to lure us into a trap. They'll probably have a number of interceptors up at all times, and have them stacked at various levels so that no matter how we attack, they can meet us head-on. With radar-guided missiles, they could knock most of us out of the sky long before we get within a hundred miles of the fleet.'

Dave nodded in agreement, and shivered at the thought.

'Could they be planning a pre-emptive strike?' Alan asked. 'They may be limited in range, but if they carried drop tanks and no bombs, they could hit us here on the ground with guns only.'

Trevor nodded. 'It's a strong possibility. With just eleven of us, we can't maintain a CAP over Honiara, and there are no long-range radars in the Solomons. We're really wide open to a surprise attack.'

'It's too risky to stay put,' Nick said. 'We have to move as quickly as possible. Dave, what's that long strip on New Georgia Island called?'

'Munda,' Dave said. 'I think it would be the only strip in the Solomons long enough for an F-15, other than Henderson. It's a good strip.'

'How come?' Alan asked. 'It's only used for local traffic, isn't it?'

Dave answered, 'Like Henderson Field, the original strip at Munda was carved out of the jungle by the Japanese in 1942. When the US Marines took it, it was extended and widened to take bombers. Decades later, it became an international airport, though that title is a little grandiose. It'll take jets, but the facilities are pretty basic. The terminal is just a corrugated iron shed.'

Their more immediate problem was that the Munda airfield had no lights. The single landing strip was bordered by jungle-covered hills on one side, and an ocean bay on the other. Landing on a black strip on a black night in an F-15 was too frightening to contemplate. As it was already close to 4.30 p.m., they had only ninety minutes of light left to get from the Honiara hotel to Munda.

The eleven pilots checked their mounts and strapped in as quickly as they could. Ten jets roared into life and taxied for take-off. One didn't. An electronic glitch in Eagle 056 interfered with its automatic start sequence, and Dave didn't recognise the problem quickly enough. The left engine's igniters had failed to fire at the correct time, and 30 or 40 litres of raw Jet A-1 fuel was pumped into the engine, to lie unburned. Dave chided himself for his carelessness. He'd have to sit for half an hour, strapped in the cockpit, waiting for the excess fuel to drain and evaporate off before he could begin the start sequence again.

He called on the radio. 'Eagle Leader, this is Eagle Zero Five Six. Trev, I've had a starting problem. I'll be delayed half an hour. I'll catch up.'

'Roger, Zero Five Six,' came the instant reply.

Ten F-15 Eagles made it into Munda just on dusk. Night fell quickly in the tropics, and as Dave descended into the Munda circuit area, he could see only two pinpricks of light in a black void. These portable floodlights – one at each end of the strip – had been hastily set up just for him by the crews of the three PNG Hercules that had preceded the F-15s. Otherwise, the airfield and the hills alongside it were indistinguishable.

His eyes flicked rapidly between his instrument panel and the two lights. Only by making a wide sweeping turn out over the invisible water, and a curving approach back towards the field, could he keep the lights in his vision. When he was in the last 100 feet of descent, the twin spotlights attached to the front leg of his undercarriage finally picked up treetops, then open ground, then smooth tarmac.

At 180 knots, Dave swept over the first floodlight. It wasn't his best touchdown, but at that moment, anything short of a crash felt good. *That's another of my nine lives used up,* he mused, as he taxied to the parking area.

That night, the pilots stayed in Munda's only accommodation, two to each small, dark room in the old single-level building. Reed mats covered the cracks in the concrete floors, and paint peeled from the fibro walls. Dave slept fitfully on the sagging mattress.

He knew it was the same for all of them.

The alarm at 3.30 a.m. came far too soon. They departed in total darkness, the only light on the strip again coming from the portable spotlights at each end. The crewmen hadn't slept: they'd laboured through the night, removing the F-15s' external fuel tanks and fitting the 950-kg Mark 84 bombs that the C-17s had brought to Honiara from Australia. Once they'd finished loading, the three Hercules had departed for Rabaul, a safe haven well to the west in PNG.

Dave had a scary moment when he lifted the F-15's nose into the inky blackness and shifted his eyes from outside the canopy to the instrument panel. For a few seconds, he couldn't feel whether he was climbing or descending, flying level or in a turn. It was a sensation feared by all IFR pilots. He had to totally trust in the fighter's instruments and ignore what his senses told him.

Within minutes, he could see the first signs of dawn. He and the other F-15s climbed to 3000 feet to give them safe height over the mountainous islands surrounding New Georgia Sound. They'd planned to drop down once they'd cleared the islands to avoid discovery by the Chinese AWACS aircraft, but just as they passed Malaita Island, a call came over the radio from the ground crew at Munda.

'Eagle Strike, this is Munda base. Scratch mission. Repeat, scratch mission. Return to Munda.'

The relief flooding Dave's body was almost immediately swamped by dread. What could cause the mission to be scrubbed? Had something gone dreadfully wrong?

They circled for a few minutes to burn off some weight, and to allow dawn light to reveal the strip. Rusting hulks of US Marine landing barges still littered the foreshore, and there were several aircraft wrecks also from World War Two that were still visible in the water. He could identify a Wildcat fighter and a Japanese twin-engine bomber, even though they'd lain there for more than eight decades.

Landing was easy this time. The pilots quickly gathered at the rough building that served as an international terminal. Fly-spotted fans powered by a small generator circulated the heavy air, but did nothing to cool it. They all rolled the tops of their sweat-stained flight suits down around their waists, and gratefully accepted bottles of cold water proffered by the ground crew.

Trevor called the group to order. 'Rick Salmon has been on the radio. He has some news for us: Henderson Field has just been bombed from about ten thousand feet. Although the bombing wasn't very accurate, and it seems there were no casualties, it has badly damaged the old terminal building, which is still burning, and has punched large holes in the hardstand where the F-15s were parked yesterday. The attacking aircraft almost certainly came from the two carriers.'

Nick and Alan high-fived each other. 'We dodged that one, boys,' Nick said.

Dave reacted quite differently. 'Jesus,' he said. 'We've dragged the poor bloody Solomon Islanders into this fight, and now they're copping the punishment. Bastard bloody Chinese!'

Trevor put his hand on Dave's shoulder. 'At least the good news far outweighs the bad, Dave. No islanders were killed, or even injured, and damage to the airport has been restricted to the old building, some parking areas, and bush outside the airport boundary. That can easily be rebuilt.'

Dave agreed. 'Yeah, Trev, you're right. Thank God for that.'

'There's more good news,' Trevor said, and grinned. 'At 4.30

this morning, probably just after the Chinese jets left the carriers, two Australian Collins Class subs intercepted the Chinese fleet. They sank one carrier and damaged another. The Chinese fleet has changed course and seems to be heading back north.'

Relieved sighs echoed around the bare metal walls of the so-called terminal, as the pilots clapped each other on the shoulders and exchanged smiles.

'*Two* Collins Class subs?' Dave asked.

'Yes, two. Apparently, the Navy dockyard at Fremantle has worked night and day to get the second sub through its maintenance early.'

Relief flooded the pilots and ground crew. Dave sagged into an old couch that served as the only furniture.

'What do we do now?' asked Alan.

'I must inject a note of caution to our optimism,' Trevor said. 'Before the carriers turned back, they refuelled and relaunched their aircraft. It could be that those aircraft are continuing to head south.'

Dave frowned. 'Where would they go? They couldn't have been carrying a full fuel load, if they bombed Henderson.'

Trevor raised his eyebrows and spread his hands. 'We don't know, but it's possible they were met by aerial tankers out of mainland China. They may be heading for somewhere closer to Australia. The word is that we'd better hotfoot it back home. The Hercs are due to return shortly, and we'll swap bombs for fuel tanks, then get going as quickly as we can.'

* * *

Sunday morning's Qantas flight 7538, a Boeing 787 Dreamliner from Seoul, South Korea, was due to land at Darwin International

Airport at 7 a.m., and it was right on schedule. As usual, the Jindalee over-the-horizon radar stations at Laverton in Western Australia and in Alice Springs, Northern Territory, had picked up its return signal not long after it passed Singapore. The operators in both stations noted an unusually strong return, but thought little of it.

Darwin's Aviation Weather Services radar was capable of detecting storms at a radius of almost 150 nautical miles, but their aircraft tracking radar wasn't very accurate. It didn't need to be to control normal civilian traffic. On that morning, the Darwin radar operator, Adrian Thorburn, also noticed an unusually strong paint from the Qantas jet. However, the transponder signal confirming its identity and height was perfectly normal. At a distance of 100 nautical miles, approval was passed to the Boeing to leave flight level 400, descend to 9000 feet, and reduce speed to 250 knots.

As it was the only international arrival in his shift, Thorburn wasn't focusing on the radar return quite as much as he might have. During his instructions to the Qantas captain on the approach, he noticed that the radar paint had split into five distinct images, while the much stronger transponder signal stayed with just one. That simply didn't make sense. As he watched, the five images separated. Only the first complied with the instructions he'd given to the Qantas flight – to continue on descent – while the four others levelled off on a heading to proceed directly over the airport. Thorburn called to his supervisor, Brian Thompson.

'Hey, Brian, come and look at this. Something very weird is happening. Maybe the computer's having a meltdown.'

Thompson's eyes widened as he peered over his colleague's shoulder. He grabbed his powerful binoculars and trained them on the incoming flight. To his utter astonishment, he saw four very large jets in close formation directly above the Qantas Boeing 787. He recognised them immediately as Airbus A380s.

The four huge airliners roared overhead. At a distance of about two and a half nautical miles past the airport, they began to disgorge hundreds of tiny black objects.

'What the hell?' Thompson shouted. 'They're dropping something over the Army barracks… shit, they're paratroopers!'

He dropped the binoculars and grabbed the nearest telephone. The number for the Robertson Barracks, home of the Australian Army's 1st Brigade, was on speed-dial, but they didn't answer for thirty long seconds.

In the space of three minutes, one thousand six hundred Chinese troops landed in the middle of the Army compound. The few sentries were overwhelmed without even firing a shot, as they thought it must've been some sort of exercise that nobody had told them about.

Of the three thousand five hundred Army regulars resident at the barracks, seven hundred were absent on weekend leave. Almost all of the others were enjoying a normal Sunday off work. The invading force captured them easily.

The Chinese paratroopers only had to drive a short distance in commandeered trucks to take control of Darwin's International Airport. Four hours later, six air-to-air tankers arrived, together with the twenty-four J-15 fighter jets that had taken off from the carriers just north of the Solomon Islands.

Of the few Australian Army regulars outside the base at the time of the parachute drop, only ten were fully armed. They'd been on a bush exercise 100 km south of Darwin, near Adelaide River, and were on their way back to barracks in three Hawkei light combat vehicles. Tired and badly in need of showers after an arduous night hike, they were listening to music on the radio when the program was interrupted by an announcer who'd been coming to work as the parachutes left the four jetliners. He excitedly described what he'd seen.

In the lead vehicle, Lieutenant Andy Moore dismissed the announcement as a prank, but decided to check in with the Army base just in case. There was no reply. He sat bolt upright and turned to the corporal driving the Hawkei.

'If this is for real, we'd better get off the main road. Take the next turn to the right and let's find some cover. We'll hold out until we get some clarification on what's going on.'

Twenty-four hours after the airborne assault on the Army barracks, three unremarkable Chinese-registered cargo ships unloaded over a thousand more troops into Port Darwin, along with tanks, field guns, anti-aircraft guns and missile batteries, and four-wheel-drive trucks. This process was repeated with the arrival of more ships in the following days. In 2015, Chinese interests had paid $506 million to secure a ninety-nine-year lease on Port Darwin. Many had criticised the deal by the Liberal Party government of the day, which had meant that a Chinese company was already in place to control the movement, loading and unloading of all shipping.

The next to arrive was the *Shandong*. Although damaged, it had reversed course yet again and brought nine ground-attack helicopter gunships. They flew off the carrier one by one.

Inside a week, the Chinese had twenty-four fighters, nine gunships, numerous transport aircraft, twenty thousand troops, and an array of army transport trucks and weaponry all based in and around Darwin's airport.

CHAPTER 10

19 SEPTEMBER 2026

The Australian Prime Minister and his cabinet had to accept that while the F-15s had chased a decoy fleet, the Chinese had succeeded in landing an invasion force on Australian soil. It was small compared to the one the F-15s had repelled in July, which had included forty troop ships and would've put even more fully equipped soldiers onshore, but it was still a strong force. The Australian Army would no doubt slow their advance south from Darwin, but without air cover, the end result was a foregone conclusion.

* * *

While the ground crew hastily removed bombs from the F-15s' underwing pylons and replaced them with external fuel tanks, the eleven pilots gathered in the deserted international terminal at Honiara to hear the news coming in from Australia.

Disgusted, Trevor threw his gloves down and ran a handkerchief around his sweaty throat. Even at the early hour, the heat was oppressive, and their khaki-green flight suits were uncomfortably warm. 'Dave, the bastards have blindsided us, and we fell for it hook, line, and sinker. *Shit!* We've got to get home as fast as we can. We'll go direct to Cairns and regroup there before figuring out our next move.'

Dave hurried to his aircraft with mixed emotions. He desperately feared for the future of his country now that the Chinese had successfully landed a force in Australia. At the same time, however, he couldn't help but savour the intense relief that he and his colleagues wouldn't have to attack the invasion fleet. He knew that it would've almost certainly been a suicide mission.

The three-hour flight to Cairns International Airport was uneventful, but as the F-15s approached the coast, they descended into a coastal tropical storm. From brilliant sunshine, they plunged into a grey soup, where strong winds buffeted the aircraft. The tower reported a crosswind of 25 knots, gusting 30, which was right on F-15's limit. *Why*, Dave pondered, *is it that coastal airstrips are always built at right angles to the prevailing wind?*

With no horizon visible, they descended on instruments, turning one at a time when instructed by the tower. The airstrip materialised out of the mist and rain at 200 feet, but even that last descent was a battle against the crosswind. Dave was immensely relieved when he could switch all systems off and climb stiffly down the side of the aeroplane.

Thankfully, airport formalities were dispensed with, and the eleven pilots were bussed in clean and air-conditioned comfort to the Novotel, a luxurious multi-storey hotel near the foreshore. Dave barely noticed the beautiful view over the huge hotel pool to the bay beyond from his fifth-floor room. He lingered under a hot shower, slipped on a hotel robe, then eased his aching frame into a comfortable chair and called Chloe.

'Hi, gorgeous. How's my favourite girl?'

'Oh, darling, so glad to hear your voice. Are you okay? Is Trev alright? You both looked so tired and drawn before you even left.'

'We're both okay. Tired, and a bit stiff, but okay. Just getting old, I guess. You've heard that the whole damn thing was a waste of time?'

'Yes. Oh my God, it's awful news about Darwin. What do you think will happen now?'

'We're still in the dark, Chlo, but I'm hoping the politicians have cleared the way for RAAF pilots to take over the F-15s. Otherwise, I could guess that we'll be thrown back into the fray fairly soon.'

'Surely not again! Dave, you can't!' Chloe shuddered. 'But if they do make you fly again, where will you go next?'

'We'll probably try to head off the Chinese moving south, I guess.'

Chloe and Dave talked for a few minutes more, but Dave badly needed some rest. He stretched out on the wide, comfortable bed and dozed off, without even turning on the TV for a news update. If he had, he probably wouldn't have slept at all.

Three hours later, Minister Rick Salmon met the eleven pilots in a small conference room. He was accompanied by several Air Force and Army people who Dave didn't know. His head was still re-flying the landing in the storm, so he didn't begin to concentrate until the briefing began in earnest.

'Like the old saying goes, there's good news and bad news,' Salmon began. 'The Chinese J-15s overflew Guadalcanal. At first light, they met up with large air tankers that had flown from one of their new bases in the Spratly Islands. Once refuelled in mid-air, they flew on with the tankers on a south-westerly heading, arriving at Darwin after it had been taken by the paratroopers.'

Sighing, Salmon rubbed at his forehead. 'Essentially,' he said, 'we're in a game of chess with five players. First, obviously, we have the Chinese. They claim they are rightly defending their assets in Australia from illegal resumption by our government — who are, second, doing everything in their power to defend our sovereignty, with limited and handicapped resources.

'Third, we have the US Government. The mutual defence treaty we've had for many decades was undermined by the Republican regime, and the current president fears backlash from voters who are against getting involved with any more wars. As we all know, since 2016, the USA has had two periods where it has become quite parochial in its interests, to the detriment of the free world.'

Salmon paused to make sure the tired pilots were concentrating on him. They were, and he continued. 'Fourth, we have the US military. We've backed them in many campaigns. Our guys always punched above their weight, and therefore earned quite a reputation. Almost without exception, the high commands of the US Army, Air Force, and Navy believe they should be in this current fight, boots and all, to help us. They're supported by many politicians, and a fair slice of the US population. Support for us seems to be growing. Some of the military heads have come as close as they've dared to flouting US Government policy. It's not to go past this room, but I can tell you that we had a lot of inside help in stealing those F-15s.'

The eleven Eagle pilots exchanged glances, wondering what covert activities there'd been.

'Right now,' Salmon said, 'the US Navy has one of their newest carriers heading from Honolulu to the Coral Sea, and they have several nuclear subs shadowing Chinese subs in both the Coral and Arafura Seas. The US Army has had a rotating garrison at Katherine, south of Darwin, for many years. They've beefed that up from about a thousand combat troops to three thousand, with more coming. The US Air Force had a squadron of F-22s and a squadron of F-15E Strike Eagles rotating through Darwin from Guam. They've just requested to bring both squadrons to Katherine for extended "exercises". So, if the US Government's position were to change in our favour, the US forces, combined with what's left of ours, could quickly deal with the Chinese invasion.

'The fifth player is, of course, your Eagle Force. I know it's been tough, and you've lost a lot of good men. But, like Churchill said… you know the quote.' He hesitated, and looked at each man in turn. *Nine of the best*, he thought, before continuing.

'The Chinese Government is squawking loudly that the US is trying to bully them. Militarily, they have a huge army and are very strong at home, but their armed forces aren't really geared for a war so far from the mainland. They obviously expected a quick victory from their first invasion fleet. As we speak, they're flying more troops and tanks into Darwin. We don't think they'll risk bringing troops in by ship now. They'll probably try to consolidate their forces before making a breakout either south to Alice Springs and on to Adelaide, or south-east to Brisbane. We have our Army preparing for both eventualities. If the Yanks don't come in to help, it'll take our every resource to prevent them from achieving either goal.

'Our greatest problem is air support. While the Chinese maintain air superiority, our troops are hamstrung. I'll let my colleagues from the RAAF and Army discuss our tactics from here. I just want to say that you continue to be crucial to us, and we'll all be praying for your safety and success.'

Wing Commander Roy Pearce introduced himself. He explained that he was an ex-Hornet pilot, who now instructed fighter tactics in Hawks at Williamtown. He looked like a typical RAAF senior officer: medium height, trim and fit, neat moustache, grey hair. From a distance, he and Trevor could've been mistaken for twins, but for the fact that Pearce was twenty-five years younger.

'You've done an amazing job under the limitations,' he said, 'some of which, I'm glad to say, we are redressing. We've pulled the AIM-9M Sidewinders and their targeting systems from the remaining derelict Hornets at Williamtown, and will progressively fit them to your F-15s. That work is starting as we speak. We'll initially fit two aircraft – it'll take a few days, so they'll remain behind while the rest move on.

'The other good news is that we're fitting bomb and air-to-ground missile systems to twelve of our Hawk trainers. They'll be ready within a week or two. Our aim, meanwhile, is to contain the Chinese. Tomorrow, nine of your F-15s will transit to Katherine, via Borroloola. After you pass Borroloola, you must descend to low level – no higher than fifteen hundred feet above sea level and five hundred AGL – and remain there right across the southern part of Arnhem Land to Tindal RAAF base at Katherine. The Chinese are certain to have AWACS aloft looking for you, and probably will have a CAP over Darwin.

'The naval J-15s that the Chinese flew off their two smaller carriers are limited in range, radar, and weaponry. Even so, they can pick you up at a hundred miles, and their radar-guided missiles are good for close to that distance. The only way to avoid being targeted is to stay low. Very low.'

Someone murmured, 'We know all about that.'

Pearce continued. 'We're still figuring out the best plan of attack, but ideally, once the Hawks are available, we can completely change tactics. The Hawks will take over the low-level attack role. Your F-15s will then provide top cover – your only task will be protecting the Hawks. Of course, that's if the Chinese don't make a pre-emptive move.'

Details followed about the current position of Australian troops and tanks south of Darwin city, and what the F-15s' targets might be. Their imperative was to knock out the Chinese fighters, on the ground or in the air.

The F-15 pilots had one night in the five-star hotel. Tomorrow, nine of them would be heading back to war.

CHAPTER 11

Ordinarily, the flight from Cairns across the base of Cape York Peninsula and along the remote coast of the Gulf of Carpentaria would've been a pleasant one. Dense bush thinned out as the east coast was left behind, and undulating hills flattened out to the gulf's low-lying coastal plains, with lazy brown rivers snaking slowly towards the sea. Nearing the Northern Territory border, the ground rose, and an escarpment ran parallel to the coast. Periodically, rocky red gorges split this escarpment. Each was full of sparkling blue water and lined with lush greenery, starkly contrasting with the dry surrounding bush. It was country that few Australians knew existed, and even fewer had seen.

But today, Trevor was too concerned with what might pop up on his radar screen to admire the scenery below. He regularly switched on the powerful radar in his aircraft's nose for a few seconds. It could scan close to 200 nautical miles ahead of the formation while at their cruise altitude of 40,000 feet. Of course, using the radar had one big drawback: it announced his fighter's presence to any AWACS listening out.

He needn't have worried. No electronic blips appeared on his screen, and the formation passed over Borroloola on schedule. It then began its planned descent.

The route from Borroloola to Katherine crossed an entirely different landscape. To the right of the track lay the virtually uninhabited Arnhem Land plateau, a vast conglomeration of rocky escarpments and sparsely treed plains. To the left was open grassland, most of which had long ago been divided into huge cattle stations. From this point, the F-15s stayed low. Even with a loaded weight of 20 tonnes, moving across the ground at nearly 1000 kilometres per hour, the F-15s were bounced around by the early morning thermals. Dave was glad that they'd left early, as by midafternoon, it would be a bone-shaking ride anywhere below 12,000 feet.

Katherine's long airstrip was shared by military and civil aircraft. They streaked across it at 1000 feet, and one by one pulled 4G turns to slow down before joining wide base turns and landing on Runway 32. After taxiing in, they were directed to revetments on the eastern side of the strip, so the F-15s were shut down under individual covers some distance apart from each other. Obviously, attack by Chinese J-15s was a possibility, and nobody wanted to make it easy by lining the fighters up close together.

Separation might work to mitigate damage from air attack, but it hadn't worked when the Chinese infiltrators had crept in three months ago. The blackened and twisted remains of RAAF 75 Squadron's F-35s lay under more revetments on the south-east corner of the field. In contrast, a squadron of visiting USAF aircraft were parked in neat rows, as if daring the Chinese to touch them. The whole base was busy, with the RAAF and Army taking advantage of the US presence, which deterred the enemy from putting in an appearance.

The nine F-15 pilots climbed from air-conditioned cockpits into hot, dry, still air that reeked of burned jet fuel. Dave wanted to get out of his flight suit and under a shower as quickly as possible – though he would've agreed that the dry heat was easier to tolerate than Honiara's heavy humidity.

In normal times, Katherine had many tourists stopping over to visit the nearby Katherine Gorge, but the arrival of the Chinese forces in Darwin had sent tourists and many locals fleeing southward. Now, the pilots had their pick of houses in the Tindal township, which was part of the airbase, or of several motels in the city some 15 kilometres north. The hotel they chose was convenient, if not anywhere near five-star.

Dave, Alan, Nick and Trevor agreed to meet for a pre-dinner drink at a bar across the street from the hotel. As they walked in, wearing casual clothes, Dave spotted a group of USAF pilots still in their khaki-green flight suits. He stopped abruptly, causing Nick to bump into him. 'Oh dear, this could be awkward,' Trevor said. 'Let's hope they don't know who we are.'

'Why, what's the problem?' Alan asked.

Trevor grimaced. 'These guys would rotate between here and Guam. They probably used to fly the F-15s we've stolen.'

'Shit, of course. Let's head to the opposite end of the bar.'

They bought their beers, and found a space well away from the Americans – who, Dave noticed, all looked like carbon copies. They were all young, of medium height, solidly built, fit, and clean-shaven, with close-cropped crew cuts. They kept glancing towards the Australian trio. After fifteen minutes or so, one of them approached.

'Hiya,' he drawled, 'you're some of the guys who brought in the F-15s at midday, right?'

Nobody answered immediately, but then Trevor nodded.

The American waved towards his friends. 'Come meet these Aussies! They're flying the Eagles.' He turned back to the Australians, stuck out his hand, and said, 'The name's Hank. I'm really pleased to meet y'all.'

After introductions all round, the Americans wanted to know if the stories were true. Were they all retired RAAF pilots, who hadn't flown fighters for years? What had it really been like to attack that Chinese convoy? How had they evaded radar detection for so long? How good were the missiles and guns on the Chinese ships? Had one of them actually shot down an FC-31?

At the last question, there was a hesitation before Trevor said, 'Dave here did. He got one.'

Dave instantly became their hero. They demanded he recount the aerial dogfight, their eyes shining as they absorbed every detail of a real-world kill. Dave was diffident. He couldn't forget that he hadn't just downed an aeroplane, but a young man, who no doubt had a father, a mother, a girlfriend or wife, and perhaps children too.

One of the Americans asked Dave if he'd placed a star on the side of his cockpit, to indicate a kill. 'No,' said Dave. 'I hadn't thought to do that.'

'Ah!' Hank cried. 'You gotta. We'll organise that for you. What's your tail number?'

'Zero five six,' Trevor replied for Dave. 'And you'd better add a ship as well. It was Dave's bombs that sunk the *Mao Tse Tung*.'

★ ★ ★

At 4 a.m. the following day, the F-15 pilots assembled for a quick breakfast in the RAAF ready-room. On the way there, they passed the black and twisted frames of the burned-out F-35 fighters. None were salvageable; they'd been abandoned by the RAAF. The partially severed tail of one twisted forlornly in the gentle breeze. In contrast, not far away sat a dozen pristine matt-black USAF F-22 fighters and a grey KC-10 aerial tanker.

Dave couldn't help remarking to the other pilots: 'There we are, guys. Twelve of the best fighters in the world – and nearby, no doubt, twelve of the best-trained pilots – here in Australia as part of our mutual defence cooperation, and the Yank pollies won't let them join in the fun. Instead, us poor old fellas are sent into battle with one arm tied behind our backs.'

In the ready-room, they hastily grabbed bacon, eggs, toast and coffee, but Dave was still disgruntled. He struggled to concentrate as Trevor briefed them on their mission.

'As you know, the broad plan is to contain the Chinese for a few days, and whittle down the numbers of J-15s if we can,' Trevor said. 'Obviously, they outnumber us almost three to one, so we're going to have to be extremely careful. In about a week, the Hawks will arrive, and they'll take over the ground-attack role, backed up by Army helicopter gunships when it's safe for them to operate.'

'The helicopters can only fly if we achieve air superiority,' Nick said. 'How the heck are we going to do that when they outnumber us three to one?'

'By being clever, and by utilising our advantages over the J-15.'

Alan raised his mug. 'When are the other F-15s joining us, the two that are being fitted with Sidewinders? And when will *we* get 'em?'

'I was coming to that,' Trevor replied. 'You'll get Sidewinders as soon as the RAAF engineers can acquire and reinstall the systems – and the first two to be equipped won't be joining us. Details are hush-hush, but I can tell you that the next Chinese troop-carrying aircraft that passes within two hundred nautical miles of Henderson Field might get a big shock.'

He gave a brief, sharklike grin, before sobering once more. 'We're getting reports from Army personnel hiding in the bush not far from Darwin. They tell us that the Chinese do have at least one AWACS up at all times, with two fighters sitting on the ramp ready to scramble. The AWACS go high, and are obviously scanning in anticipation of a bombing attack. All of the remaining J-15s are on alert. The Chinese will have civilian observers in the bush between Darwin and Katherine, probably put in place long before the invasion. So, no matter how careful we are, they'll know when we're coming.'

Again, Dave began to experience the feeling of total inadequacy for the task ahead. He couldn't help but think that his luck could only take him so far. He shook his head and focused on Trevor's briefing.

'Five of us will go in very low, two hundred feet above terrain, so the Chinese radars won't be able to pick us out of the ground clutter. The other four F-15s will be flying high cover at about fifty thousand feet. Those decoys will probably be spotted a hundred miles out, maybe even further. We expect that the Chinese will scramble all their fighters. The five low-level fighters must reach Darwin at about the same time as the Chinese scramble. But instead of bombing, we'll be travelling light – guns and main fuel tanks only – so we'll have maximum performance. With them just taking off, we'll hopefully be able to knock down one or two in a single pass before hitting full afterburner and climbing out.

'The decoy F-15s will turn and run as soon as the Chinese scramble, so they'll always be out of range of the enemy. Any pursuing J-15s will have their radars looking ahead, so unless they get a warning from their base, they won't know about our second wave coming up behind them. That gives us a second chance at knocking out a couple more. The decoy F-15s will only return to Katherine when any pursuing J-15s have run out of endurance.'

Dave repeatedly told himself not to think about his chances of survival, and to just concentrate on flying the aeroplane. He was allocated his customary position: last in the low-level flight of five. As they headed out to the waiting Eagles, he remembered the old military saying that grand battle plans last until the first shot is fired. He hoped this one might be an exception.

The bright lights inside the shelter were harsh on Dave's tired eyes. He hadn't slept well, and rising at 4 a.m. had been brutal. Clambering up the ladder to the cockpit of his F-15, he was startled to see a red star and an outline of a sinking ship painted just below the cockpit sill. 'Blow me down,' he muttered, 'those Yanks must've organised this while we were at dinner last night.'

Some pilots loved night flying. Dave never had. After take-off, he struggled to keep Number Four – Alan – in sight. He relaxed a little once he'd closed up into his position in the tight right-echelon formation. First light was now just visible on the horizon to their right. Trevor, who was in the lead, would've set his forward-looking GPS to give 200-foot terrain clearance, so he'd receive both audio and visual warnings when the ground ahead forced a climb or descent. Dave and the other three wingmen had to stay with him, following his flight path exactly, without monitoring surrounding terrain. It was essential to trust the leader implicitly, and Dave did. Otherwise, thundering over those low hills, just higher than the treetops, would've been too scary. Particularly when covering a kilometre every four seconds.

The sky was turning from black to deep blue as they approached Darwin's airport. Five miles out, they changed from the tight echelon formation to line-astern, with six-second intervals between aircraft. One after another, they pulled up to 2000 feet, and from that height, they could make out the airport directly ahead. Dave immediately saw that Trevor's plan was working. The Chinese jets were racing along the runway and launching into the gradually lightening sky. With impeccable timing, the F-15s swooped down on the unsuspecting enemy.

Dave could see Trevor's twin afterburners converging with those of a J-15 that was just entering a steep climb. There was a flash, and for a second, he thought the two aircraft had collided. Then he saw Trevor's F-15 pitch into a climb, leaving large pieces of the enemy tumbling earthwards, trailing smoke and fire. Another J-15, about to lift off the runway, suddenly spewed flames. The pilot ejected, and his rocket-powered seat narrowly missed the F-15 that had shot his J-15 to pieces. Alan's F-15, just ahead of Dave, stitched lines of explosive shells across some taxiing J-15s. One spewed burning fuel, but the others miraculously avoided damage.

The picture was changing too fast for Dave to select his own target. He was midway down Darwin's main runway before he realised there were two intact enemy fighters still on the ground.

'Shit, I've stuffed it up!' he cried. Then he saw an orange dot ahead: the glowing exhaust of a jet beginning a climbing turn to the left. F-15 or J-15?

Hoping it wasn't one of his own colleagues, he slammed the thrust levers all the way forward and yanked the control stick back. G-forces dragged at his face and arms, his vision narrowing, as the big fighter pitched into a steep climb. The glowing dot resolved into the twin afterburners of a fighter, but the Eagle and the J-15 both had twin engines and twin upright tails, so weren't all that different from the rear. The most obvious difference was that the J-15's engines were further apart. As Dave hurtled towards it, he recognised that it was a J-15.

His adrenaline went into overdrive. He was approaching it rapidly, and the enemy pilot had no idea of the imminent danger. The F-15's 20mm Vulcan cannon fired at the rate of six thousand explosive rounds per minute; a three-second burst converted the sleek J-15 into a twisted mass of burning metal. There was no ejection from the fireball.

Dave turned hard to avoid the debris, and kept his turn going until he was headed south-east. He'd lost sight of all other aircraft, friend or foe, so he flicked on his radar briefly, scanning for any J-15s that might be returning to Darwin. It showed multiple targets, some going his way, some coming north towards him. Too many for one lone F-15 to handle, so he nosed over and headed for the deck at well over the speed of sound. He kept going at a very low level, right past Katherine and on for another ten minutes. Fuel was getting low, but he knew that any J-15s still airborne would be even worse off, so he judged it was safe to throttle right back and sneak into the base. As he touched down, the low fuel warning lights were blinking.

Dave's was the eighth F-15 to come back. Four of the low-level flight had each bagged a J-15 at or near Darwin. Initial jubilation at their success died when they heard that the decoy force had been successfully targeted by the pursuing J-15s' long-range radar-guided missiles. One F-15 may have been lost. It was Nick's.

They waited anxiously, but when there was no possibility of the missing F-15 still being in the air, they had to face the fact that one more of their thirty-six was gone. He was not just another pilot. He'd been their friend, and he left behind a wife and family. They could only hope he'd ejected and survived, but late in the evening, their worst fears were confirmed.

The 'five' were now three. Nick was dead. Wayne was still recuperating from his back injury, a bout of Dengue fever, infected mosquito and leech bites, and recurring malaria. At least he was alive.

Dave rang Chloe as she was about to get into bed. She sobbed when he told her what had happened. 'This is so crazy,' she cried. 'Why are you out there when we have hundreds of young pilots that are trained for this sort of fighting? I can't bear this much longer.'

'Politics, Chlo,' Dave replied sadly. 'The pollies argue, and we fight to survive.'

It was now eight Australians against twenty invaders – just slightly better odds than yesterday. That night, the Americans painted another star on Dave's F-15.

★ ★ ★

On that same night, Trevor Mayer opened the briefing by reading from an ABC News bulletin: '*In another indication of the growing groundswell of support for Australia from the US military, and in defiance of US President Stuart Ainsworth's edicts, USAF aircraft and support personnel based at Katherine appear to be creating a "shield" for the F-15s against aerial attack by the Chinese. The Government of the People's Republic of China appears anxious to avoid any inadvertent damage to US assets, because they fear such loss or damage might prompt the US Government into reversing its policy of staying out of the conflict between Australia and China.'*

'Let's make the most of our semi-protected situation,' Dave said. 'It might not last.'

They discussed tactics for two hours. Trevor summarised the discussion by simply saying they wouldn't get away with using the same tactics twice. The Chinese would plug every gap as the F-15s exposed it. They had to try something different on the following day, and they were told to expect a briefing at 4 a.m. Leaving Trevor pondering over charts, the other pilots shuffled off tiredly to their rooms at 8.30 p.m.

At 10 p.m., each pilot received a phone call. Dave sagged back on the bed and breathed a sigh of relief as Trevor spoke. 'The early-morning mission is scrubbed. A severe thunderstorm is expected to hit Darwin in the early hours, and a reassessment will be made at 7 a.m. tomorrow. The briefing is rescheduled to 8 a.m.'

A sleep-in! The others were probably just as relieved as Dave, but all were under such strain that nobody showed any emotion.

* * *

Powerful floodlights lit the terminal and maintenance buildings of Darwin's international airport. Lights marked every runway and taxiway, every road and parking area. Moving patrols, both on foot and in vehicles, regularly combed the complex. Two sentries were allocated to each and every parked military aircraft. The Chinese were determined not to be caught in the same way they'd caught the Australians.

Lieutenant Andy Moore knew the layout of the airport like his own backyard. His men regularly used the facility for training exercises, and he'd located and memorised every ditch, every drainage pipe, and every pool of shadow. To get anywhere near the terminals, he and his men would first have to approach through bushland, then pass through open fields south of the runways, as the other three sides of the complex were bounded by residential and commercial buildings that would almost certainly now be occupied by the Chinese.

Even in peacetime, it was hard to get anywhere near parked aircraft without being detected. In wartime, when the enemy expected some sort of attack, it was all but impossible. Moore needed a miracle, and he hoped that Darwin's unpredictable weather just might provide it. Normally, the 'pre-wet' season didn't begin until October or later, but this year, the thunderstorms seemed to be arriving early.

Moore and his men were camped in a small, treed gully well to the south of the airport. They'd strung up mottled khaki-coloured camouflage sheeting to prevent detection from above. They huddled together, eating cold rations, as they couldn't risk lighting a fire.

'We might get a ripper storm tonight,' Moore said to Sergeant John Crane, as he looked at the sky from their makeshift campsite.

'Yessir,' said Crane. 'I think you could be right. It's been hot enough today to fry an egg on my hat, so we sure could do with a cool-down.'

'With those clouds, we'll get one hell of a lightning show, even if we don't get rain. Organise the boys to break camp – we'd better make the most of it.'

In similarly mottled camouflage clothing, with blackened faces, the ten Australian soldiers left their truck hidden in the scrub and hiked towards the airport. They reached the southern boundary fence a little earlier than expected, but a lightning storm had already begun. By 11 p.m., they sheltered under scrubby trees as bright flashes revealed towering cumulus clouds above the city, and all other sounds were drowned out by the almost-constant rumble.

Moore whispered to his men, 'It would've been suicide to try to cross the airfield with all these spotlights on. Our moving shadows would've stood out like granny's tooth, but the flickering from this lightning should mask our shadows. Let's go. Pray that the storm doesn't stop before we do the job and get out.'

Crouching low, using the ditch and the lightning flashes as cover, they crept the two kilometres to the intersection of two runways. Here, they huddled against a fibreglass marker.

Now, here's the tricky bit, Moore thought.

During a particularly violent flash and boom, the troop sprinted across the tarmac. To Moore, it seemed like they were fully exposed for minutes before they reached the next three-metre-long fibreglass taxiway marker. In reality, it was just fifteen seconds. Beyond this marker and to the left were two rows of J-15 fighters, each aircraft separated by hastily dug earth mounds. To the right was a row of dark green four-engine jet transports, all with their rear cargo ramps open. Moore could see soldiers sheltering from the electrical storm beneath their wings.

They would be totally exposed if they tried to get to all of the enemy aircraft, and would very likely be wiped out. But there were five fighters and three transports that they had a chance of reaching while the lightning kept Chinese heads down. With hand signals, Moore allocated his team individual targets.

'Throw your grenades right on 11.30,' he whispered, 'then get the hell out the way we came in. Good luck.'

Right on cue, large drops of tropical rain began to splash down. The last few guards who'd braved the lightning retreated to take shelter. As ten synchronised watches hit 11.30 p.m., five grenades were thrown into J-15 tail pipes, and another five grenades were pitched into the cargo holds of three Xi'an Y-20 transports. Ten simultaneous explosions were barely heard above the rumble of lightning, but flames shot many metres into the air, galvanising the Chinese guards. None seemed to realise that grenades had caused the damage: they apparently thought lightning had ignited the aircraft. Fire bells rang, sirens wailed, and ten extremely lucky Australians retreated from the cacophony and disappeared into the night without a single challenge. Much later, the true cause of the damage became apparent, and a number of soldiers were marched off, under arrest for dereliction of duty.

While the F-15 pilots slept, the odds against them had changed again. Now, it was eight of them against fifteen of the enemy.

* * *

Huang Bai knew that the radars aboard their fighters weren't performing as they should, but he felt that poor tactics during that first clash with the Australians were more to blame for their problems. Even the airfield security had let the cause down that night, allowing five aircraft to be destroyed. With the wild and unseasonal storms that lashed Darwin all of the following day, no action had been taken by either side, but Huang Bai knew that stalemate wouldn't last for long. Now it was forty-eight hours after that attack by the F-15s, and there hadn't even been a discussion on tactics to counter the Australians. He searched for the man who'd taken his leadership role, Captain Cheng Hou, and found him lounging in the luxurious office he'd commandeered from Darwin's civil airport manager. Huang Bai was apoplectic. The precious J-15s and their even more precious pilots were being squandered, and this man was acting as if he were on holiday!

Huang Bai stood at attention in front of an impressive desk while Cheng Hou lazily examined his phone, ignoring him. Huang Bai felt his resentment rise with every minute that he waited to speak. Eventually, the captain looked up, pretending to be surprised to find him there.

'Yes, Huang Bai. You wanted to see me?'

'Captain, you're allowing these mongrel Australians to dictate when and where we engage them. We must draw them into a fight on *our* terms. Please let me lead an attack on their base. Divide our fighters into a low-level attack force and a high-level cover. They'll be forced to defend their base, and for once, we'll have the advantage of both height and surprise.'

'You've had your opportunity to lead, *Commander*,' Cheng Hou sneered. 'Look where that got us. You're very lucky to have a second chance, but don't think your presence here allows you to order me around, as you've repeatedly tried to do. I shouldn't have to remind you that I am now your senior officer. Nor should I have to remind you that an aerial attack on the enemy base carries many risks. A single bomb going astray and damaging the USAF aircraft there – or worse, killing USAF personnel – could trigger the American imperialists to join with the Australians against us. Then we could never succeed.'

'But,' Huang Bai said, and hesitated, before reluctantly adding, 'sir, we're being slowly destroyed. We must–'

'There is no *must!*' Cheng Hou shouted, and stood up so suddenly his chair thudded into the wall behind him. 'I'm tired of your attempts to undermine me! Today, you'll be my wingman. You will protect my tail, not attack the enemy. You will only fire your guns or missiles if I am in danger. That is all!'

Huang Bai was silent. His chances of being an ace, and therefore resurrecting some face, were already receding daily. Now, he was to play nursemaid to a man he couldn't respect.

He returned to the ready-room and sat a little apart from the other pilots, who were loudly swapping stories about the bar girls of Shandong's ports. He wanted to warn them that today, the Australians would probably try a variation on their successful tactics from that first day. However, he knew that if he tried, Captain Cheng might sack him from the flight line altogether.

The warning klaxon sounded, interrupting one man's vivid description of his last night of leave. Fifteen pilots raced for their waiting aircraft. Huang Bai cursed Cheng Hou's stubbornness as he plugged the twin leads from his helmet into the communications panel of his J-15. With a crackle, the radio came to life, and he heard the controller stating that two enemy fighters had been detected by AWACS radar, approaching from the south-west at low altitude. He knew immediately that they must be decoys. The terrain to the south-west was flat, so they would know they'd be detected. That meant others were probably approaching undetected from the hills to the south-east, at very low altitude.

Huang Bai hesitated, then pressed his transmit button and shouted: 'Captain Cheng, they must be decoys. Others will attack from the south-east.'

The call wasn't acknowledged, but he knew that even Cheng Hou had to realise he was most likely correct. Just as they began to take off, Cheng Hou shouted a command over the radio. 'Ong Qihan, Zhao Lina, follow the AWACS heading to confront the attackers. The rest of you, stay with me. We'll climb and head south-east.'

Minutes later, the main force of Chinese fighters was streaking south-east in a clear blue sky. Ong Qihan and Zhao Lina reported that the two attackers the AWACS had detected had turned tail and run long before getting close to Darwin, confirming Huang Bai's prediction.

His radar picked up one blip, then another. Six targets were emerging from the protection of the hills about 30 nautical miles ahead, approaching at very low altitude. *Gotcha*, he thought, and grinned under the tight-fitting oxygen mask.

Immediately, the Chinese pilots slammed their thrust levers forward and nosed over into a 20-degree dive. Their speed quickly surpassed Mach 1.5. The attackers were still far too far away to see by the naked eye, but Huang Bai saw one of Cheng Hou's radar-guided missiles drop away from its pylon. Immediately, its motor ignited. With a huge plume of white smoke, it tore away at over three times the speed of sound, three missiles from the other pilots rocketing after it.

Huang Bai watched the blips on the radar screen suddenly divert from their tracks. The F-15s' defensive electronics must've picked up the incoming missiles, and they turned tightly in attempts to evade the danger. Several did so successfully, but one blip faded off the screen. He thumped the canopy with his left fist when the remaining blips accelerated away and disappeared into the ground clutter.

'We got one of the mongrels,' Cheng Hou crowed over the radio. 'But there are still more to kill!'

The J-15s wound off altitude rapidly as they pursued the Australians. In less than ninety seconds, thirteen Chinese and five Australian jets were in whirling dogfights. The F-15s dropped flares and chaff to deflect close range missiles while trying to bring their guns to bear on the J-15s. Huang Bai saw one F-15 climb steeply away then turn and dive towards a Chinese fighter, and Cheng Hou rolled hard left and accelerated to intercept it. Huang Bai turned with his leader, scanning for threats. He burned with the desire to pull away and make his own attack, but then an irresistible picture flashed into his consciousness.

As Cheng Hou straightened to attack the unwary Australian, Huang Bai allowed his jet to drift into a position directly behind the one he was there to protect. For a few seconds, as Cheng Hou opened fire on the F-15, he grappled with his own traitorous thoughts. Then, as if without conscious input, he felt his forefinger tighten on the firing button. He watched a short burst of cannon fire leap from his own jet and into the tail of Cheng Hou's. Sparks flew, pieces of the aeroplane peeled off, then its internal fuel tanks erupted. Huang Bai rammed the control stick to the right to barely avoid the resulting fireball. He circled the falling chunks, watching for a parachute. There was none. Nor could he see another jet; the Australian fighter had gone down, and the sky was deserted. He set course for Darwin at an economical cruise speed.

After landing, the Chinese pilots gathered in what used to be a RAAF crew room. They shouted and laughed as they related their versions of the combat. Two Australian jets downed, for the loss of only one: their commanding officer. Huang Bai noticed that nobody seemed particularly upset by that. He didn't join the celebration, but sat alone and considered the possibilities. He knew he was the logical choice to replace Cheng Hou, but he also knew his papers had been marked 'Never to be promoted'. Would circumstances overrule that edict?

The base commander interrupted the rowdy pilots. 'With the

unfortunate loss of Captain Cheng Hou, Commander Huang Bai will assume the role of acting leader of this J-15 squadrons. He will not assume the rank of captain, but will remain commander. I expect a permanent replacement for Captain Cheng will be announced shortly.'

So, Huang Bai thought, as he fought to control a grin, *fate has decreed I should have another chance of realising my dream.*

* * *

The third aerial attack relied on the F-15's one big advantage over the J-15: much longer range, even when carrying a good weapon load. This time, the Australians took off in daylight, as they wanted local Chinese observers to notify Darwin's occupiers that they were about to be attacked. By now, Dave was getting a little less uncomfortable flying 'in the weeds', and even had a few seconds to take in the changing countryside that flashed beneath his wings: low hills, rocky escarpments, blue billabongs, grassy valleys, and glimpses of broad brown rivers. But as soon as they received a radio message from one of the Special Forces soldiers that the Chinese had launched ten of their fourteen fighters, the F-15s turned tail and ran. They flew on a heading of 180 degrees for thirty minutes, then reversed course.

The pursuing J-15s sensed the trap. They hedged their bets. Ten of them, including Commander Huang, turned back to land and refuel as quickly as possible. The other four continued flying south at 20,000 feet, scanning with radar ahead and to 30 degrees each side, hoping to catch the F-15s. They didn't detect the low-flying Australian fighters and passed them directly overhead. As soon as the two forces crossed paths, the Australians went to full afterburner and pitched up into the vertical. They passed through

30,000 feet in thirty seconds, pulled over inverted to 30-degree dives, rolled out and accelerated to over one and a half times the speed of sound. That put them above and behind the J-15s.

Six F-15s hit the four J-15s with Vulcan cannons blazing. All four of the Chinese died without knowing what hit them.

Now it was just ten Chinese fighters against six Australians. The confidence of the F-15 pilots was growing. Dave let himself think that there was just a chance that they might win this uneven war, and that he might even survive it. That night, the Americans painted a third star on F-15 tail number 056.

Events of the fourth day of the war in Darwin crushed any optimism they might've felt. Dave cradled a steaming coffee cup as he sat in the starkly furnished briefing room. He shook his head dejectedly. 'The Chinese had us cold,' he told the intelligence officer. 'They had the height advantage, and the weapons to make the most of it. We went in low as usual, but of course, they knew we'd taken off from Katherine. They must've scrambled – they had aircraft circling at various heights, from a few thousand feet to forty thousand feet or more. As soon as we emerged from the cover of the hills about thirty miles out of Darwin, they were on us.

'We blew past the first couple that were circling down low, but had to evade the next pair coming down from above. By the time we'd evaded them, there was another pair diving on us. We had the choice of climbing up and facing them or staying low and trying to outrun them. As they outnumbered us almost two to one, we chose to scatter and run. After that, it was every man for himself.

'I turned hard, barely avoiding the mangroves, and went to full afterburner. I ignored the airspeed limits for low altitude flight, so I hope I didn't do the aeroplane any damage. I ran, hugging the coast until I was over a hundred miles east of Darwin, then turned east on a course for Katherine. I lost sight of everybody else.'

Dave had been the third F-15 to land. Two more had followed within minutes, but one was missing. Trevor, their leader, the driving force behind them all, Dave's friend of over forty years, wasn't coming home. His wingman described how he'd been a half-mile behind Trevor when they both came under radar-guided missile attack. He'd been fully occupied evading two missiles when he saw Trevor's F-15 take a hit and, seconds later, go into the trees at over 700 knots. There had been no attempt at an ejection.

After the debrief, they drank a quiet toast to their lost comrades. Dave was usually the first to leave drinking sessions, but that night, he was one of the last. He dreaded the call he had to make.

His iPhone felt as heavy as lead as he scrolled through his contact list and selected Jenny Mayer's number. Dave had known Jenny since she and Trevor first got together, and considered her as much a friend as Trevor had been. When she answered, her flat tone told Dave that she'd already been informed of the tragedy.

'Hello, Dave... are you okay?'

Despite their closeness, he didn't know what to say to her. He could barely speak. Typical, he thought, that her first concern was his wellbeing, not her own devastating loss.

'Listen,' she said, 'even if Trev had survived this terrible business, he would never have come to terms with it. He was so distressed at having brought his friends into war, only to see them killed.'

'But Jenny, he's a hero,' Dave cried. 'Without Trev—'

'It didn't matter to him, Dave. He loved you, Nick, Wayne, and all the other pilots, and would've wished himself in the place of everyone who was lost.'

CHAPTER 12

24 SEPTEMBER 2026

Over a subdued breakfast the following morning, the five remaining Eagle pilots discussed who should be their new leader. Dave's old friend Alan Taylor was chosen. He was the obvious option, as he'd been a wing commander in the RAAF before joining Qantas twenty years previously. Although only of average height, he was a charismatic figure, with dark, wiry hair, a prominent nose, and bushy eyebrows. He was always friendly and keen to assist his fellow pilots, and was an excellent pilot himself. He'd been one of Trevor's closest confidants on all tactical matters from the first day at Henderson Field.

Despite Dave's respect for his new leader, Trevor's loss continued to cast a deep shadow over him. Alan and the other three remaining members of the F-15 force were ex-fighter pilots, and those three were two decades younger than he was. While they made every effort to include him, he felt old, inadequate, and alone.

* * *

It was now just five F-15s versus ten of the enemy J-15s. Alan Taylor was no fool. He knew that the Chinese wouldn't fall for the same tactics again. It was going to be very hard to take the offensive; in fact, he expected that the boot might be on the other foot.

On this sixth day, he knew that the five F-15s couldn't risk being caught at low level against an enemy that would be stacked at various levels above. They would have to stay high this time.

At first light, as the five Eagle pilots were preparing to start up, Alan saw a flight of four USAF F-22 Raptors depart. He could also see that four more were being prepared for flight. It puzzled him, but he didn't think much of it.

At 50,000 feet, he led the five Australians towards Darwin. On his radar, he could see, at about the same altitude, ten blips that his electronics identified as J-15s. *Looks like it's going to be the gunfight at the O.K. Corral,* he thought.

A moment later, the radar showed that missiles had been launched at a range of 80 miles, and that those missiles would impact in ninety seconds. The F-15s had to pull high-G turns and drop chaff to evade them. Guns against missiles at altitude had only one ending, so the F-15s ran. The J-15s, scenting blood, followed.

Just as they did, over the area frequency came a clear message: 'Tindal traffic, this is Raptor One-Three-Seven, currently orbiting Katherine city. Be advised that the airspace for ten miles radius of Tindal airbase is closed to all traffic for a live fire exercise. Any unidentified aircraft will be fired upon.'

It was a stalemate. The Chinese jets turned, thwarted, back to Darwin.

* * *

Rick Salmon's RAAF VIP jet landed in Katherine before dawn on the sixth day of the air war over Darwin. He explained to the five pilots that the governments of Great Britain, Germany, France, India, Vietnam, Thailand, Malaysia, Singapore, the Philippines, the Solomon Islands, Vanuatu, and Indonesia had put out a joint communique. It condemned the military action by China against Australia, and decreed that Chinese civil and military aircraft were formally denied access to airspace in all listed countries until it ceased all hostile action.

Furthermore, it announced that Great Britain's Royal Navy was despatching an aircraft carrier, the HMS *Queen Elizabeth,* to the Philippine Sea. The carrier, its escort of destroyers, and its fifty F-35 fighters would patrol the territorial waters off the Philippines to enforce the closure of the country's airspace. The governments of Thailand, Singapore, Malaysia, and Indonesia would also all be conducting extra air patrols to enforce their closure.

'So,' Rick said, 'instead of just two F-15s based at Honiara, there will shortly be a regional armada of fighter aircraft forming a barrier against the Chinese reinforcing or even resupplying their forces in Darwin by air. Our two submarines now patrol the same area, and they're aided by non-combatant US subs. With their supply chain cut off, and mounting pressure within the USA to enter the conflict, time isn't on the side of the Chinese forces here in Australia.'

Alan put himself in the Chinese position. He could see that with the more overt American protection they'd received the previous day, the Chinese would soon have to either withdraw or make a breakout from Darwin, regardless of the risk of accidently hitting the USAF aircraft at Katherine. That breakout had to be through Katherine, then either to the east towards the coast of

Queensland, or down to South Australia via the desert city of Alice Springs.

'Rick,' he said, 'how much longer do you think the Chinese will wait before acting?'

'Hard to say, Alan. They've built up a force we estimate at about twenty thousand infantry soldiers, and they have tanks, guns, and mobile short-range missile units, as well as helicopter gunships for troop support. Their obvious weakness is control of the air. However, now that you're down to only five jets, and the air war is at a stalemate, they might take the risk at any time. They probably know we'll have the RAAF Hawks joining the fray quite soon, so the break-out could happen any day.'

Salmon went on to describe how the Australian Army had hunkered down in two places. The 3rd Brigade from Queensland had formed a barrier on the highway, halfway between Tennant Creek and Mount Isa, just west of the border between Queensland and the NT. The 5th Brigade from NSW and the 6th Brigade from Victoria had set their front line on the hills on the northern edge of Alice Springs, 1000 km south of Darwin. Altogether, four thousand troops guarded the two locations, and they were supported by another three thousand non-combat personnel.

Alan looked worried. 'We'll have to move the instant the break-out starts. We can't mount a defence from the base itself, as there'll be too much risk of being overrun. The presence of the USAF has given us a shield against air attack, but if the enemy is as desperate as you say, they might take their chances. We just can't rely on that shield any longer.' Dave and the three other pilots nodded in agreement.

Alan made doubly sure that everyone was prepared to abandon Katherine at the first sign of Chinese troop movement towards them. The five remaining Eagles were readied, and every member of the support crew knew what to do to aid in the escape south.

* * *

General Xu Zihao was fuming. The planned departure for his break-out force had been midnight. The assembly had begun the evening before, but hadn't gone at all smoothly. Many of his troops and support staff were scattered all over Darwin's airport and surrounding commercial buildings, camping in passenger lounges, offices, and anywhere else they fancied. A number of officers had taken over the airport hotel. More troops and officers were still at the Robertson Barracks, where they'd been guarding the Australian prisoners. Coordinating the scattered forces was proving to be a nightmare. Unseasonal rain didn't help, either.

The road out of Darwin was a good highway, mostly straight except where it snaked through the hills, but it was narrow. A single lane in each direction limited vehicles from overtaking each other to get in the correct order, and that was critical. Xu Zihao wanted one squadron of main battle tanks at the point of the spear, immediately followed by his best troops in their trucks. They were to be followed by mobile anti-aircraft guns, missile batteries and their operators, and a second squadron of battle tanks on low-loaders. After that came support staff and equipment, which included signallers, fuel tankers, food and water carriers, caterers, mechanics and their tools and parts, medics, and a complete field hospital and its staff. Weaving through this melee were light all-wheel drive trucks carrying officers who added to the confusion by giving conflicting orders on who was to follow whom.

Many of the troop-carrying vehicles had been taken from the Australian Army barracks. Those they didn't want had been disabled or destroyed. The Chinese drivers, often the least educated and experienced of the troops, were unfamiliar with the Australian vehicles, and many stalled at the worst possible time, creating a stop-go caterpillar-action for kilometres. With ten fully equipped soldiers per truck, it took two thousand trucks nose to tail, occupying more than 20 km in length, just to carry them. Once the convoy did begin to move, the total distance, including all the guns, tanks, tankers, and support gear, stretched to a slow-moving 100-kilometre traffic jam!

Justifiably fearing a night attack by the F-15s, all vehicles had hastily-taped-on headlight hoods. The resulting dim light and close tailgating caused a number of rear-end shunts. The more severe shunts holed radiators, thus disabling vehicles, which could only be pushed to the side of the narrow road and abandoned. Occupants had to then find another vehicle with space enough for them and their equipment.

General Xu Zihao knew that the next few hours might determine the future of the entire Australian campaign.

* * *

The five Eagle fighters had been prepared with a light load of Mark 84 bombs, napalm canisters, and sufficient fuel to make a brief low-level attack on the expected advancing troops, before making a dash to Tennant Creek, some 200 nautical miles south. They knew that the Chinese were very likely to have figured out exactly what they'd do. It was a dangerous game for both sides.

There was no moon, so it was another pitch-black night, with light rain from a uniform cloud cover at about 4000 feet. Unusual for the 'Top End' of the Northern Territory, Dave thought. At this time of year, the rain usually came in quick and heavy downpours from isolated storm clouds.

The F-15s switched on their navigation lights only long enough to form a loose trailing formation, then made another nerve-wracking scud at little more than tree-top height. Multiple times, they had to pitch up suddenly to avoid high ground, their GPS screens flashing yellow warning lights. Even after all the low flying he'd done in the past weeks, Dave still found it terrifying. He kept reminding himself that the fifteen remaining Chinese fighters would be expecting them, and their only chance of success, or even survival, was to remain undetected. At least the rain would make it even more difficult for the Chinese radars to pick them up.

The lead F-15's two 900-kg bombs and twin napalm canisters, hastily aimed in the darkness, created a fearsome sea of death and destruction for the leading vehicles in that convoy. As fifth in the flight, Dave had difficulty avoiding gouts of flame and debris from the other F-15s' explosives, let alone the Chinese weapons.

He was uncertain how accurate his aim was, but he thought at least some of his ordnance hit the line of trucks as he banked hard left away from the carnage and pulled till the g-forces hurt. Momentarily blinded by going from the harsh glare of exploding napalm to inky blackness, Dave fought the urge to pull up into clear air and away from the hills and rain. He knew that if he did, the enemy fighters would pounce.

* * *

Huang Bai's eyes nervously danced from scanning the sky to the fuel gauges on his instrument panel. He felt physically ill. He'd prayed for a second chance at leading the force, but so far under his command, they'd lost four J-15s and four pilots for just one

F-15 destroyed. Only in the last two engagements had his tactics proven superior. There were still five F-15s out there, and he had to provide air cover for the crucial breakout. He couldn't afford to fail.

He had had set up a CAP of two fighters over the assembling convoy. Two more J-15s were ready to scramble, and all remaining aircraft were fuelled and armed. With the cloud solid from a base of 4000 feet to about 7000 feet, the CAP had a difficult job. Patrolling at low level used a lot of fuel, which meant a relatively short endurance.

Huang Bai and his wingman had taken the third shift. Just as fuel was getting critical, he called for the next pair of J-15s to launch. As he dropped the undercarriage of his jet and configured the flaps into the approach setting, he saw the glowing tails of the replacement CAP lifting off the runway into the night sky.

Ten seconds later, he heard the panicked call over the radio: the convoy was under attack. The bastard Australians had struck at the worst possible time for him. Yet again, Huang Bai cried out in frustration, knowing that by the time he landed and refuelled, the enemy would've already wreaked their destruction.

★ ★ ★

After their attack, the F-15s avoided radar lock from any J-15s above by staying low. When they'd gone far enough to feel safe, they climbed to 40,000 feet for an economical cruise into the airport at Tennant Creek, and Dave began breathing normally again.

For once, they landed too early to be bothered by the usual heat and swarms of flies that greeted visitors to the area. Dave enjoyed the feeling of the cool desert air on his face when his canopy cracked open. The airfield had plenty of fuel in its underground storage, and an advance ground crew had prepared for the fighters' arrival. Each aircraft took 10,000 litres of Jet A-1, then the ground crew pumped water into the storage tanks to deny the oncoming invaders the use of the remaining fuel. Their J-15s would have to wait for their own road tankers.

Within an hour, the F-15s were taxiing for departure to the airfield at Uluru, while their ground crew followed in trucks. As soon as they left, Army engineers blew craters in the runway to make it as difficult as possible for the Chinese pilots to land.

The F-15 formation overflew Alice Springs airport. There were no US assets there to provide a shield like they had at Katherine, and Uluru was another 200 nautical miles south-west, out of range of any J-15s flying out of Tennant Creek. They hardly needed to use their GPS navigation systems to find it. It stood out for many miles, looking like a giant brown pebble dropped onto a red plain.

The nearby hotels, which were normally busy with tourists, were all but deserted. That suited the pilots and crew, as it left them with their choice of luxurious accommodation. Dave and his colleagues were picked up by a small bus and dropped off at a stylish single-level hotel, which boasted a large swimming pool and a twenty-four-hour restaurant that was opened just for them.

Not long after he'd settled in, Dave heard the RAAF Hawks arrive: a dozen of them, supported by Hercules transport aircraft loaded with ammunition and other supplies. This meant the five F-15 pilots were no longer alone in their aerial battles against the Chinese. Nevertheless, Dave couldn't shake the depression that had overtaken him since Trevor's death.

That afternoon, he phoned Chloe. Not normally one to add

to his wife's worries, he admitted that his chronic back pain was getting to him. 'Honestly, Chlo, it's hard to concentrate on flying when my spine feels like it's locked rigid. Even climbing in and out of the cockpit is becoming difficult. Sometimes, I can't stand up straight after a flight. At least the hotel has decent mattresses, but we probably won't get much time to enjoy them.'

Alice Springs was the obvious target for the enemy, who would most likely reach it sometime the next day. It had a big airfield with two runways, and it sat on the north-south road and rail corridor through the centre of Australia. While the Australian Army occupied the town, it formed a barrier against the Chinese – but if they failed to hold it, there was nothing to stop the invasion force from reaching the city of Adelaide, South Australia's capital.

Late that afternoon, the five F-15 pilots met Wing Commander Roy Pearce and his eleven 76 Squadron pilots. Dave couldn't help noticing that he and his four colleagues looked tired and worn, presenting a stark contrast to the newcomers. The RAAF boys were decades younger, immaculate in new khaki flight suits, and eager to join the fight.

After an hour of discussion, Roy Pearce summed up the situation. 'Our Hawk trainers make a handy light attack bomber, but they're much smaller and slower than your F-15s or the Chinese fighters. If we were to make the initial attack, it's likely the enemy interceptors would pounce on us from altitude and wipe us out before we could deliver our ordnance.'

He paused, looking squarely at the F-15 pilots. 'My squadron has had practice missions in Alice Springs, so we know the area quite well. The town has some very handy natural barriers to aid the Army's defence. Namely, the last thirteen kilometres of the road from Darwin pass through some very inhospitable terrain.

It's hilly, dry, rocky, and impassable for any tank or truck, except on the narrow highway itself. Even foot soldiers would have a tough time there.

'That means the enemy really only has one practical choice: their armoured vehicles and troop-carrying trucks will motor down the highway, probably with air support from helicopter gunships, which will aim to take out the Army's artillery. Then, once through the hills, they'll fan out and outflank the infantry. You fellows in your F-15s must make the initial strike as they bunch up to penetrate that last thirteen kilometres. By hugging the deck, you should get very near the anticipated battle zone before being detected.

'You have the speed to complete an attack before the Chinese can intercept you, along with the ability to carry a big enough bomb load to make a dent in their force. We'll carry a relatively light load in our Hawks and full internal fuel. After dropping your bombs, you are to climb at max rate to intercept the J-15s, which will presumably be coming down fast from their loitering altitude. You'll have to keep them busy while our Hawks come in as a second wave. It's not ideal, I know, as the Chinese will have the height advantage – but hopefully, you'll have the benefit of surprise.'

'Surprise?' Dave exclaimed. 'Hardly. They'll be expecting us, alright.'

Pearce nodded, acknowledging this comment. 'The J-15s might have the height advantage, but your F-15s have the range. If the Chinese can be denied from taking the town and airfield for long enough, they'll have to break off to return to the north. That will leave their army without air cover. We'll only have to contend with short-range ground-to-air missiles and guns.'

'*Only*,' Dave heard one Hawk pilot mutter. It was going to be like flying into a hornet's nest.

Later, the Australians cooled their heels in the plush common area, listening as ABC News reported on worldwide condemnation of the Chinese invasion. In the USA, public opinion was swinging in Australia's favour. Optimistic views on US military intervention were expressed by a couple of the reporters, but Dave knew that any action by politicians would take its time. Too much time, as they expected to be called into action within the next eighteen hours.

Sure enough, RAAF intelligence officers rang with an update that evening. Based on the reports of ground observers, US satellites, and RAAF AWACS aircraft, they expected the enemy to be within sight of Alice Springs by 9 a.m. tomorrow.

★ ★ ★

It was still dark and cold when the five Eagle pilots arrived at the airstrip. The wind had been strong enough during the night to make the surrounding desert oaks sigh, and to deposit a fine coating of red dust over the fighters. In the light of a row of spotlights, ground crew were busy polishing canopies and removing bungs from air intakes, exhausts, and pitot tubes.

At first light, they awoke their dormant mounts. The quiet of the desert was broken by the electronic hum of each big bird. Dave had by now committed the start-up checklist to memory, so the procedure was routine until the last item. The left engine tested up to a hundred and five percent RPM, but the right engine refused to go higher than ninety-eight percent. Dave checked and rechecked. All else was as it should be. A valve somewhere might be failing, or perhaps there was damage to turbine blades. Maybe he'd ingested a small bird on the approach into Uluru, or even a stone on the strip itself. Whatever the cause, an engine change was almost certainly needed, but that required a spare engine, as well as the facilities and time to install it. They had none of those.

Every ounce of his professional being, as an engineer and as a pilot, screamed at him to declare the aircraft unairworthy and shut it down. He was already fighting a premonition of doom, and his survival instincts clutched at this justifiable excuse not to fly. However, as his turn came to throttle up and release the brakes, he didn't hesitate. He wasn't going to let his mates down.

Despite his preoccupation, the incongruity of the sleek and deadly F-15s taxiing within sight of the ancient monolith of Uluru didn't escape him. As he turned his fighter from the hardstand onto the taxiway, he saw the F-15 and Hawk ground crews forming a line along it. Every man saluted before quickly covering their ears as each aircraft passed by. Dave lifted his chin, straightened his back as much as the tight harness would allow, and returned the salute.

The first rays of sunlight struck the top of Uluru as the five F-15s reached the end of the taxiway, their huge engines whining impatiently. They rolled at ten second intervals. Eagle 056's turn came, and almost without conscious thought, Dave pushed the twin thrust levers forward, through maximum military power to full afterburner. The earth shook. His 22 tonnes of metal, glass, fuel, and weaponry hurtled towards the horizon, pushed by 25,000 horsepower. Well, not quite that. He could feel the swing to the right as his problem engine failed to deliver full power.

With tiny movements of his stick and thrust levers, Dave manoeuvred into position behind Alan's lead aircraft. They were close this time, not in a loose battle formation, with each aircraft less than a wingspan apart, slightly below and behind the one before it. Although the morning air was still cool, the F-15s rose and fell as one as they rode increasingly turbulent air just above desert scrub, white gum-lined dry creeks, red sand dunes, and rocky ridges at the speed of sound.

Captain Pete Grutzner commanded the battery of six 155mm Howitzers that had been dug into the rocky hills north of Alice Springs. He had the guns firing at the enemy column as soon as it was in range, but they were never going to hold back an army – especially not without air support.

His radio was linked to the F-15s via a RAAF Boeing 737 Wedgetail AWACS holding at 45,000 feet above Uluru. He keyed the mike and yelled into it above the staccato boom of his own guns. 'The Chinese must've sped up their convoy. The first elements are now in view of Alice Springs. We are engaging, but they're coming on fast.'

The Chinese had arrived two hours earlier than they'd expected, and the F-15s were still fifteen minutes away. Flying over Mach 1 just feet above the desert floor was already enough mental load for them all, but Dave had the additional worry that his right engine might fail at any moment. The urgent radio report added even more to their anxiety. If the defending Army units were overrun before the F-15s reached Alice Springs, their mission was already over. The Chinese would take the town and the airfield, and Uluru would be well inside the range of the J-15s.

Another radio report came from the RAAF AWACS: 'There are eight interceptors circling at various altitudes from ten to forty thousand feet above the motorised column.'

What happened to the other two? Maybe the cratered runway

at Tennant Creek had caught a couple of them. Whatever the case, Dave knew that it meant there were now five F-15s against eight of the enemy.

Grutzner's guns quickly knocked out several lead vehicles in the invading column, but here the terrain was so flat and featureless that following vehicles simply drove around them. In minutes, the battery would be overrun.

The loaders had stripped to their waists. They glistened with sweat even in the chill of the morning. Grutzner tried to remain calm as he made another broadcast, but he couldn't prevent his voice from rising an octave. 'Aussie aircraft. We can see contrails from high-flying enemy fighters above. Attack helicopters are seconds from hitting us. Tanks and mobile guns are coming up fast, and their troops are just behind. If you can't reach us in a minute or two, don't bother coming. It'll all be over.'

Dave saw a hand signal from Alan Taylor, and the five fighters moved out of echelon formation into line astern, spreading the distance between each to about a half mile, or three seconds. The radio was silent, as to alert the patrolling J-15s now would've been suicidal.

Dave could see the hills surrounding the town. A line of green ahead must've been the Finke River, and smoke billowed on the far side of the city. The call came from Alan – 'One, two, three, *go*' – and one by one, they pulled into 6G climbs. G-forces dragged at Dave's face and arms, and vapour streamed from his wingtips. They were all now exposed to the radars of the patrolling J-15s. At 4000 feet, they rolled inverted and pulled, diving towards the Chinese army.

Grutzner had all but given up hope. His men had extracted a fearsome toll from the enemy, but the best effort by artillery alone was always going to be too little, too late. He had a choice to make for his men: abandon the guns and retreat into the rocks behind them, or keep firing until they were killed.

He tried to yell to keep firing, but he never got the words out. A few hundred metres away, the first part of the oncoming Chinese column disappeared in a sea of flame that was quickly topped by rolling black smoke. A moment later, his ears were assaulted by a roar that was clearly discernible above the noise of his own guns. He fell back and gaped as the five F-15s demolished the spearhead of the Chinese attack force.

* * *

Huang Bai anxiously watched the ground forces approach Alice Springs from the bubble canopy of his fighter, high above the northern edge of the small city. His wingman hung in the air over his right shoulder. All eight J-15s were in position, paired and stacked at 10,000 steps in the cloudless sky. Each pair orbited in a race-track pattern, throttled back to 200 knots to conserve fuel, radars switched off to avoid detection. They relied on an AWACS aircraft orbiting nearby to alert them to the threat Huang Bai expected to materialise at any moment.

He thumbed the transmit button on his joystick. 'Nighthawk, this is Red Leader. Confirm you are active and watching for enemy attack from the south.'

'Red Leader, this is Nighthawk. That's affirm.'

'Remember, when they come, they'll have at least some of their aircraft down in the weeds. Others may be at altitude. We must have warning enough to intercept *before* they attack the troops.'

'Affirm, Red Leader. No bogies high or low at this time.'

Huang Bai's fighter was equipped with several radios. In addition to listening out to two frequencies for the AWACS and his pilots respectively, he was also trying to monitor the Australian Army's broadcast. They made listening in difficult by constantly switching frequencies, but he did hear a plea for aerial support. He could picture the panic amongst the outnumbered defenders below as the Chinese force rumbled along the highway towards them.

In one instant, all three radios came alive. He fumbled with the selector to silence all but the AWACS, and as he did so, he banked into another right turn in the race-track pattern.

Almost 16 kilometres below, a row of bright red dots suddenly punctuated the line of tanks, trucks, guns and men. Frozen momentarily, Huang Bai saw the head of the army column disappear as the red dots grew into black mushroom-shaped clouds.

'*Diu!*' he shouted. The AWACS had failed to detect the low-flying F-15s, and they were killing his troops while he was still at 40,000 feet.

Huang Bai jabbed at his transmit button. 'This is Red Leader!' he screamed. 'Attack, attack, *attack!*

★ ★ ★

Bits of metal soared above Dave's head, trailing smoke. Below him, explosions rippled through the Chinese column, their artillery ammunition going off like fireworks. He had to fly into that cauldron.

Ignoring the two helicopter gunships out on his left, he banked hard right to swing around the massive fireballs obliterating the road below. Smoke trails passed his left wingtip. *Shit, ground-fired missiles!* he thought. *Lucky I jinked when I did.*

Back in line with the road, he pressed the ordnance release. Bombs and napalm canisters fell away in split-second intervals.

The aircraft leapt as it was relieved of the load. He hit full afterburner and pointed the nose straight up. Above 10,000 feet, there was no danger from ground-fired missiles or small arms fire – now it was the J-15s he had to worry about!

Air-to-air missile contrails criss-crossed above him. An F-15 to his right pulled into a collision course, vapour pouring from its wingtips, and he rolled to avoid it. As he began to level out, a J-15 flashed past his nose. The pilot didn't even see him, too intent on locking onto the F-15 he'd dodged. He chopped power and banked hard enough that he greyed out momentarily. Seeing the F-15 and pursuing J-15 diving away to his right, he rammed the throttle lever forward, following them. The Chinese pilot was still fixated on the F-15 ahead. Easy shot. He fired a two-second burst, and pieces peeled off the J-15, smoke erupting from its tail.

Forget him, he's done, Dave told himself. *The one you don't see is the one that will get you.*

An F-15 shot past him with two J-15s on its tail in a vertical spiralling dance. He banked after them, but the hunted F-15 turned the wrong way, and he was still out of gun range of its pursuers. The lead J-15 fired a heat-seeking missile. A white streak of smoke accelerated towards the F-15, which ejected flares and pulled hard right. The missile followed the flares and exploded amongst them. If he'd turned left, he would've brought the two J-15s within Dave's range.

The lead J-15 fired another missile, then another. The F-15 evaded the first but the second exploded just beneath his tail. He spiralled out of control. The two J-15s pulled up and slowed down to watch. In seconds, the wingman was directly ahead of Dave. A two-second burst obliterated him, and the lead J-15 went into a vertical dive.

Dave's missile warning system shrieked. An enemy fighter was locking onto his tail. Turning hard, he pulled into a climb, and the warning stopped. Directly ahead, two J-15s were trying to out-turn an F-15. Dave couldn't read his tail number, so just shouted a general warning over the radio: 'Two behind you. Turn hard left, *now!*

He did. Below, the Hawks had arrived, and were decimating the enemy column. They'd deal with the helicopter gunships too. Dave and the other F-15 pilots had done their job – they'd kept the J-15s busy while the Hawks did theirs.

The two J-15s continued their chase, with Dave speeding after them. Every minute was taking them many miles north-east of Alice Springs. The F-15 made a shallow-banked turn to the south, towards Uluru, and the two enemy jets broke off. *They must be fuel-critical by now,* Dave thought. His own fuel was disappearing at nearly ten litres per second, but the wingman was almost in gun range, so he kept his throttles jammed to the full.

The lead J-15 pulled up and over in a tight loop. The wingman swung right. Dave followed him.

Shit, it's a trap!

The lead J-15 was head-on and closing fast. Red orbs flashed over Dave's canopy. He opened fire too, getting at least one hit. Smoke burst from under the J-15's wing: it had fired a missile.

The world went dark. Dave was surrounded by a terrible roaring, as the control stick went slack in his hand. The bird was dying around him. He was defenceless. Any second now, he'd be blown out of the sky.

From the first day of combat, he thought, *this is how I'd expected it would end.*

* * *

When Huang Bai, in pursuit of another F-15, glimpsed the tail number of 056 sliding past as it banked steeply to follow him, he felt twin stabs of excitement and fear in his gut. He shouted to his wingman, 'This one is out to kill me. Get him off me!'

He turned to run to the north, pushing the nose down to gain maximum speed. Breathing in grunts, he began to take control of himself. His wingman had, stupidly, stuck so close to his tail that 056 was able to swing down behind them both.

That gave Huang Bai just one chance. He pulled up into a half-loop, rolling out at the top, as his wingman shot past, heading for home. The pursuing F-15, intent on the wingman, kept coming. They hurtled towards each other at over 2000 kilometres an hour.

'Now we'll see who is best,' Huang Bai whispered, as he pressed the firing button. Orange fire from 056's cannon whipped past. His fighter bucked as it took several hits. Both his engines began to die, and the controls grew sloppy as the airspeed decayed. The nose fell. He reached up to the ejection handles behind his head, took a deep breath, and pulled.

Immediately, Huang Bai's arms were pinned to his sides, and his face felt as if it were being pulled from his head as he momentarily came under the force of 13G acceleration. When he regained consciousness, he was well clear of the stricken J-15, dangling under the white canopy of his parachute. He watched his jet spiral down to hit the desert floor. The remaining fuel ignited, and he was buffeted by the heat of the expanding fireball.

Huang Bai drifted down a few hundred metres from the crash site, hitting the ground and rolling amongst the sparse and prickly bushes that grew on the red-brown plain. The buzzing of flies was the only sound in the stillness of the desert. His initial elation at having survived quickly faded, his stomach lurching as he pondered the fact that he'd been defeated yet again. His small force had failed to protect the troops from air attack. He had been shot down. He had no future, whether he was rescued or not.

The only consolation was that he'd hit that cursed F-15, tail number 056. He hoped he'd killed the pilot as well as the aeroplane.

Huang Bai activated his emergency locator by pulling out its aerial. It broadcast on a Chinese military frequency, or it could be switched to an international frequency, which all nations monitored worldwide. He then sat down on his folded chute to await rescue.

Will they come and get me? he asked himself. *They might be too busy looking after themselves.*

* * *

Seconds passed like an eternity, but Dave was still alive. From his right eye, he could make out a blurred horizon. His helmet's visor was shattered. An icy gale was pouring through a hole in the canopy. Fumbling for the thrust lever, he pulled it back until the blast of air was fierce, but bearable. He still couldn't make anything out from his left eye. Was it gone altogether?

Keep calm, he told himself. *Just fly the aeroplane.* One engine was all but dead, and the other vibrated badly. He shut the first down, bringing up the second's power, pushing hard with his right foot to keep a constant heading. There must've been some airframe damage – the jet was flying like a pig. He couldn't see well enough to read the directional gyro, even if it still worked, but his location was the least of his worries. He was descending at a couple of thousand feet per minute, and the vibrating engine howled in protest.

Now, he could make out individual scrubby trees. There was a low ridge directly ahead and a plain bare of trees to the left. A dirt road angled across the plain, possibly the Plenty Highway. If it was, help wouldn't be far away. He should eject, but with his back the way it was, it'd likely leave him crippled for life.

Dave turned towards the plain. Hopefully, the surface was firm, otherwise the F-15 could dig a wheel in and cartwheel. But he had no other option. He was committed now.

Would the undercarriage extend? The emergency generator light was glowing, so he must have some electrical power. He moved the lever and felt the *thunk* as the gear locked down. His one working eye wasn't focusing properly, so he couldn't see the indicator. He'd just have to trust that the gear really was down.

At this rate, Dave was going to overshoot the bare area and crash into mulga scrub, so he lowered the nose, reducing the thrust. He couldn't afford to get this wrong. The engine shrieked and vibrated. *Please hold together for a few more seconds!*

The low ridge disappeared beneath him, and he pulled back on the stick, touching down heavily on red dirt thinly covered by sparse dry grass. The tyres sank into the dirt, slowing him quickly. He closed the thrust lever, and the working engine rattled as it wound down.

He'd stopped. Another 50 metres and he would've ploughed into the scrubby trees.

Dave pushed the canopy button. Nothing happened. He tried again. The aeroplane felt dead without the usual whine of generators, inverters, and fans. The air was still. He couldn't breathe, so he ripped his oxygen mask off. He jabbed at the button again and again, the confines of the cockpit suddenly claustrophobic. He banged his fists on the canopy, but it was designed to withstand two and a half times the speed of sound.

He couldn't move it that way. It was getting hot – the bubble canopy was like a glasshouse, and the air conditioner had shut down like everything else.

Get a grip, Dave told himself. *Think it through.*

The circuit breaker panel was on his left side, down low. He couldn't see from his left eye, and his back was so stiff he couldn't get his head around to use his right, so he felt for it blindly. *Got it!* Several circuit breakers had popped. He pushed at them, and some popped again. One stayed in. He tried the canopy button again. With a whir, the canopy unlocked and slowly opened above him. Even strapped in tightly, with his helmet and flight suit on, he could feel a flood of fresh air. Then there was silence, apart from the tinkling sound of cooling metal.

Dave carefully unfastened his harness and reached for his helmet. A big chunk of it was missing, and his fingers met sticky blood. Fear that his left eye was gone bubbled in his stomach. A fierce stab of pain came when he gingerly eased the tightly fitting helmet off, followed by another when he touched his bloody cheek. His head ached, and his throat was parched. He needed water.

Slowly, he climbed out of the cockpit, using the handholds built into the aircraft, along with the single-step strut, which had extended automatically when the canopy opened. Halfway down, he could see that a missile had exploded close to the nose, peppering the canopy with shrapnel.

His foot slipped from the small step. He collapsed into a heap under the fuselage, lying on the red sand until flies found his bleeding wounds. He staggered to his feet.

An emergency locator beacon was fitted to the aircraft, and should be emitting a signal, but with the damage the F-15 had sustained, he couldn't be sure it was working. There was another in a pocket of the ejector seat.

Dammit, Dave thought. *I'll have to climb back into the cockpit.*

* * *

The bulk of the Chinese ground force had been converted into a long column of charred wreckage. Flames still flickered in places, and there were occasional explosions from overheated fuel drums or ammunition. The road itself was black with melting tar, and the dry and prickly foliage either side was gone, leaving only twisted stumps. The stench of scorched paint, oil, fuel, and human flesh was appalling. Whole platoons of troops sat motionless in derelict open trucks, many melted into unrecognisable shapes. Wedgetail eagles began to congregate above, circling in thermals created by the burning machinery. They were ready to feast, if only the few surviving humans would get out of their way.

This ghastly scene stretched for more than 20 kilometres, but a number of troop-carrying trucks at the tail end of the Chinese force had escaped the wrath of the Australian jets by scattering on both sides of the highway, leaving tyre tracks across the barren plains. By midmorning, there was a scattered convoy fleeing back towards Darwin, and more than a thousand less-fortunate stragglers following behind on foot.

Intent on escape, the Chinese soldiers ignored the single column of black smoke that spiralled upwards just a couple of kilometres further east – except for one young captain, who, elated at having avoided the fate of so many of his compatriots, ordered his driver to divert in that direction. He soon found the wreckage of Huang Bai's fighter, which was nothing more than a metallic skeleton surrounded by smoking ash. Then he saw a lone figure striding towards him.

'Ah, Mister Pilot, it looks like you could use a ride.'

Huang Bai flushed with anger at the captain's derisory tone, but curbed his retort. 'Yes, that would be greatly appreciated. Otherwise, I might be in for a long walk.'

The captain laughed. 'I'm Captain Chen Chao. Come sit with the driver and me. We can't have an officer stuck with this motley bunch.' He gestured towards the four morose soldiers sitting in the back of the truck.

As they bounced across the gibber-strewn plain, Chen outlined their options. Huang Bai agreed that escape to the north was their best chance, but stipulated that they must keep off any roads where the Hawks might patrol. They both knew that if their positions were reversed, no mercy would be shown to the enemy, and every soldier and every truck would be hunted down. They assumed, incorrectly, that the Australians would do the same.

* * *

With both the Chinese army and its surviving jets in disorganised retreat, the three remaining Australian F-15s and ten Hawks were able to safely land at Alice Springs Airport, just south of the battle zone. Stores of fuel and ordnance that had been air-lifted to Uluru were reloaded onto RAAF C-17 transports for immediate relocation to the new base of operations.

Under the strong morning sun, Roy Pearce climbed out of his Hawk and strode to where Alan Taylor and the other two F-15 pilots were standing. About to give them a big 'well done', he saw that the trio were anything but elated at the success of the strike. Instead, he simply shook the hand of each man and said: 'Your job is done. You can leave it to us from here. The bastards are on the run.'

With no time to lose, Pearce then called his nine remaining Hawk pilots for a hasty briefing while they awaited the arrival of the C-17s. They used the vacant domestic terminal at the airport. 'Okay, boys,' he said, 'we've lost two to ground-fired missiles, but I understand both Jos and Terry were able to eject, and the Army is bringing them in. The F-15 boys have lost two: one pilot apparently never ejected, and sadly, he has been killed. Nobody knows what's happened to the other guy. He's down somewhere, and we don't know if he's alive or dead.

'We'll now patrol the highway, and hit any tank, missile launcher, or artillery piece they take with them. We'll ignore troop-carrying trucks – leave them to the Army. We'll also ignore all the troops and trucks fleeing to the east of the highway. The Army guys believe that for a while, they'll head east up the Plenty and Sandover Highways, then try to cross the country due north to rejoin the road to Darwin. They can't do us any harm. The poor bastards will probably all get lost in the desert and die of dehydration or starvation!'

* * *

Dave used his handkerchief to carefully dab at his face. He had two parallel scrapes along his cheek and a long, deep gash over his left eye that was still open. The congealing blood had glued his eye shut, and it was aching horribly. He didn't know if the eye itself was damaged. The whole side of his face was swollen, so he'd given up on trying to open it.

He'd managed to get at the emergency locator beacon and supplies in the cockpit. Beacon transmitting, his thirst temporarily quenched, he'd used the emergency canister as a pillow and stretched out under the wing. Small, buzzing flies seemed determined to crawl into his eyes, mouth, and ears, so he covered his face with his dampened hanky.

Despite his wounds, he felt a glimmer of positivity for the first time since Trevor had been killed. He'd survived, and it looked like they'd managed to stop the Chinese advance. The RAAF was here now; the rest was up to them. Injured or not, he'd be home with Chloe in a few days.

Mentally and physically spent, Dave fell into a dreamless sleep, but not for long. The sound of a distant engine penetrated the fog in his head. He rolled over and pushed himself up, wincing as pain shot through his back. An army truck emerged out of a cloud of red dust.

'Boy, they didn't mess around,' Dave muttered. 'I thought I'd be here all day.'

He hobbled out from under the wing. He couldn't help but imagine the sight he presented: grey-haired and stooping, half his face scarred and swollen, one eye caked in dried blood. Hardly the picture of an Air Force fighter jock.

The truck pulled up with a squeal of brakes. One man climbed down from the cab, and four more jumped from the canopy-covered tray. Dave's head still throbbed, and his vision was fuzzy, but he could see that something wasn't right. Their uniforms were an odd shade of green, and they all carried rifles. They shouldn't need rifles to rescue him.

A harsh command confirmed what his brain had refused to recognise. He hadn't been rescued. He had been captured by the Chinese army.

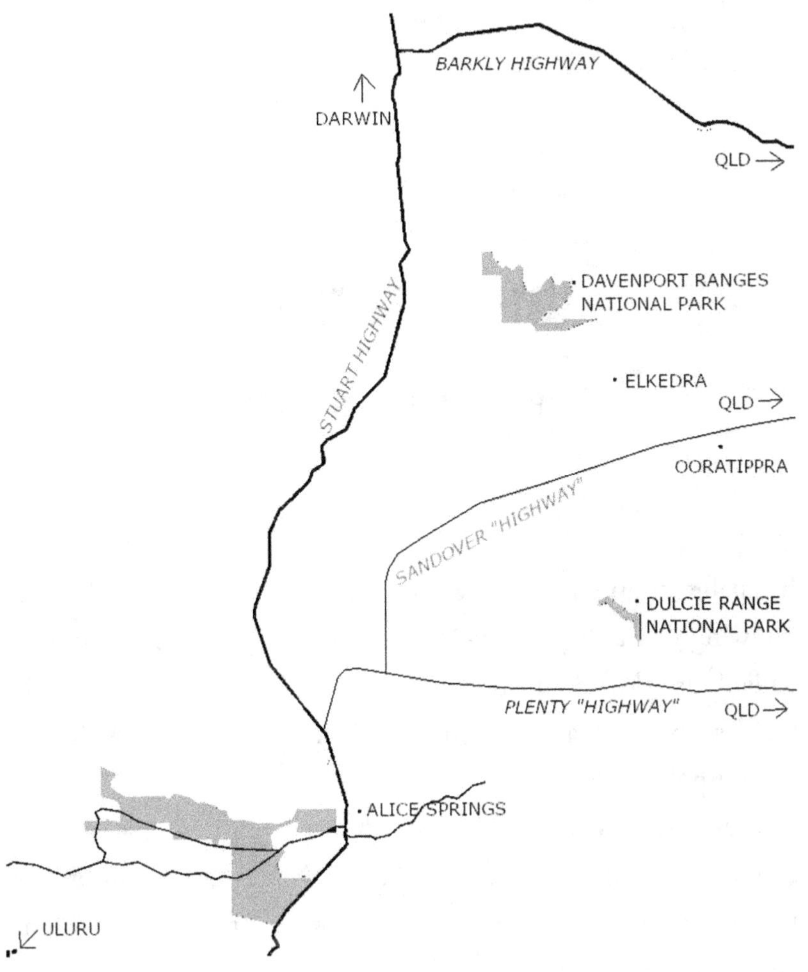
BARKLY HIGHWAY
DARWIN
QLD →
STUART HIGHWAY
DAVENPORT RANGES
NATIONAL PARK
ELKEDRA
QLD →
OORATIPPRA
Sandover "HIGHWAY"
DULCIE RANGE
NATIONAL PARK
PLENTY "HIGHWAY"
QLD →
ALICE SPRINGS
ULURU

CHAPTER 13

Incapable of attempting any sort of resistance, Dave stood under the wing of the downed F-15. He was confronted by an officer, while four soldiers surrounded him. The officer began speaking in Chinese, but all Dave could do was shake his head and say: 'I only speak English.'

The officer, a short man in his early thirties, appeared to consider this for a moment, then tried again, this time in broken English. Dave could understand very little. 'At least you're doing better in English than I could in Chinese,' he said. After several attempts, Dave got the gist that this was First Lieutenant Fang Liang of the People's Liberation Army, and that Dave was now his prisoner.

Dave was shoved away from the F-15, and the soldiers began poking him with their rifles. Then one lashed out with his boot, catching Dave just under the kneecap. He crumpled. All four soldiers began kicking him. He tried to stand but was slammed in the neck with a rifle butt. When he collapsed back, gasping and coughing, the soldiers fell on him, holding him down while

Lieutenant Fang retrieved leather straps from the truck. Dave was tied tightly around the ankles and wrists, his arms behind his back. They picked him up bodily and threw him into the canvas-covered back of the truck.

Trussed that way, Dave couldn't prevent his head from slamming into the unyielding metal frame of a row of hard seats. After a few minutes, he'd recovered enough to take in his surroundings. He lay on a hardwood floor between two rows of seats, one on each side of the tray. Bags of supplies were stashed against the back of the cab. He squirmed into a corner, then levered himself onto one of the seats. He sat there for a time, listening to the Chinese soldiers talk, until Lieutenant Fang climbed into the cab beside the driver and made a radio call. He kept looking at Dave through the back window of the cab while he spoke, and after terminating the call, he began shouting at Dave. One of the soldiers jumped up onto the tray and yelled at him too. When Dave didn't respond, he was clouted over the head with a rifle butt. The soldier then made it clear that Dave was to lie on the floor.

The other three soldiers climbed in, the engine started, and the truck lurched away from the F-15. Dave now lay between the feet of the four soldiers. Every now and again, one would prod him with a boot and laugh.

My future isn't looking rosy at all, Dave thought.

* * *

They drove for several hours, but to Dave, it seemed like days. Red dust swirled into the truck through the open rear, so both prisoner and captors were soon covered in it. All began coughing, and Dave's eyes felt gritty. He ached in every possible way.

His wrists and ankles burned from the tight straps, his throat was parched, and his stomach growled with hunger.

Late in the afternoon, the truck stopped, and the Chinese soldiers all climbed out. They ignored Dave, but as he was desperate to urinate, he began shouting. They continued to ignore him, so he squirmed to the back of the tray. He could see that the truck was sitting on an open, stony, red-brown plain dotted with tufts of thin, dry grass, stunted bushes, and sparse mulga trees. His captors had started a fire with bits of dead mulga and were boiling something on it. Quickly, one picked up his rifle and threatened to hit Dave with the butt. When Dave said, 'Piss, piss,' the soldier understood.

The straps were removed long enough for Dave to relieve himself, though standing up was a torture. They gave him some water but didn't share the food they were preparing. In minutes, they'd trussed him up again. Fortunately, his hands were in front this time.

Back in the truck, alone, he was able to able to gather a few empty sacks to lie on. He fell asleep almost straight away, hardly waking when the soldiers climbed in to get their bedrolls. They slept that night under a sheet of canvas strung between the side of the truck and some low bushes.

At dawn, the soldiers roused. Dave was given a swig of water that tasted like it had been in a canteen forever. He was even able to splash a little onto his face and gingerly explore his wounds. The gashes on his face stung like the devil, and his eye was still firmly glued shut, but it wasn't hurting, so that gave him hope that he hadn't lost the eye itself.

They drove all of that morning, bouncing over rocky ridges, plains covered with thin grass tussocks, and mulga scrub. There were frequent sharp dips as the truck negotiated dry watercourses. Every bump was magnified by the harsh springing, and with each one, Dave was tossed into the air to crash down onto the unyielding floor.

At midafternoon, the truck drew to a stop. The soldiers dismounted, but he was ordered to remain where he was. Minutes later, he heard another truck drawing to a halt alongside, then the sound of raised voices.

A different face peered at him from the open back. More harsh words in Chinese followed, and he was unceremoniously dragged off the truck. It looked as if there was a stand-off between his captors and a new group, which consisted of two officers and four soldiers. Dave couldn't understand a word, but he gathered that the disagreement was over him.

After some emphatic shouts and gesticulations, Lieutenant Fang threw up his hands and stalked away. One of the new officers strutted to and fro before Dave. He was taller than Fang Liang, lightly built, and good looking. He wore a grey flight suit instead of the army fatigues of the others, and carried an automatic pistol on his hip. Dave had a sinking suspicion about him even before he spoke.

'I am Commander Huang Bai of the People's Liberation Army Navy Air Force. What is your name and rank?'

Dave knew that admitting to being a civilian might not go well. 'I am Flight Lieutenant David William Pentreath of the RAAF.'

Huang Bai sneered. 'You lie. Say your rank, and this time, tell the truth!'

Dave repeated his statement, using the rank he'd held during his RAAF service long ago. Huang Bai stepped forward and slapped him hard across his injured face. He staggered back.

'Stand to attention! Tell the truth, or you will be punished most severely.'

'Sir, I am a retired flight lieutenant, David William Pentreath.'

'*Liar!*' Huang Bai screamed. 'You have no rank. You are a civilian, an engineer! You aren't even a real pilot!'

Dave was stunned. It was obvious that Huang Bai already knew altogether too much about him. Rather unwisely, he retorted: 'Your intel isn't entirely correct, but I wasn't a fighter pilot until we beat the crap out of you guys back in July. I didn't do too badly, though, did I?'

The comment appeared to infuriate Huang Bai. 'You had the luck of the devil himself,' he spat, 'and you killed many good sailors and airmen.'

'Could've done it with one arm tied behind my back!'

Huang Bai launched himself at Dave, landing several blows with his fists and a kick to Dave's knee. Ankles and arms still bound, Dave tripped and fell backwards. Huang Bai lashed his boot into Dave's ribs.

'Commander Huang!' the other new officer shouted, rushing forward. 'Control yourself!'

Huang Bai did appear to make an effort to calm down. As the three officers began to argue again, Dave warily got to his knees, but couldn't stand. The other new officer seemed angry with Huang Bai. He called to his four soldiers, and they strode to their truck, got in, and drove away. Lieutenant Fang hesitated for a moment, then walked away into the bush. With growing fear, Dave realised that he was about to be left with Huang Bai, a driver, and four ordinary soldiers. There was now no other officer to moderate Huang Bai's behaviour.

As the sound of the departing truck faded away, Huang Bai

barked orders at the soldiers. One immediately drew a knife and cut the straps around Dave's ankles. He struggled to his feet and stood, swaying, face-to-face with Huang Bai. When Dave looked into his eyes, Huang Bai struck him again and yelled, 'Look down!'

Dave focused on his feet, and Huang Bai began an interrogation. He spoke in passable English, but his pronunciation of some key words made the questions hard for Dave to understand, and that made Huang Bai angrier by the minute. When asked to list the names of the Eagle pilots, both alive and dead, Dave could only shake his head. He didn't dare look up. Huang Bai struck him several more times, until, tiring of it, Dave looked directly at him and said: 'I don't understand you.'

Two soldiers snickered as more blows fell. The other pair turned and walked a few yards away, keeping their backs to the scene. The driver retreated to stand beside the cabin of the truck.

Huang Bai drew his pistol, yelling and gesticulating. Dave understood that he was expected to kneel, but didn't comply, because he had a fair idea that he'd be shot in the back of the head if he did. With one hand, Huang Bai tried to spin him around and push him down, but again, he refused to cooperate. Huang Bai jammed the pistol back into its holster and tried again with both hands. *No way am I going to make it easy for this ponce,* Dave thought.

Face red, spit flying from his mouth, Huang Bai turned to yell at the two watching soldiers. Dave saw an unlikely opportunity. The pistol on Huang Bai's hip was just centimetres from his bound hands. He hadn't fired a pistol since early in his RAAF training days, but he reached for it without hesitation. He knew nothing of Chinese arms, so as he grasped it, he hoped that the safety catch would be on the trigger guard. If it wasn't…

It was. His right forefinger slid over the safety, pressing it off. Huang Bai began to swing back around. The pistol barrel was almost touching his chest when Dave pulled the trigger. Huang Bai collapsed as if his legs had turned to jelly. The two nearest soldiers, just metres away, froze. Dave didn't hesitate. He swung the pistol around and shot one, then the other.

The two who were standing back took a couple of seconds to turn and understand what was happening. Dave made good use of those seconds. He took careful aim on the first as he stooped to pick up his rifle, hitting him high in the chest. The last soldier was bringing his gun to his shoulder as Dave swung the pistol towards him. Dave shot first, and he dropped the rifle, screaming.

In the few seconds since the first shot, the unarmed driver had leapt into the truck's cab and swung the door shut. The engine cranked. Dave ran to the cab, jumped up onto the side step and pointed the pistol through the open window, yelling for the driver to get out of the truck. The driver likely didn't understand the words, but he certainly understood the command. With voluble appeals, his hands on his head, he slid down from the cab. Dave made him stand by Huang Bai, who was bleeding on the ground, gasping for air. Two of the soldiers were rolling around and moaning loudly, but the other two were still and silent.

Dave collected their rifles and threw them into the truck. Earlier, he'd seen a first-aid pack in the back, so while watching the soldiers carefully, he found it and pulled it out of its canvas pocket. He threw it to the driver.

At that very moment, he heard a motor approaching from the south. It was probably another Chinese truck retreating along this track. Quickly, he kneeled over one of the soldiers and pulled a large knife from the scabbard on his hip, then ran to the truck and climbed in. He dropped the pistol and knife on the seat beside him. It wasn't easy for him to turn the key, with both his hands still strapped tightly together, but he managed it.

Dave willed the engine to start. It cranked, but wouldn't fire. The sound of the approaching vehicle grew louder.

'It's a diesel,' he muttered to himself. 'Maybe it needs pre-heating.' He turned the key partway, and a yellow light came on. He counted to five then turned it again. After few cranks, the engine burst into life, emitting a cloud of black exhaust smoke. He didn't hesitate. He engaged first gear, and with an ungainly jerk, the truck began to roll.

The terrain was rough. He had to dodge mulga trees every few metres, and to change gears, he had to take both hands off the wheel, so his progress was slow. He worried that if another truck followed, it might be able to go faster than him just by following his wheel tracks. Judging by the position of the sun, he was heading east, which would hopefully take him out of the Chinese fugitives' path, as they were coming from the south and heading north.

Twenty minutes later, he came to a flat area of red-brown clay. It was bare but for a sprinkling of small, smooth stones, burnished almost black by the desert sun. He brought the truck to a halt. To move any faster, he had to get his hands untied.

He picked up the knife, jammed it between his knees, and sawed the straps restraining his wrists against the sharp blade. It was hard to hold the knife firmly, but he found that he could stop it from falling away by bracing the back of the blade against the steering wheel. With that, for the first time in almost forty-eight hours, his hands were free.

★ ★ ★

Lieutenant Fang was expecting to hear one shot. When he heard five in quick succession, he ran back through the scrub towards the truck. His jaw dropped when he saw it lurching away, engine roaring, leaving five prone figures plus one confused driver. The driver seemed to be frozen in shock, as was Fang Liang.

Seconds later, the appearance of two more trucks coming from the south galvanised Fang Liang into action. He frantically waved them down.

'We had an Australian prisoner!' he shouted. 'He's stolen our truck and escaped. There are injured men here. Please help!'

One truck full of armed soldiers immediately turned to follow Dave's tracks to the east. The occupants of the second truck included a medic, who quickly assessed the five who'd been shot. Two were already dead. Huang Bai was unconscious and bleeding heavily from a chest wound, while the others had what looked to be survivable injuries. The medic treated all three the best he could, before they were loaded awkwardly aboard the now-crowded tray and the truck roared off northward.

Fang Liang had been told that Huang Bai likely wouldn't live for more than a few hours, but when the truck stopped that night, he was still breathing. The medic rigged up an intravenous drip for him. A few hours later, he gave a drawn-out groan, and Fang Liang sprang to his side.

Huang Bai whispered just one question: 'The prisoner… did he escape?'

Fang Liang shook his head. 'I don't know, sir, but one truck went after him. It hasn't returned to the convoy. Not yet, anyway.'

Huang Bai's face contorted in combined rage and pain.

* * *

Just as Dave shoved into first gear, the motion now far easier with his hands cut free, he glanced at the outside mirror and saw a truck emerging from the mulga scrub. It was about 500 metres away, and it was coming straight for him.

Dave dropped the clutch and pressed the accelerator to the floor. Just ahead was a low ridge, little more than a pile of fractured stones, out of which sprouted some scrawny bushes and a few stunted mulgas. He swung sharply around it and jammed on the brakes. The truck skidded to a dusty halt. Praying he was sufficiently hidden by the scrub, he leapt down from the cab, leaving the door wide open and the motor running. He grabbed one of the rifles from the back of the truck, then ran to the edge of the ridge.

The pursuing truck was barely 100 metres away and approaching fast. Dave fumbled with the unfamiliar rifle, sliding the bolt back and releasing it so a cartridge slid into the chamber. He moved clear of the scrub and took aim. His arms felt weak after being severely restricted for so long, but desperation made the almost impossible merely difficult.

He pulled the trigger. The rifle had been set to fire automatically, so instead of the single shot he'd expected, a burst ripped through the desert air. The truck's radiator gushed steam and hot coolant — his initial aim had been good. The recoil caused the barrel to rise, and the stream of bullets smashed into the windscreen. The truck veered left and kangaroo-hopped to a halt. Soldiers began leaping from the back, so Dave sent another hail of bullets their way. He didn't wait to see a result. Still holding the rifle, he ran for his truck and climbed aboard.

Soldiers rounded the edge of the ridge. He mashed the throttle and the truck leapt away, the bellow of the straining engine drowning out any other sound. The back window exploded into a thousand glass shards, some hitting his neck and swollen cheek. More bullets struck the metal of the cab. One outside mirror disappeared, but the engine didn't falter.

Dave didn't slow down until long after the sun had fallen below the horizon. With not much light left in the sky, he pulled into a patch of scrub and switched off the hot engine. He slid tiredly from the cab and looked back along his wheel marks. The desert was silent and still. He sat heavily on the bumper of the truck and sighed with relief. There was no sign of his pursuers.

Not only was he totally exhausted and sore from the top of his head to the tips of his toes, but after a few minutes' rest, he realised he was ravenously hungry and as dry as a chip. He hadn't eaten anything since breakfast the day before, and he'd had little water to drink. In the fading light, he searched the canvas-covered tray.

He was in luck. Quickly, he found bags of rice, boxes of packaged food, and plastic drums full of water. There were a few cooking utensils and, thankfully, matches. He hesitated before lighting a small fire in the lee of the truck, hidden from anyone who may have followed his tracks. Not that there was much chance of anyone surprising him. Even the slightest glimmer of a headlight would've been visible for miles.

The desert night was black and freezing, so the glow of that little fire was an enormous comfort. Dave wasn't usually a fan of rice, but the steaming dish of boiled rice with a few rehydrated vegetables was right next door to heaven. He savoured every mouthful. After eating, despite his bone-weary tiredness, he found his brain going into overdrive. He knew he'd have to be on high alert to evade his pursuers. He considered his options, then decided to head due south. That should keep him east of the retreating army.

His thoughts switched to the events of the last few months. He'd always considered himself a peaceful person, yet he'd no doubt killed people in aerial combat, and by bombing the Chinese ships and army column. A few hours earlier, he'd shot five people with a pistol, then sprayed a truck with an automatic rifle, probably killing more.

He was shocked by his own actions. He desperately wanted this nightmare to be over, and to be the old Dave Pentreath again. For hours, he sat and stared into the glowing embers, before he finally succumbed to his weariness.

* * *

Aches and pains woke Dave long before first light. The cold night air made his facial injuries sting, and he was still very sore from being kicked and bounced around on the tray of the truck. His face and hair were covered in the all-pervading dust, and he longed for a change of clothes. Not that there was much chance of that anytime soon.

It was the third day since his capture. The night was silent, gin-clear, and ablaze with the stars of the Milky Way, so dense that it looked like a giant paintbrush had sprayed the sky with glitter. He soon had the fire going again. With some hot water, he swabbed his swollen eye, removing the dried blood and dust. For the first time in days, he was able to open it a little. He could even see with it. The confirmation that he still had two working eyes made him more confident that he would survive. He promised himself that he would, eventually, return home.

The menu was limited in variety, but at least there was plenty of rice and dried vegetables. By the time he had food ready, the very bottom edge of the eastern sky was turning from black to indigo. While he ate, distant clouds on the horizon began glowing silver and gold, and the sky above lightened to blue. Soon after, the golden rays of the sun were lighting up the tops of the scrubby trees around him.

He felt even better after eating. Once again, he went through his situation. Number one, the Chinese squadron he'd escaped from must surely have more on their minds than pursuing him further across the desert. They would be hell-bent on retreating to the north.

Number two, his nearest safe destination was Alice Springs. Problem was, where exactly was he, and where was it from his location? Somewhere sou-sou-west, he suspected. If he went far enough in that direction, he'd eventually hit the Stuart Highway, which ran from Alice Springs to Darwin. As long as he didn't run into any Chinese soldiers along the way, he would be home free.

Number three, remnants of their army might still be retreating from the battlefield, following the same tracks he'd been taken on. That meant he'd have to keep well east to avoid running into them.

Number four: supplies. There was plenty of food and water in the truck. How about fuel? The gauge in the truck had showed it was full yesterday, but was that accurate?

The truck had two large diesel fuel tanks, one on each side, mounted on its chassis. Dave removed the cap from one, but couldn't see a fuel level. He found a thin stick and poked it inside. The tank was almost empty – there couldn't have been more than 20 litres in it. The other tank was full. It was large enough to hold roughly 200 litres, so altogether, he had about 220 left. A truck of this size would use about 25 litres an hour, meaning it would last eight, maybe nine hours. It might not take him all the way to Alice Springs, but he hoped he would find a cattle station along the way, which would have diesel fuel.

Just then, Dave caught a distant sound. He stood stock still. After a few minutes, the sound came again, louder this time. Quickly, he doused the fire with sand. With no further warning, a Chinese truck, unmistakable in its green and brown camouflage paintwork, emerged from scrubby trees about half a kilometre away from him. It was heading north, leaving a thin trail of red dust behind it. The canvas top of Dave's truck must've been visible over the low scrub, but the vehicle trundled on, passing about 200 metres from where he crouched. Before it disappeared, another truck emerged, following the tyre tracks of the one ahead. It ground on past Dave, its occupants again seeming oblivious to his presence.

Dave's new-found optimism took a big hit. He clearly wasn't beyond the tracks of the retreating army. He waited for half an hour, listening out anxiously, until the flies buzzing around the remnants of his breakfast made it hard to pick up any distant sound.

Starting up the truck, he set his course a few degrees east of due south, or what he figured was due south. In front and to his left, the plains were flat, treeless and featureless, with a thin, patchy covering of dry native grass over red-brown stony ground. A few kilometres to his right were low, rock-strewn hills, some bare, some sprinkled with grassy hummocks and mulga trees, their thin leaves and black trunks barely shading the sunburned ground.

Periodically, dry and sandy watercourses crossed his path. Some were little more than gutters, while others were more than a metre deep. The larger ones supported scraggly river gum trees, their white trunks providing relief from the harsh colours of the desert.

Each watercourse had to be taken carefully, as the eroded edges were near vertical in most places.

After a couple of hours, Dave stopped at one of the dry watercourses, one that had a few sparse trees to shield him from view. He built a small fire and made a cup of the Chinese tea. How he longed for coffee!

Climbing back into the truck, he noticed that a folded piece of paper had been shaken out from beneath the seat on the passenger's side. As he carefully unfolded it, he was amazed to find that it was an Australian Government publication: a World Aeronautical Chart, Alice Springs area, scale one to one million.

The chart had pencil lines roughly marking some tracks, and notes written in Chinese in the margins. The lines started about 75 kilometres north of Alice Springs. An arrow marked a right-turn from the Stuart Highway onto the grandly named Plenty Highway. Dave knew from taking charter flights over it in past years that it began as a sealed development road, suitable for the road trains that carried cattle to market in Queensland, but the asphalt ran out after 30 or 40 kilometres. The further east it went, the rougher it got. The pencil lines followed station tracks that left the Plenty Highway after about 50 kilometres to head north, always keeping 50 to 100 km east of the highway to Darwin. North of a cattle station named Elkedra, the map showed no roads or tracks. Here, a pencilled arrow skirted the remote Davenport Range, then pointed due north. If the Chinese army followed that route, they'd eventually hit the Barkly Highway. Turning left would take them back to Tennant Creek, where they'd probably try to rejoin the Stuart Highway to Darwin.

Dave must be somewhere along that pencil line. Next to a cup of coffee, a GPS would've been most welcome. By the time he'd stolen the truck, the Chinese soldiers had been making their own tracks across the desert, so they must've made it north of Elkedra Station. If his guess was correct, it confirmed that his best option was to continue heading due south, while keeping far enough east to not run into the retreating enemy. By the time he hit the Plenty Highway, they'd surely have all gone north of it, and he'd just motor into Alice Springs.

But first, Dave had to confirm his location. If he was where he thought he was, by continuing south, he would cross the Elkedra River. If those hills he could see to the west were in fact part of the Davenport Range, the river wouldn't be too far away. Once he crossed it, it would be about 175 kilometres across country to the Plenty Highway. Easy!

Dave resumed what he hoped was a southerly course. He only drove a little above walking pace, fearing a puncture from either stones or mulga roots, which were nearly as tough as the rock they'd grown in. They stuck out of the ground like tyre spikes. Occasionally, he'd hit 20 kph on a sandy patch, but then, every bump exacerbated his aches and pains.

Around midday, with the sun beating down from a cloudless sky, he saw a line of a different green ahead. Instead of the dull olive of mulga, it was apple-green, the colour of ghost gum foliage. That could only mean a significant watercourse. As he neared it, he could see the pearlescent white of the tree trunks. A small mob of red kangaroos, the first wildlife he'd seen, were quietly grazing beneath them. The big males, some up to two metres tall, stood up, resting on their tails, to watch the approaching truck. With a degree of reluctance, they turned and slowly hopped away from the shade they'd been enjoying, stopping periodically to ensure Dave wasn't following.

The sand in the dry riverbed was even redder than the surrounding plain. Dave found a place where the banks on either side weren't too steep for the truck to negotiate. After walking across the sand to check its stability, he drove into the creek.

To his surprise, the sand slowed the truck quickly. Despite Dave gunning the engine, within seconds, the vehicle was straining to keep moving. Then, with a jerk, it was bogged. The sand was much softer under the weight of the truck than he'd expected.

'Fuck!' Dave shouted, frustrated with himself for his misjudgement. He had two choices: try digging it out, or let the tyres down to improve traction in the sand. Digging out a truck that probably weighed over ten tonnes would be hard work for a fit man, and all but impossible for him in his condition. He opted to try deflating the tyres first.

It worked. The problem was that he had no way of pumping the tyres up again. The bulging sidewalls were now even more susceptible to damage by rocks and stakes, and the tyres could overheat at any higher speed. He would have to be extra careful.

Once safely on the south side of the riverbed, Dave stopped under some dappled shade. Laying the map out on the truck's bonnet, he compared where he thought he was to the features around him. The river looped a bit, but its general direction was unmistakably east-west. Some dry debris caught up on a dead branch indicated that the water flow would be to the east. The highest point of the hills he'd been passing were to his west. All of it matched. He calculated that he was probably between 40 and 60 km east of Elkedra Station. If he crossed an east-west station track within half an hour of leaving there, it would be further confirmation.

Sure enough, twenty-five minutes after leaving the dry river,

Dave crossed a track. It was so unobtrusive he was on it before he saw it. It was simply a grader cut across the landscape that removed scrub, stones and the occasional ant hill. It didn't look like any vehicles had used it for a while, as only the footprints and tail marks of kangaroos, birds, rodents, and small lizards marred its loose surface. This had to be the station track marked on the map. He was now pretty sure of his position, which improved his confidence enormously. If he continued on a southerly course for another 60 or 70 km, he should cross the Sandover Highway, and just beyond that, the Sandover River.

Dave drove even more carefully for the next three hours. The further south he went, the sandier and redder the ground became. He certainly was in the aptly named 'Red Centre'. Despite his caution, about midafternoon, the steering began pulling to the left. Jumping down from the cab, Dave immediately saw that he'd staked a tyre. It was badly holed. Extracting one of the two spares from under the rear of the tray meant squatting in the dust to heave the heavy wheel from its cradle, dragging it clear of the tray, then rolling it into position. By the time he'd tightened the last of six big nuts on the hub, he was hot, tired, and so rank he could barely stand his own smell. More importantly, he worried that he was now left with only one spare wheel.

Dave made camp early, in a patch of mulga that gave him some thin shade and plenty of dry, gnarled firewood. He made a good fire this time. Using the cooking utensils to heat up some water, he stripped stark naked and washed himself all over for the first time since the night at Uluru. It felt good, although he was horrified to see the extent of the purple bruising all over his chest, shoulders, sides, and thighs. *No wonder I'm so stiff, sore, and tired,* he thought.

At dusk, a flock of galahs flew over, then settled in a nearby lone dead gum tree. Their sharp calls replaced the buzz of flies as the day cooled. *The sound of the outback*, Dave thought.

CHAPTER 14

1 OCTOBER 2026

At a 9 a.m. press conference in the White House, President Ainsworth announced that in a review of US policy towards the Pacific and Southeast Asia, its allies in the region, and its commitment to world peace, the ANZUS treaty of old and the more recent AUKUS treaty were to be renegotiated and reinstated. As an immediate show of goodwill towards its partners in the old treaty, US troops, ships, and aircraft would be immediately deployed to aid Australia in its war with China.

Right-leaning Australian newspapers reacted with large headlines proclaiming the announcement as the confirmation of Australia's certain future in a new world order. Even left-leaning papers grudgingly accepted the American entry as good news, but reminded their readers that the US had a history of joining conflicts late then proclaiming the victory as their own. *It happened in World Wars One and Two, and it will happen here*, one editorial claimed.

Whatever the politics, the Australian public reacted joyously. The cloud over Australia's future, still very much in evidence despite the defeat of the Chinese invasion, evaporated immediately. The stock market recovered all lost ground within days, then continued the upward trend into record highs.

Very quickly, everyday life began to return to normal. Instead of exclusively occupying the first half-dozen pages of most newspapers each day, articles on the war and its aftermath were suddenly relegated to page seven and after. On the day of the president's speech, there was a short report on page eight that the missing F-15 had been found some 100 kilometres north-east of Alice Springs. It said that there was no sign of the pilot, but an air and ground search would continue. What it didn't say was that the search party had found Dave's broken helmet, and a cockpit spattered with dried blood.

* * *

At first light on the fourth day since his jet had crashed, Dave checked his supplies again. He still had plenty of food and water, but the fuel level in the tank was a shock: he only had 40 or 50 litres left. The going had been slower than he'd imagined it would be, and the under-inflated tyres must've increased fuel consumption. It didn't take much calculating to establish that he wasn't going to get as far as he'd hoped. However, he should have enough to reach the Sandover, and sooner or later, someone would surely come along.

Spirits restored, he cranked up the truck. The next few hours were uneventful. In the early afternoon, he was gratified to make out a line of grey and green on the horizon, just around the time he'd expected to be within sight of the river. As he got closer, the line transformed into white-trunked river gums that shimmered in the heat haze.

Before reaching the river, he crossed the so-called Sandover Highway, a dirt road that once again didn't seem to have borne any traffic for some time. That confirmed his belief that the Chinese army hadn't come this far east. He gratefully turned onto it, and for the first time was able to get the truck into fourth gear. The under-inflated tyres whined at the higher speed, reminding him to slow down. He couldn't afford to destroy another tyre now.

Just as indicated on the map, the Sandover road and river converged after he'd driven about 20 kilometres. The width of the dry riverbed was a surprise. *Boy, there must be some volume of water flowing when it does rain,* Dave thought. The river was not just formed of one channel, but a half-dozen of them, each separated by sand banks studded with white gums and twisted logs. These channels added up to a riverbed at least a hundred and fifty meters wide, but there wasn't a single drop of water in sight.

Dave followed the river for a few more kilometres as it snaked towards the Stuart Highway, but as the map indicated, the road and river then diverged again. Dave picked a spot to camp where a clump of gum trees provided passable shade, and thicker low scrub shielded his camp from the road. The nearer he got to the Chinese escape route, the more cautious he needed to be. As the afternoon light faded, he did risk another roaring fire to heat up water for a good wash, and to soak his filthy shirt and undies.

Dressed in only a pair of boots to keep his feet clean, and to avoid the numerous thorns and three-cornered jacks, Dave hung his clothes over some low branches. He heard no sound, but suddenly sensed that he wasn't alone. He froze, staring into the scrub a few metres away. He remained motionless for a minute before seeing two pairs of eyes watching him. Two faces materialised out of the shadows: two grinning faces, topped by fuzzy black hair.

The Aboriginal youths emerged from the scrub and walked into Dave's camp. They were tall, skinny, and dressed in old T-shirts and shorts that had once probably been brightly coloured, but were now so dusty and faded they acted like camouflage. Their bare feet were almost the same colour as the sand they stood on, but above their ankles, their legs and arms were black. They seemed oblivious to the thorns that lay everywhere, and to the flies that crawled around their eyes. They didn't appear to notice Dave's nakedness, but he pulled on his wet undies anyway.

'Hey, boss, what you doing out here? What you doing with that army truck?'

Dave had initially been startled by the soundless approach of the two boys, but quickly relaxed in their easy-going company. He gave them a very brief version of the last five days, saying only that he'd stolen the truck from Chinese soldiers, and omitting that he'd shot anybody. He also said that he wanted to get back to Alice Springs, and asked if they knew what the road was like from here.

'Oh, boss,' the taller and older of the two said, 'them Chinese fellas still been hanging about on this road not far from here. Some trucks got away from the big fight at the Alice, also lots of Chinese fellas are walking. They're still coming. They got guns. Hungry. Steal anything. Shoot anything. We live Amaroo, but take off. Everyone from Amaroo take off. White fellas, black fellas all go. Scary guys, those Chinese.'

Dave looked at the map, and asked if they could confirm his location. They were reluctant, so he didn't press them further. *Maybe they couldn't read maps*, he thought. He found Amaroo on the map. It was about 90 or 100 km east of his estimated position. 'Did you guys walk here?' he asked.

'No, no. Our dad, he got old Landcruiser ute. We all camped near old bore over there.' The younger one pointed vaguely to the east.

'What's at Amaroo?'

'Big station house, workshop. Our camp. Nobody there now. All gone till Chinese go.'

'I need to get back to Alice Springs. Is there another way? What's the country like south of here?'

Their eyes rolled, and they looked at each other. 'Ooh, long way thataway,' said the older boy. 'Rough country. Hard to find water between here and Plenty Highway.'

Dave tried to get more information, but they'd clearly never been into the rough country between there and Alice Springs, except along the road. Dave offered them some hot boiled rice, which they eagerly consumed. As dusk fell, without another word, they stood up and wandered off along the road.

Dave rolled himself up in the four bedrolls to ward off the cold, and lay awake digesting this news. He now had a new choice to make. He could sit and wait right there until the Chinese left or were rounded up. Or, he could strike out across country, directly towards the Alice. Common sense said to sit tight, maybe even wander over to the Aboriginal camp, if he could find it. He could give them some of his supplies, in exchange for any change in the menu they could offer. He could even give them the truck when he didn't need it anymore. Happy with that decision, he went to sleep.

Dave slept soundly until bright sunlight woke him. There seemed little point in getting up early, as he wasn't planning on going anywhere that day. He had a slow breakfast, then sat back to enjoy the sounds of the desert. The galahs and corellas were calling, and the wind was rustling the leaves of the white gums. As the day grew hotter, the buzz of flies drowned out everything else.

He was bored by midmorning, as he had nothing to do, and nothing to read. By early afternoon, he'd had enough of inactivity. He decided to explore a bit to the south. But to do that, first he had to cross the Sandover.

Dave walked along the bank for a mile or so. The river was wide and dry, and consisted of several channels separated by sand banks and occasional islands of trees and half-buried logs. The sand was soft and undulating. The banks were mostly steep, but there were a few places where the truck would be able to descend onto the riverbed without much trouble.

After firing up the truck, he nosed it between ghost gums and down the bank. The moment the front wheels hit the sand, he knew he was in trouble. The truck was all but bogged in seconds. With his foot hard down, revving in first gear, Dave was just able to keep moving until he reached the first sandbank. As soon as the front tyres hit it, the vehicle stopped with its rear wheels spinning.

Once again, Dave clambered down from the cab and saw that all four wheels had sunk deeply into the sand. He had no option but to deflate the tyres a bit more. Already low in pressure, they were worse after Dave let more air out. The wider tyre footprint did work, however, and with a lot of revving, he inched the truck forward. He could smell the clutch burning. When he reached a firmer patch, he stopped to reassess, and to allow the motor, tyres, and clutch to cool. It was obvious that there was no going back now.

Dave gathered dead branches and twigs and laid them in front of the rear tyres. He clambered back behind the steering wheel, and with a look to the heavens, let out the clutch. The truck made it a few metres, then stopped again. Dave repeated the process over and over for the next three hours. By then, dusk was approaching, and he'd made it about halfway across the dry river. He was tired to the bone and exceedingly frustrated, so he quit for the night. The only compensating factor was that there was plenty of dead wood around to make a roaring fire, and again, he used some hot water to give himself an all-over wash.

Dave guessed it was about midnight when he heard the wind pick up, becoming gusty enough to make the canvas shudder. Looking out from under the canopy, he found that the usual brilliant display of stars had disappeared. He went back to his cosy bundle of bedrolls, but lay awake listening to the wind. After some time, he drifted off, waking to find the drumming of the canvas had been replaced by sporadic plops of rain on the roof. Within minutes, it had intensified to a torrent.

He jolted wide awake. The middle of a dry riverbed was no place to be in heavy rain. Then common sense calmed him. This part of Australia probably averaged less than 100 millimetres of rain annually, although it varied greatly from year to year, and it could come in any season. Once in a decade or so, the heavens opened, and all the rivers flooded, cutting off roads and even the north-south rail line for days. Flash floods had killed many people in the area. But this didn't sound like one of those big rain events. Sure enough, it began to ease after a few minutes, and Dave relaxed.

CHAPTER 15

Prime Minister Roger Quick wasted little time in following up on the announcement by the US President. The press conference in Parliament House, Canberra, was packed with TV, radio, and newspaper journalists. Cameras and microphones were trained on the raised podium.

After welcoming the attendees, Quick read from a prepared statement. 'I am pleased to announce that my defence minister is already in discussion with the defence attaché from the US Embassy here in Canberra regarding resurrecting the ANZUS and AUKUS treaties. Meanwhile, as previously announced, American troops and aircraft already based in Katherine have become active in the mop-up operations against the Chinese Army.'

He braced his hands on the edges of the podium. 'Right now, both US and Australian troops, with air support from helicopter gunships, are moving on two fronts against the remaining Chinese ground forces. The first contingent is proceeding north along the road to Darwin to capture the retreating troops. The second has formed a barrier along the Tennant Creek-Camooweal

Road. They will imprison all surviving troops who make it that far north.'

A reporter interrupted Quick with a shouted question: 'What's going to happen to the captured Chinese soldiers?'

'I was coming to that,' he replied. 'All will be identified, treated for any injuries they may have sustained, and held in Darwin pending arrangements to ship them home to China. Now that the Chinese Government has formally announced the cessation of hostilities, we will begin negotiations to facilitate that evacuation.'

'Has there been any development on the missing airman?' called another reporter.

'Well, yes and no,' said Quick. 'The aerial search did locate his aircraft, but he hasn't been found. It is possible that he's been taken prisoner by Chinese soldiers. Our search of the area continues for the dual purpose of finding him and pinpointing the location of the retreating forces.'

'Can you tell us the identities of the F-15 pilots yet?'

'We are about to release the names of all those civilian pilots who so bravely came to their country's aid. That is, except for that of the missing pilot. We've learned from interviewing a captured soldier that the Chinese forces have a particular interest in his identity, as rightly or wrongly, they blame him for the bombing of the carrier *Mao Tse Tung*.'

* * *

Dave was woken before dawn by the screech of galahs and the more musical calls of little corellas. He shivered as he pulled on his flight suit, pondering the long day ahead of digging the truck out of the sand. However, when he jumped down from the tray, he found clear skies overhead – and that, to his surprise, the overnight rain had settled the sand, so it had a firmer crust.

He knew it would soon dry out. Quickly, he fired up the truck. With surprisingly little effort, he got it moving again, inch by inch. It did bog down a couple of times, but after about an hour of straining the engine and tyres, Dave steered the heavy truck over the far bank. He stopped for a while to let the truck cool, and to boil up the usual unappetising meal of rice, dried vegetables, and weak tea. The tyres looked sadly under-inflated, but he could do nothing about that. He'd also burned a lot of fuel in the riverbed.

It was a straightforward trundle over the familiar type of flat grassland for the next hour, until large expanses of low, dense mulga became more frequent. Progress through these was tortuous, twisting around the thicker and taller trees, scraping over coarse bushes, and trying to avoid staking a tyre.

Dave's heart sank when he heard the engine misfire a couple of times. When it died altogether, he banged the steering wheel in frustration. The truck rolled to a halt in the middle of a barren plain. Dave tried restarting, but he feared that he was wasting his time. 'Can't be fuel, not yet,' he muttered. 'We should have enough for a few more hours.'

He jumped down from the cab and immediately saw the cause. The end of a gnarled and brittle mulga log, which must've been kicked up by his front tyre, had neatly pierced the bottom of one fuel tank. As he watched, the last drops of precious diesel fell onto the bare red surface. 'I'm in the shit now,' he said. 'Jesus, just when I thought I might have a chance!'

After walking around the truck two or three times, he resigned himself to the situation. He spread the map out on the seat. By his calculations, he was halfway between the Sandover and a place called Arapunya, with roughly 25 kilometres to go. There was an airstrip there, so there had to be some sort of settlement, either there or nearby.

Easy, Dave thought. *I can walk twenty-five kilometres.* Hell, he and Chloe had walked over 100 kilometres along the Galana River in Kenya a few years ago. They'd averaged 20 km a day. Of course, they'd had a safari guide, armed guards, and porters, but they'd done it. And here, he wouldn't have to dodge lions, elephants, crocs and hippos.

Dave knew that the chances of finding water along the way were virtually nil. He was putting all his eggs in one basket, but he didn't have much choice. The Sandover was dry, so there was no point in going back there. If the worst happened and there was no water at Arapunya, it was only another 25 or 30 km to the northern tip of the Dulcie Range. There'd have to be some rock pools in the foot of the mountains.

He carefully considered what to carry. Taking one of the backpacks from the tray of the truck, he filled it with a bag of rice, a small cooking pot, matches, and a plastic bottle of water. He tied one bedroll and a nylon poncho on top and clipped five water canteens onto the waist strap. Thinking that middays would probably be hot, he ripped a piece from a shirt to cover his neck. He jammed a cap on his head to hold it in place, then hoisted the pack. It weighed about 15 kilos. Not too much for a fit young bushwalker, but Dave's injured back protested.

Leaving the automatic pistol and rifles in the truck, he slapped its bonnet, said 'Thanks for the ride,' and set off towards what he calculated was due south. After walking for a few minutes, he stopped and looked back. The truck looked small and forlorn, the only feature on the dry plain.

As he set off again, a buzzing cloud of flies gathered around his head. They concentrated on the still-oozing wounds on his cheek, so he wrapped the ends of the torn shirt around his face and tied a loose knot. By midday, the heat of the sun made him strip off his flying suit. He walked on in just a T-shirt and undies, but that left his legs irritated by the frequent spiny bushes that made his track an obstacle course.

There wasn't much point in stopping for a rest, as there was no shade anywhere, and if he took off the backpack, he knew he would struggle to hoist it again. He was in constant pain from his bruised ribs and thighs. His only consolations were that soon after midday, clouds rolled in and reduced the glare, and that as he drank from the canteens, the weight he carried became lighter and lighter.

Dave stopped at dusk. There was no proper firewood, but he made a short-lived fire from twigs and dry grass, which was enough to heat some rice. He refilled his water bottles from the large plastic bottle, leaving just a few litres in it. After dark, it began to rain. The poncho wasn't big enough to cover him if he lay down, so he sat huddled under it all night, shivering, dozing and waking in cycles, but never sleeping properly.

He was wide awake long before dawn. The cold had seeped into his bones, and he had difficulty moving at all. The coming of first light was a relief; it had been the most miserable night he'd ever experienced. The clouds had disappeared, but the thin grass was too wet to light, so he had no breakfast. In low spirits, he trudged on.

This day was a repeat of the previous one. He trudged across the same endless plain. Nothing broke the horizon. He had to take care to keep the sun in the right position, otherwise it would've been too easy to walk in a big circle. His lower back became more painful by the hour, until it felt like the discs in his spine were grinding, bone on bone. No clouds gave any relief from the heat, and he drank from the canteens constantly. At least he was able to rest that night in the first patch of mulga he came to. He got a small fire going and ate some rice. Exhausted, he sank onto the hard ground, covered himself partially with the poncho, and slept for a few hours.

Hunger pains woke him, and he was anxious to move on by first light. He began to worry that he'd already passed Arapunya. If he'd gone too far east, he could've missed it altogether.

After an hour or so, he came to a low ridge that supported some scrub. From it, he could see a track just 100 metres ahead. He stumbled forward. It had to be the path to Arapunya. If he followed it to the east, the airstrip should be there.

Ten minutes later, Dave came to a graded gravel airstrip about 700 or 800 metres long. It was barely discernible from the surrounding treeless plain but for a couple of cracked and faded fibreglass cones that marked each end. There was nothing else. No building, no water tank, no windsock, and no sign of recent human activity. The only sound was the buzzing of flies.

For the first time, Dave despaired. He pictured himself a desiccated corpse, lost forever in this pitiless, arid desert. He dropped his backpack onto the ground and looked for somewhere to rest a moment. There was nowhere. No shade from the sun, no escape from the tormenting flies, and no clue as to what he should do next.

Although he'd already memorised every detail of the area, he dragged the map from his backpack and squinted at it once more. He confirmed what he already knew: there was no likelihood of finding help closer than a couple of cattle stations that were 70 or 80 km to the east. He'd never make it, because his water wouldn't last.

That left just one course of action. He'd have to pray that he'd find water in the foothills of the distant Dulcie Ranges. He plodded on towards the south, aided only by his ever-diminishing load of food and water, and tried to pick up the pace.

Soon, he came to a clay pan fed by a dry watercourse made up of several small channels. 'Must be Ooratippra Creek,' he muttered, after a glance at the map. It came out of the Dulcie Range, so at least his navigation was correct. He walked on for another hour, keeping the shallow creek bed in sight, until he came to a small patch of mulga scrub, then another. More patches of dry grass broke the monotony of the gibber plain. Dave squinted, took another swig of water, and brushed a fly off his cracking lips. He saw a blue line on the horizon.

'That's the Dulcie Range,' he croaked. Spurred by new confidence, he increased his stride.

The sun was already hot by the time he reached some small white gums that grew on the narrowing but deeper banks of the creek. He dropped the backpack with a grunt. As these were the first decent trees he'd seen for a couple of days, it looked to be a good shady spot to camp for a couple of hours. He wandered along the red-soil bank, picking up scattered wood. As he stepped over a gnarled branch, he glanced down to see that his foot was coming down on the scaly body of a coiled brown snake. He yelped and threw himself forward. His boot missed the sleepy snake by centimetres. It reared and struck at him, but he jumped away and the deadly fangs missed. It scythed past, its head held high. Dave recognised that it was a king brown, one of the world's most venomous snakes. This one was big: close to two and a half metres long.

'Shit, that was close. Too fucking close,' Dave muttered as he hastily retreated, taking his firewood well away. He hoped he wouldn't come across any of the snake's friends or relatives when he camped that night.

His water store was now down to a few litres. Less than a day's supply, even if he was careful. According to the map, there were several bores on the other side of the range, not far as the crow flies, but at least a day's walk. More likely two. He was relying totally on finding a waterhole in the rocks at the foot of the range. He hadn't seen signs of cattle on the plains, but midway through the next day, he saw what looked like a worn cattle trail coming towards the creek bed from the east, then meandering along the bank. A few minutes later, a huge flock of green and yellow budgerigars swooped past, wheeling as one high into the sky, then back down to near ground level. There had to be water somewhere.

Along the old trail lay the remains of a dead horse. Its dry, brittle skin was holed in several places, revealing that the carcass was hollow. It seemed to have fallen, and in its struggle to stand, had kicked up a ring of stones, from near its nose to behind its tail. A pitiful sight. Nearby was the desiccated body of a feral cat. Dave couldn't help but think that he could end up looking like those two creatures if he didn't find water within twenty-four hours.

Dave camped early and built a big fire. He used some water to boil his usual meal, but despite feeling gritty and uncomfortable, couldn't risk using any for a wash. That night, he rolled out his bedding on coarse sand, against a steep section of bank, which served to shelter him from the night breeze. The sand was soft under his hip. The bank reflected heat from the blazing fire, so he was warm all night. Above, the black sky was ablaze with countless stars, enough that he could've walked along the river under starlight alone.

At dawn, sunrays created a silver glow on clouds far to the east. The sky above was crystal clear. Even before the sun slanted into the tops of the small trees along the watercourse, many birds became active. Corellas announced their communal activities with screeches, and several types of fearless finches darted near Dave. Later, a pair of wedgetail eagles with wingspans of two and a half metres circled high above.

The walk that day began easily, as there were scattered trees along the creek banks to provide periodic respite from the hot sun. Dave guessed that cattle too found the shade enticing, and had eaten bare the tussocky grass that would've otherwise crowded his track.

He plodded past big red kangaroos lying under the shade of a white gum. In the distance, he saw emus; they took fright at his approach and rapidly strode away. A goanna that looked to be close to one and a half metres long regarded him with disdain, and there were small mammal tracks in patches of sand. They all needed water, but where was it?

In the foothills, there were many small, dry watercourses that appeared to coalesce into what would become the Ooratippra Creek. However, none looked remotely like they held water. As the day wore on, it became more and more apparent that his only chance was to find a rock pool in the range, the size of which became clearer with every step. It extended across his path and as far as he could see.

Dave made it into the low, barren foothills of fractured

sandstone by last light, leaving trees, bushes and grass behind. He was dog-tired, having walked over 25 kilometres that day. His stony camp was bearable only because he found a lone, decaying mulga tree that had grown in a crevice. It provided plenty of firewood, and he slept that night certain that he was on track.

With a degree of trepidation, he pressed on towards the crest the next morning. As the climb gradually steepened, and the rocky surface became more and more difficult, his rate of progress dropped to a crawl. He panted with the effort. The large red-brown boulders in his path were sharp-edged, and the smaller ones formed a loose scree. The only vegetation amongst the rock was dry, spiny spinifex grass. Soon, his ankles were red and itchy. The higher he climbed, the larger the boulders he had to negotiate became, and the further away the summit appeared.

Climbing 300 or 400 metres hadn't sounded high to Dave that morning, but he hadn't factored in the heat, scarcity of water, limited food supply, or his protesting body. He now realised reaching the bores on the western slopes over the far side of the range would be an immense challenge.

By late afternoon, Dave had begun to despair. It was hard to appreciate the harsh beauty of this arid land when he faced dying of thirst. He'd seen no sign of water: no rocky pools, no springs. Nothing. Then, as he heaved himself over a ledge, there before him was the pool he'd dreamed of.

It was only small, the size of a large bathtub, but it was clear and cool. With shaking legs, Dave unbuckled his backpack and let it drop to the ground. He sank to his knees. Slowly, he leaned forward until he could bury his face in the life-saving water. He drank until he could drink no more.

Unable to bear leaving it, he made camp by the waterhole.

There was no shade, and the sun was still powerful, but there was a single stunted mulga bush in a crevice just below the pool, which over decades had shed enough dead branches to provide a small fire.

That night, Dave was startled by loud howling from a pack of dingos. Once, they came close enough for him to see their fleeting forms in the flickering firelight. He supposed that they'd come for a drink, only to find him in possession of the waterhole, and were too nervous of humans to risk getting any closer. Rightly so. There was still a bounty on dingos across much of inland Australia, despite research showing that dingoes did little harm to cattle, and were effective in controlling feral cats and foxes. He hoped they knew of an alternative water supply, because he hated the thought of them going thirsty.

CHAPTER 16

6 OCTOBER 2026

News broadcasts across Australia announced that the official search for the missing F-15 pilot had been called off. A government spokesperson commented that there was now little hope of finding him, and unless he was a prisoner of Chinese soldiers yet to be rounded up, it must be presumed that he was dead.

Ken Newstead, Dave's fast friend and owner of a certain recently repaired North American SNJ, switched off the radio in disgust. From the comfortable study in his harbourside house, he rang Chloe Pentreath. 'Chloe, I just heard they've called off the search for Dave!'

'Oh, Ken, it's terrible,' she said, her voice thick with tears. 'Such a shock. I thought they'd look until they found him, but they rang last night to tell me they were suspending the search. Our son Adam and I have been calling charter companies to see if we can hire an aeroplane and pilot to do our own search. We haven't had any luck – they'd all been shut down during the crisis, and none are able to supply an aeroplane for another few days. I'll keep trying until I find someone. I don't know what else to do.'

'Try no more, my dear. My old Twin Comanche is ideal for this job. It's sitting in its hangar at Bankstown, primed and ready to go. I'm throwing some clothes and a toothbrush into a suitcase right now. I'll take off for Alice Springs by lunchtime. It's a fairly long flight at a hundred and seventy knots, but I'll be there early tomorrow, and will start in the search area by midday.'

Chloe gasped. 'Ken, that's so wonderful! You've answered my prayer. I just can't bear the thought of him being lost out there with nobody even trying to find him. Of course, I'll pay all your expenses. Could you use an observer?'

'Don't worry about money, Chloe. I couldn't stand by and do nothing while Dave is still missing. And yes indeed, an observer would be great!'

'Adam would love to be involved. He's beside himself with worry. We'll both come, if that's okay with you?'

'Having Adam as an extra observer would be fantastic, but I suggest you wait at home in case there's news from elsewhere. Adam and I will find him.'

Ken put the phone down and grabbed his maps and a small suitcase. *We'll find him if he's still there to be found,* he thought grimly.

* * *

Huang Bai lay in a portable army cot, wracked with chest pain and physically spent, but fully alert mentally. He cursed the fate that had befallen him. He blamed all of his setbacks on three factors: sheer bad luck, the failures of others, and the devilish fortune of that bastard Australian who'd shot him. He'd been given responsibility for all fighters in the first invasion force, only to have the carrier sunk under him. Then, he'd lost authority to a man whose incompetence allowed the Australians to dominate during the second invasion. Finally, when re-installed as squadron leader, his fighters had lost to civilian pilots. This was the ultimate humiliation, and it festered in his brain. He could think of little else.

Huang Bai wouldn't acknowledge, even to himself, that he'd also had some extremely good luck. When he'd been shot, only minutes had passed before a truck with a medic aboard had arrived. Moreover, that medic, Corporal Meng Wang Fei, was dedicated to medicine, and had studied well beyond the normal syllabus of a field medic. He'd also been careful to hoard scarce medical supplies so he could treat serious injuries like Huang Bai's.

Corporal Meng tended to several injured soldiers during the retreat, but Huang Bai was by far the most seriously wounded. Meng Wang Fei devoted every available minute to him, and after seven days, during which he was treated with IV fluids and antibiotics, Huang Bai had begun to recover physically. But mentally, his dark depression only intensified as he relived events of the past few months.

* * *

Almost 500 kilometres to the south, his nemesis, Dave Pentreath, was at last feeling optimistic. The morning of October 6th was clear and bright, he'd refilled his canteens, and he wasn't far from reaching the top of the Dulcie Range. The map showed two bores on the western side of the ridge, less than ten kilometres away as the crow flies. Beyond that were well-known cattle stations like Huckitta, Mount Swan, Dnieper, and MacDonald Downs. He had enough food for a day, maybe two if he stretched it, so he'd make it to one of those stations. It should be easy going, once he got to the top of the ridge.

It looked to be only a short climb, but it was midmorning before Dave neared the top, when the spectacular view to the west was suddenly revealed. His stomach lurched, and his body recoiled: another few steps and he would've plunged over a vertical cliff. He stumbled back and dropped his backpack. Breathing heavily, he edged forward on hands and knees, peering over the precipice. The sheer wall fell about 35 or 40 metres, before sloping steeply away to the plain far below. This escarpment ran unchanged into the distance either side of him.

'Oh, shit,' he groaned, and pulled back from the edge. He felt like he'd been hit by a sledgehammer.

The plains below the escarpment were very different to the barren sandstone behind him. Small trees dotted the red soil, interspersed with grassy patches. In the middle distance, he could see two lines of darker growth that indicated watercourses, and the map showed that the two bores were probably near them. They may as well have been on the moon, as he had no chance of ever reaching them.

Defeated, Dave lay in the narrow strip of shade provided by a crevice near the ridge. He might've lain there all day but for the constant irritation of a growing swarm of flies that refused to be deterred by his swatting. Eventually, he decided that he had to keep moving, no matter how hopeless his situation. But which way? He could retreat and try to skirt the range at its northern end, or follow the ridge to the south, where the cliff face must eventually peter out.

The thought of retreating was unbearable, so he had to go south. He hadn't gone far when he came to a crevice that started right at the top of the ridge. His tired knees made the clamber over boulders and loose stones painful, and in a moment's inattention, he didn't notice that one flat rock was like a loose tile.

He put his weight on it. It slid sideways, and he went with it, falling heavily on his side. He cried out as needle-sharp pains knifed upwards from his ankle. Winded, he took a minute to reassure himself that no skin had been broken by the ragged stone, but when he tried to stand, the sharp pain returned with a vengeance. He fell back with a groan.

If he'd broken his ankle, he was stuffed. He lay still, willing himself to try again. The only sound was his own breathing. Even his gaggle of flies had deserted him. He lay amongst the rocks all afternoon.

That night, he looked at the rising moon, and he wondered for the hundredth time if his wife might also be looking at it and wondering what had happened to him. No doubt he'd been classified as missing, presumed killed, and she would be hurting. He longed to reach out and tell her that he was doing his best to come home, and not to give up on him yet.

The dawn of the twelfth day was clear as glass, so Dave knew it would be hot by midmorning. He tried hobbling along, but his swollen ankle made it impossible to negotiate the rough terrain. He sat in the sliver of shade from a large boulder, his leg propped up to ease the throbbing pain, and looked at his water bottle. People died out here if they went without water for a day or two, even at this time of year.

★ ★ ★

News bulletins on the morning of October 7th carried the story that there was still no sign of the missing pilot, despite extensive searching by a privately owned light aircraft over two and a half days. A spokesperson for his friends and family admitted that their hopes of finding him were fading fast.

'We'll be up again today, but that will complete our cover of the search area. If we don't have any luck by then, I'm afraid there will be little point in continuing,' Ken Newstead said.

Meanwhile, the Chinese Government had denied all knowledge of the missing man. 'If we had captured him,' they added, 'he would face court, charged with multiple cases of murder.'

The truck carrying Huang Bai, Meng Wang Fei, four injured soldiers, and four young privates was almost out of fuel. There was little food or water left, and they were battered and bruised from the truck's constant jolting across the desert. When they ran into a US Army patrol as they attempted to cross the Camooweal to Tennant Creek highway, they were beyond any form of resistance. Expecting to be treated harshly after being disarmed, to their surprise, they were given fuel, food, and water, and placed in a convoy returning to Darwin under escort. As Huang Bai was still stretcher-bound, he was moved into a US Army ambulance, which was taking other serious cases to an AIF medical centre that had been set up in Tennant Creek.

Before the ambulance drove away, Corporal Meng bent down to speak to Huang Bai. 'Good luck, sir. You're in good hands now, and you should be home to your family in China soon. And, if I may, please forget your past disappointments, and start a new life of peace now that this war is over.'

'Thank you for all that you've done for me,' Huang Bai whispered. He still found it difficult to breathe, let alone talk. Grateful as he was to Meng Wang Fei, he made no promise to forget the past.

* * *

At first light on his thirteenth day in the desert, Dave tested his ankle. It was still badly swollen, and each time he put weight on it, excruciating pain shot up his leg. Despite that, he knew that he could wait no longer, as he was on his last dregs of food and water.

Crossing the crevice took an hour. Past it, however, the ridge was relatively flat. With an ancient mulga branch for a walking stick, he toiled on. Each step was agony. When the sun at last slipped behind a glowing line of clouds on the far horizon, he estimated that he'd covered barely five kilometres in the whole day.

He dropped his pack against a red-brown boulder. It wasn't the ideal campsite – it was exposed to any breeze that might come that night, and thin, decaying sticks of mulga constituted the only firewood. He was restless, cold, hungry, and utterly depressed, because the end of the escarpment wasn't yet in sight. In trying to find a way down, he was actually moving further and further away from the bores down on the plain. He was fast running out of energy, and his last few litres of water wouldn't last more than a day. He knew what it was like to be thirsty, and feared that soon, he'd find out what it was like to run out of water altogether.

He heard a distant noise: a low drone. He held his breath and listened carefully. Nothing. Had he imagined it? Seconds later, he heard it again, much louder this time. Two engines. A light twin, flying low, he was sure of it.

Despite strong protest from his twisted ankle, Dave scrambled up the last few metres to the top of the ridge. He stood on the edge of the sheer rock face, with all his weight on one leg, and scanned the sky to the north. At that moment, the very last rays of the sun penetrated a gap in a far distant cloudbank, and both he and the top of the ridge were lit by golden rays. The aircraft was also lit up, just above and perhaps half a mile off the ridge line.

Dave waved his arms furiously. Even knowing nobody would hear, he couldn't stop himself from shouting hoarsely. He was momentarily blinded as the twin flew between him and the glowing orb of the dying sun. Then it was past, and the sound of its engines faded quickly. He recognised it as a four-seat Piper Twin Comanche. He'd flown one of those, years ago.

Two thoughts tumbled in his brain. One was that the Chinese didn't fly Twin Comanches. It was a private aeroplane on track towards Alice Springs, and that meant the city was in safe hands. His second thought was that it had disappeared all too quickly. His only salvation had just flown by, and he couldn't see it anymore; only its wingtip strobes were still just visible, winking in the fading light.

Then the strobes begin to turn to the right, away from the ridge, gently at first. *Just altering course,* his logical mind said, but he held his breath. The turn continued. It was more than just a course change. Although the sun had now deserted the hilltop, the Piper was still brightly lit. Its unmistakable outline, with its wingtip fuel tanks, was now silhouetted against the darkening mauve sky. Dave didn't dare hope that it was coming back. But it was!

This time, the aircraft levelled its wings as it paralleled the ridge line, barely above Dave's position and just 100 metres away. He felt that he could see the pilot's face looking at him, but perhaps it was just his imagination. The aircraft hummed past, went a mile or two, then turned again, repeating the fly-by, even closer this time. This time, Dave could clearly see the pilot and passenger waving, and he read the registration number. ZRO. Zulu Romeo Oscar

He knew that plane. He knew its owner. His friend, Ken Newstead, was at the controls.

The Piper began to climb back on its original course, waggling its wings as it did so. Dave was still grinning widely, holding his arms in the air, even after the aircraft had disappeared into the night sky and its sound had faded altogether. Collapsing back beside his backpack was painful, but he barely noticed. Even the last handful of soggy rice was bearable.

He awoke while it was still very dark. He was cold, and his swollen ankle was throbbing. Putting a boot on that foot was agony, and he couldn't do up the laces. He had no firewood, nor any food, but his spirits were high. Ken was searching for him. They'd come, and soon, he hoped.

They did. As the first rays of sun highlighted the eastern horizon, Dave heard the *thud-thud-thud* of a helicopter. A big one. One minute later, an Australian Army Blackhawk materialised out of the dark southern sky. It flew a slow orbit around Dave, its navigation strobe lights rhythmically exposing the rocky ridge in brilliant white light. From the open doorway, a crewman in helmet and visor guided the pilot to settle the big machine on a boulder, balancing on one main wheel, its tail boom projecting over the cliff face. Dave had to shield his eyes from the swirling dust, and he didn't see three figures emerge until they had almost reached him.

Two were crewmen in their RAAF flying suits. The third was tall, well-built, and dressed in casual clothes. Dave recognised the build before he saw the face. It was his son, and he was there to take Dave home.

The roar of the twin jet turbine engines and the thumping beat of the rotor blades drowned out their cries of greeting, but the grins on all four faces said everything. Dave had to be pulled aboard the Blackhawk, whereupon he was handed a set of earphones and a steaming cup of coffee from a crewman's thermos flask. So many questions from the RAAF crewmen hung in the air, but Dave was too drained to talk. His eyes rolled and his head lolled back as he gave in to the exhaustion that had threatened him for the last two days.

The chopper took him directly to Alice Springs Hospital, where a carpark had been cleared for his arrival. Chloe waited there to meet him with his two beautiful blond daughters, having been flown in by a RAAF VIP jet late the previous night. Silver-haired and slightly stooped, Ken Newstead hung back behind them, until Chloe noticed his reticence and, looping her arm through his, pulled him into their welcome party. They all had to cover their eyes and squint as the chopper touched down in the dusty whirlwind of its own making. As the engines began to wind down, two helmeted crewmen emerged. They turned to assist Dave, one on each side, and held him as he gingerly made his way to his family.

Chloe and the girls were shocked by his sunburned skin, scarred face, and matted grey hair and beard. His flying suit was stained and dusty, and he didn't smell all that great, either, but as he grinned widely and hugged them tightly, they knew that their Dave was back.

* * *

Dave spent twenty-four hours at the hospital. The doctors, who found nothing more serious than a severely sprained ankle and mild dehydration, could do nothing but clean his facial wounds, as it had been too long to stitch them. He slept for the first twelve hours and was restless to get out for the next. When they cut his filthy flying suit off him and unceremoniously dumped it into a rubbish bin, he was a little saddened. He felt that he and the suit had gone through a lot together. Chloe had brought some of his casual clothes with her, so after a shave and haircut, with his ankle strapped, he looked little the worse for wear.

While Dave was in the hospital, a representative from the Foreign Affairs Department called on him. Immaculately dressed in a grey woollen suit and dark blue tie, he explained why, despite intense media interest, a lid had been kept on Dave's identity.

'We'd suggest you keep a low profile to avoid antagonising the Chinese Government,' he said. 'As far as they're concerned, civilians who took up arms against their military are nothing more than mercenaries and murderers. That's how they see you. What's more, some American officials are still smarting over the theft of the fighter jets. So, if you go anywhere overseas where either the Chinese or the Americans can get to you, you'll be at risk. There's also a rumour that the Chinese Government has placed a two-million-dollar reward on your capture.'

Dave was startled by this news, but he had no inclination whatsoever to travel outside Australia in the immediate future, and was therefore perfectly happy to take the representative's advice. After they flew back to Sydney by courtesy of the RAAF VIP jet, he settled in at home, resting, reading, and taking a five-kilometre walk each morning. Within weeks, he'd recovered most of the weight he'd lost, and his back pain had eased considerably. His scars looked less angry, and he soon forgot about them except when he looked in the mirror while shaving.

While his physical health improved quickly, he sometimes struggled mentally. At times, he was buoyant with the prospect of happy and carefree years ahead, but then would sink into depression when he thought about the events of the past few months. He was haunted by the loss of his colleagues, particularly of his best friend Trevor, and he had periodic nightmares in which he saw both friends and enemies dying. He had no desire to go flying ever again, so avoided contact with old friends in the aviation industry, apart from Ken.

Chloe had been ecstatic when Dave returned home, but after a month or so, she noticed that he was sometimes moody. He'd worked hard all his life, and wasn't accustomed to having time on his hands. He was thinking too much about those dark days that were now behind them. However, she knew what the answer was: he needed a hobby. A few years ago, he'd built a big shed on their property, and had restored a couple of old cars in it before the Chinese invasion. He'd accumulated lots of tools and equipment, and he knew how to use them.

'Dave,' she said, one morning over breakfast, 'it's wonderful to have you all to myself, and to have you home all day. But we do need a bit of our own space sometimes. Now you're feeling healthy, why don't you build your own aeroplane, or restore an old one? You've talked about doing something like that over the years, but never had the time. Now you do. Working for yourself and without a deadline, you'd enjoy it. You also need a challenge to keep that brain of yours active.'

Dave shook his head, poking at his eggs with his fork. 'I simply don't want to fly again. What's the point in building or restoring a plane?'

'You mightn't like flying anymore, but you'll always love aviation. You're lost without being involved in it.'

Chloe was right, of course, and Dave knew it. However, he feared she might come to resent all the time he'd commit to a project. Both of them knew that once he got his teeth into something, it would be hard to drag him out of his shed.

'I want a happy husband,' she told him, when he voiced this worry. 'Not one moping around the house all day.'

So, Dave started asking around. Within weeks, he'd found the ideal project: rebuilding an eighty-one-year-old World War Two P-51 Mustang fighter. It had suffered a landing gear failure while being flown by a private owner, and had a damaged prop, fuselage, and wing. It was quite a big task, but old WWII fighters were bringing big money from wealthy enthusiasts, and he calculated that he'd likely be able to make a profit while saving the historic aircraft.

Dave immersed himself in the Mustang project, in helping Chloe develop the house's gardens – which was her passion – and in spending time with his children and three grandchildren. The part of Sydney that he and Chloe lived in was green, peaceful and pretty, and with his days fully occupied, Dave now considered his life just about perfect. His physical health continued to improve. His sadness over his lost colleagues gradually diminished, but didn't disappear altogether. Occasionally, and with no warning, he would still see vivid mental pictures of his colleagues being shot down, of the sailors aboard the *Mao Tse Tung* burning or drowning, of the Chinese soldiers disappearing in a maelstrom of explosives on the road near Alice Springs. 'Poor bastards,' he would utter aloud, sometimes when he and Chloe were sitting quietly together. She never commented on it, but would just touch his arm gently.

Dave and Chloe did remain close to Trevor's wife Jenny. He became almost a surrogate father to Jenny's two boys, taking them to weekend sports, and offering suggestions when they needed help.

Periodically, the press raised the question of why no awards or official recognition had been given to 'the Eagle Group', as they'd dubbed the thirty-six pilots. Each time such an article appeared, there was a flurry of public interest that generally condemned the government for not having done something. After a year or so, Dave was contacted by a representative from the prime minister's department, who requested a meeting. As the tall, formally dressed young man sat in Dave and Chloe's lounge room, he explained that the situation had cooled somewhat, and the government now felt that due recognition could be given to the Eagle Group without stirring up either the Chinese or the Americans too much.

'A sum of one to three million dollars is going to be paid to each of the families of Eagle Group members who were killed, the exact amount depending on individual circumstances. Consideration would be given to a payment to yourself and the others who survived. You would need to submit an application. The PM wishes to award all, including those lost, with a high citizen's award for bravery and service to the nation. He would like to make the award personally to the survivors, including, obviously, yourself. A ceremony at the prime minister's Lodge is being planned.'

Dave was silent for a moment. Slowly, he leaned forward and looked into the man's eyes. 'I'm pleased to hear that my dead colleagues' families are to be compensated for their losses, little enough as it may be, but I am frankly incensed that a civilian award would be suggested. We carried out a military operation with military equipment against a superior military force. For our own government to offer us a civilian award only supports the Chinese claim that we were civilians who murdered their soldiers, sailors, and airmen – and payment for what we did just makes us mercenaries!'

'But Mister Pentreath, we cannot honour civilians with military awards. It is simply against the regulations under which the award system operates.'

'Bugger the system!' Dave exploded. 'I'll bet you lot are *mighty* glad some of us didn't stick to the rules.'

Later, when the official had gone, Dave related the conversation to Chloe. She was initially disappointed, as she thought all the Eagle pilots should be publicly lauded. Dave put his arms around her and said, 'Chloe, you and I would have to get dressed up in our best clobber, then stand around while the PM rabbits on about what brave little chaps we were, when all he really wants is another photo opportunity.'

She laughed, then nodded. 'Let's have our own celebration tonight instead. We'll have two glasses of wine each, instead of one!'

Later, they found out that all surviving Eagle pilots had declined the civilian award offer – for much the same reason, Dave assumed.

CHAPTER 17

5 JANUARY 2027

Like all officers who'd been captured in the desert, Huang Bai had been asked by Chinese-speaking interrogators if he had any information on the missing Australian pilot. He'd said nothing. After triage at the field hospital in Tennant Creek, he'd been transferred by Australian Army ambulance to Darwin, where he'd been admitted to the Darwin general hospital. A week later, he'd flown, with other ambulatory cases, direct from Darwin to Guangzhou in a China-Southern Boeing 757 chartered by the Chinese Government. There, he'd spent a month convalescing.

When he was released from the military hospital, he was able to walk and talk normally, and the only reservation that doctors noted was that he appeared to suffer from deep depression. A cab had been arranged to take him to the PLANAF headquarters, and upon arrival, he was greeted by the base commander, Captain Jian Zhi.

The two old friends saluted, then clasped hands. 'Huang Bai, it's good to see you. You're looking well despite your ordeals, but you've lost some weight.'

'I'm afraid the gods were against us from the beginning.'

Captain Jian held up a finger, then ushered Huang Bai into his office, quietly closing the door against anyone who might overhear their conversation. He spoke softly. 'Between you and me, we shouldn't blame the gods. I think our illustrious leaders made a bad miscalculation. They thought they could take that minnow country with a small force. They forget that when people have their backs to the wall, they come out fighting, and don't always follow the rules of war. Not that we did when we started it, either. But perhaps it was a lesson well learned, and if there is a next time, the PLANAF will allocate all the resources it needs to do the job properly.'

'I certainly hope so,' Huang Bai murmured back. 'However, I've heard rumours that this setback has made those illustrious leaders of ours think twice before the next military expedition, the retaking of Taiwan. They've managed to alienate almost every country in the region, so now it'll be harder than ever. I'm just keeping my fingers crossed that they haven't lost sight of the ultimate aim – a unified China that dominates the Pacific. I'll be waiting for the day when we can fight our enemies on an equal footing. I'll take my revenge on those bastard Australians then.'

'My friend, I hate to say this, but I don't know if you'll ever have that opportunity. It seems that the failure to achieve aerial superiority has been passed all the way down the chain of command to you. You, my friend, are their ultimate scapegoat.'

Huang Bai listened, open-mouthed. He tried to speak, but Captain Jian shook his head and continued. 'I just want to say that I've enjoyed working with you in the past, and I would've liked to continue doing so. But I'm afraid that, as you know, I have no influence over who runs the fighter squadrons. The man who's replaced you is here already. Captain Ping Luo is sitting in your chair, in your office, right now. He's expecting you, and no doubt will have orders for you. I'd better let you go. I'm so sorry to be the one with these bad tidings, but I thought it would be easier if the news came from a friend.'

Huang Bai walked the concrete path from the command offices to the fighter squadron training building with the same feeling of dread he'd experienced before his very first meeting with Admiral Shen. The lawn on each side of the path was now brown, killed by the first snows of winter, and he found coming back to this brisk temperature a shock after his time in Australia. He shivered. Each step took him closer to the reveal of his destiny. He so badly wanted his old job back, but he now knew that there was no chance of that.

The new naval fighter squadron commander was cool, formal, and scrupulously correct in the manner he greeted Huang Bai. 'Commander Huang, come in and sit down. Would you like tea?'

'No thank you, sir,' Huang Bai replied, despite his mouth being parched. He wanted to get to the nub of the meeting immediately.

As if reading his mind, Captain Ping said, 'You must be anxious to know what the PLANAF has in store for you, so without further ado, I'll let you read these orders. They come from Admiral Shen Jun himself.'

He handed a sealed envelope to Huang Bai, whose fingers shook slightly as he ripped the envelope open. He read it quickly. When he finished, he couldn't trust his voice, so he remained silent as he folded the orders and replaced them in the envelope. He looked up at Captain Ping, willing himself to appear inscrutable.

'I am sorry, Commander Huang. I'm sure you did your best, and being grounded permanently after such trauma in the service of our country is not the reward you would've desired. However, I understand that the medical evidence is clear – you will never fly military aircraft again. I believe that those orders made mention of a possible administrative position within the PLANAF, but at reduced rank and, obviously, reduced pay. You do not have to make that decision now.'

Huang Bai's world had crumbled. He left his old office for the last time and checked into a cheap hotel. That night, despite usually being only a social drinker, he walked to a bar in a run-down part of town. An hour later, he did something he never had before: he took back to his drab room a bottle of whisky and a young prostitute.

In the morning, he woke with a foul mouth and a headache, and wondered if his life could fall further. The offered administrative position in the PLANAF was so low that it would've been humiliating for him to take it. He had to accept that he'd been hung out to dry by his superiors. Nothing would alter that.

Huang Bai resigned from the PLANAF and received a modest payout. With nowhere else to go, he retreated to his family farm. Huang Jianguo was surprised and extremely pleased that his only son had returned, as his declining health had made running the farm a real struggle. Alone, he'd maintained a small piggery, several duck pens, a modest orchard, some vegetable beds, and an area used to grow fodder for the animals.

Huang Bai loved his father, but hated the work. He hated being out in the field at first light in the cold. He hated being constantly dirty. He hated the smell of the pigs and the ducks. He hated living in a small, ramshackle dwelling with only his aged father for company. He hated the long hours of hard, physical work without mental stimulation. He hated plodding home in the dark with his gumboots caked in animal shit and straw.

But he knew that the time on the farm was doing him good. His resentment over his wartime defeats and subsequent treatment by the PLANAF was slowly fading. The hard work made him physically fit and kept his appetite good, and he rapidly regained all the weight he'd lost during his long recovery from the gunshot wound.

Huang Bai hid his dislike of the farm from his father and pretended to be content. Huang Jianguo knew better than to pry too much into his wartime experiences and demotion, and he avoided talking about it, so they worked comfortably together. Only once, when trying to fix a leaking hose on his father's tiny and ancient tractor, Huang Bai slipped and cried 'This shitty old machine is no substitute for my beautiful J-15!

Six months after Huang Bai had returned home, he and Huang Jianguo sat at their rickety wooden table after a long day of tending the animals. He knew they both smelt of pig shit, but was too tired to wash before he ate. Idly, he watched his father's cigarette smoke curl and rise, adding to the fug in the poorly ventilated cottage, and to the staining of the already blackened ceiling. The amiable silence was broken when Huang Jianguo coughed, looked at the remains of his cigarette, and shook his head. 'One day, I will give up these coffin nails. But not today.'

He leaned forward, looked at Huang Bai, and said, 'Son, you've been a great boon to this poor old man, and I've enjoyed our time together immensely. The farm is looking better than it has in years. Our production is up substantially. For the first time in a decade, I have a little cash left over each month after I've paid my bills, and I can afford a few small luxuries. It would give me great pleasure if I thought you were truly happy here and would stay forever. However, anyone could see that your heart isn't in it. You're an educated man, and you should be building your own life. It's time for you to forget the past and instead look to the future. You must find a new career, find a loving and faithful wife, and make a family of your own.'

Huang Bai's eyes widened. He hadn't realised that Huang Jianguo could see through his feigned contentment. 'Father, I wish I could, but I've been wronged by fate, by my superiors, and by a man who had the luck of the devil. I can't take revenge on the gods or the navy, but whenever I close my eyes, I see the face of that damned Australian. I dream that one day I can take my revenge on him, even though I know I'll never be able to. It's hard for me to concentrate on anything else.'

Huang Jianguo shook his head. 'Huang Bai, I'm old. One day soon, I will be gone. You're my only child, and with your mother dead five years ago, I have nobody else to leave this farm to. You should go from here and seek a new challenge. Forget the navy. Forget the Australians. When I die, do not return. Sell the farm, and use your inheritance wisely. Perhaps start your own business. You are smart. You can find success.'

Huang Bai knew his father was right, but he had no idea if he could take another major upheaval in his life. He did decide that it was time to re-enter the modern world, so began riding an old bicycle into the village periodically to buy a national newspaper. One day, he saw an article on new careers within the airline industry. It said that after years of contraction through the Covid-19 epidemic and the action against Australia, the airline industry was expanding again, and was therefore looking for new pilots. Initially, he rejected the idea, but over time, the image of a fresh, clean uniform and a seat in the cockpit of a shiny new airliner began to appeal more and more.

Huang Bai bid his father a tearful farewell, thinking that he may never see him again. He travelled to Guangzhou by train, and wearing his only civilian suit, began knocking on airline doors. He was surprised to find some reluctance by international airlines to hire ex-military pilots. Even if he'd managed to get around that, he would've joined at the bottom of a long ladder of seniority, below many other pilots who had far less flying experience than he.

After a number of rejections, he was eventually offered a captain's position in a new regional airline called Panda Air. It was setting up to fly ten of the Comac C919 jetliners made in China as replacements for the Airbus A320 and Boeing 737. The pay wasn't great, being less than half of a major airline captain's salary, but it was adequate. Huang Bai rented a small flat near the company facilities in Wuhan. However, he soon found himself spending about half the week away from home, as Panda Air's routes criss-crossed the country.

As an ex-naval fighter pilot with combat experience, Huang Bai enjoyed some notoriety amongst the mostly younger Panda Air crew. When he became aware that he had a following, his confidence improved, and he developed a new persona. The suggestion of a swagger entered his walk. Slowly, he regained some of his youthful good looks. He began courting a pretty flight attendant named Yuan Xue, and not long after they met, she moved in to share his tiny flat.

During a break of a few days, he took Yuan Xue home to meet his father, who was delighted to meet her and to see the improvement in his son's wellbeing. In contrast, Huang Bai was horrified by the obvious signs of Huang Jianguo's rapid decline, but he did his best to hide his dismay.

Yuan Xue was slender, with delicate features, a city girl born and bred. However, to Huang Bai's surprise, she took immediately to the farm, its animals, the smells and the mud. She quickly formed an easy and comfortable rapport with Huang Jianguo, and seemed to enjoy staying in the dimly lit and crumbling cottage. She didn't appear to notice that its once-white stone walls were streaked with green algae where the broken roof gutters leaked rainwater, nor that it lacked the modern amenities she was accustomed to. Even the outside toilet didn't bother her.

It seemed like a turning point for Huang Bai. For the first time since he was a child, he appreciated the slow pace of rural living. When he and Yuan Xue left to return to work, Huang Jianguo seemed content in the belief that his son had at last found his way to a prosperous and fulfilling life.

Life did only get better for Huang Bai over the following months. Once again, he was in a position of authority and responsibility. He was respected by his colleagues and, after a recent pay rise, was moderately well-paid. He began to believe that he and Yuan Xue could be very happy together. Even the dark thoughts about his downfall in the military, and the revenge he had so badly wanted, receded into the back of his mind.

CHAPTER 18

2 FEBRUARY 2029

Early the following year, Huang Bai entered the cockpit for a routine flight and met a new first officer, already settled in the right-hand seat. As Huang Bai hung his uniform coat, the younger man looked up from the checklist he was studying and grinned.

'Hello,' Huang Bai said. 'I don't think we've met.'

'Sir, we have, actually – I was in my first year of training at the PLANAF when you were heading the fighter wing. My name is Wong Tao.'

Momentarily wrong-footed, Huang Bai said nothing until it was time to run through the checklist. No other chitchat was possible in the busy day that followed. However, both flight and cabin crews spent that night in a cheap hotel in Guangzhou, and as was their custom, they shared a meal at a nearby restaurant. Somewhat against his will, Huang Bai found himself drawn by Wong Tao into talking about their days with the PLANAF.

'What made you leave the PLANAF, Wong Tao?' he asked, as they enjoyed a glass of wine after the meal.

'Ah, I was a naughty boy, sir. Twice, I got bored in the J-6 jet trainer. I thought I was out of radar cover, so I did a bit of low-level flying to add some excitement. I scared a few farmers and their horses, and there were complaints. The first time, I got a rap over the knuckles. The second, they busted me down a rank and suspended me from flying for six months. I quit and applied for the job with Panda.'

Huang Bai laughed. 'Well, don't do any low flying here with me, or I'll bust you from Panda myself.'

A new roster meant that the two pilots regularly flew together, and over the following months, they became firm friends. One evening, during another stopover, they had more than the usual single glass of wine each, and the discussion drifted to people's strange habits. Wong Tao was quick-witted, and always had humorous comments about their colleagues that Huang Bai found particularly entertaining. After a brief lull in the conversation, Wong Tao hunched forward, swirled his wineglass, grinned, and said: 'You know, these Australians make rather nice wine. It's a pity we didn't succeed in taking them over. I'd go there and get a job as a wine taster!'

'Don't talk to me about Australia. You'll spoil my mood,' Huang Bai responded darkly.

The atmosphere of the evening changed. Somewhat reluctantly, Huang Bai allowed his tongue to loosen under the effects of the alcohol. He began to tell Wong Tao of the obsession he'd once had with taking revenge on a certain Australian. Wong Tao listened attentively.

'Perhaps now's the time to seek your revenge,' Wong Tao said. 'You know our government put bounties on the Australians who flew the F-15s?'

Huang Bai sat bolt upright. 'No,' he said. 'When was this?'

'Just after the war finished. They posted the notice in all military bases, apparently. The six surviving F-15 pilots are regarded as mercenaries and murderers, and anyone able to bring any one of them to face justice in a Chinese court will receive a reward of two million dollars. As far as I know, nobody took it seriously, and it's all but forgotten.'

Huang Bai was astounded. The hand holding his wine glass shook, spilling a few drops. 'I'm sorry, Wong Tao. I need to rest.'

With that, he hurried back to his hotel room, where he hunched over the stained basin in the tiny bathroom cubicle and retched until he'd lost his dinner, along with most of the Australian wine. He splashed cold water on his face and rinsed out his mouth. Looking up, he met his own eyes in the mirror. As he did, all the shadows of revenge, suppressed for many months, re-entered his mind with a vengeance.

* * *

One week later, Huang Bai and Wong Tao again shared the cockpit of a late afternoon flight into Guangzhou. As they drank Australian wine in a restaurant after finishing work, Huang Bai said, 'I've made enquiries. You were correct about that reward. It's pretty much forgotten, but it still stands. Two million to bring one of those Australian bastards to China.'

'Then let's do it,' Wong Tao said lightly.

'Wong Tao, I'm not joking about this. I don't really care about the reward, but there's one Australian I'd like to bring to justice. I've thought of a plan. I'd need three others – we'd have to raise some money up front, and we'd need time off to travel to Australia. It wouldn't be easy. If you're serious, let's talk. If not, let's change the subject right now to planes, women, or fast cars.'

Wong Tao sobered up instantly. 'I missed going to the war with Australia. I'd love to have a crack at those bastards. How dare they bloody the nose of our great leader! But I'm only a first officer, so I have no money to spend on such a venture.'

'Neither do I, at the moment.' Huang Bai sighed. 'But something might turn up. Meanwhile, we need two others who'd be interested in this reward. Keep your ears open, but don't tell anyone what we're thinking yet.'

The very next month, Huang Bai received the news he'd been expecting but dreading for years. Huang Jianguo was dead. Neighbours had noticed that his pigs and ducks were unsettled one morning, and seeing that they hadn't been fed, they'd knocked on the door of his cottage. He'd died in his sleep.

Huang Bai hadn't expected to be so affected by his father's passing, but he felt the loss deeply. He was now, apart from his girlfriend Yuan Xue and a very small group of friends from the airline, alone in the world.

The farm was sold. For the first time in his life, Huang Bai was financially comfortable. Common sense said that he should buy his own apartment, or a house, even, and invest the balance. Yuan Xue expected he'd do exactly that, and she hoped a proposal of marriage would soon follow. She was keen to begin a family.

Huang Bai was torn between that same image and his recurring dream of revenge. In May, Wong Tao invited him to a meal at a friend's apartment. There, Huang Bai met two of Wong Tao's drinking buddies on the third floor of a grimy building in a run-down suburb, and it was quickly apparent why Wong Tao had arranged the meeting.

'Huang Bai, this is Lek Lin and Zou Ning. They're aware of the reward offer, and would also love to take some revenge on

Australians. They have a little money saved. We propose that we pool our resources, and when we succeed, reimburse our expenses, then split the balance.'

Huang Bai's immediate reaction was that the whole thing was a bad idea. The three young hopefuls were clearly thinking of it as an adventure, and had no concept of its realities. Nevertheless, as details of the plan were discussed, he found himself being drawn into it. By the time he returned home, he knew that his demons had resurfaced, and couldn't be denied. That night, he told Yuan Xue of his decision.

'There is nothing I can say,' she whispered, turning her back on him to hide her tears. 'Go, then. Slay the dragon, and perhaps you will come back to me, and we can be happy.'

* * *

Huang Bai spent every moment of his free time planning the venture, which he dubbed 'Operation Kangaroo'. Language wouldn't be a problem. As English was the international language of aviation, all four had attended regular English lessons paid for by Panda Air, and Huang Bai's command of the language had improved substantially. The easiest way to get into Australia was a on a tourist visa, as travel between China and Australia was becoming common again.

The first major obstacle was his identity. He was concerned that he might be refused an entry visa if the Australian authorities identified him as a participant in the recent war. It took him weeks to locate an expert forger who could produce a new identity for his visa application. He waited until a road accident claimed the life of a Wuhan man of similar age to himself, then took the details to the forger. Two weeks later, and significantly out of pocket, Huang Bai had a second identity: Chong Tengfei, a lecturer in engineering at a local university.

The second obstacle was the biggest of all. Assuming that they successfully captured one of the Australian criminals, how would they transport an unwilling passenger from Australia to China? Eventually, Zou Ning suggested a method.

'My father is a retired fisherman. He used to work the boats that went all through the Pacific. Periodically, they would carry extra cargo, like drugs and firearms, near the Australian coast. There, the cargo would be offloaded at night into smaller boats.'

'But doesn't the Australian border security monitor all Chinese vessels as they approach?'

'Yes, they do. But there is a way…'

* * *

Huang Bai, masquerading as Chong Tengfei, and his three colleagues boarded a China Southern flight to Sydney via Singapore on 1ˢᵗ September 2029. They'd all received a tourist visa for a stay of one month. They were each carrying the maximum allowable cash of $10,000, plus another $5000 hidden in the linings of their clothes.

Their first two nights were spent at the five-star Sydney Hilton. On the third day, they moved into an Airbnb rental house in the suburb of Eastwood. The house was built with dark red-brown brick, with a faded blue-tile roof and a semi-open veranda in front. There were four bedrooms and one bathroom, a lounge room with separate dining area, and a spacious kitchen. The land was large, about 1000 square metres, with areas of lawn in front and behind the house. A driveway passed along the left side of the house to a double garage. All four were delighted with the house and yard: it was so roomy compared to the tiny apartments they lived in at home.

Huang Bai rented a small Nissan hatchback, which he used to go to several boat dealers. He was looking for an inflatable boat with an outboard motor, one that was fast and could carry at least six people. After visiting the first few dealers, he was somewhat dismayed by the cost of a decent boat. His final call was to a run-down marina in Woolwich.

The boatshed itself looked rough, but it was crammed with expensive-looking craft of all descriptions. In a corner of the front yard, under a large Moreton Bay fig tree, Huang Bai found a craft that met his specifications. Or, at least, the price did: just $20,000. It sat on an old gal steel trailer, surrounded by fallen and decaying fig leaves. Neither boat nor trailer looked very attractive, but Huang Bai couldn't afford the $60,000 that it would take to buy a new boat. The salesman explained to Huang Bai: 'This is an unusual opportunity. It's a Zodiac-brand RIB – an ex-water police boat. It can carry ten people easily, and it was made in France of superior fabric. None of your cheap Chinese rubbish.'

Huang Bai frowned at the last comment, but let it pass. 'The fabric looks very dull. There's even bird shit all over it.'

'Well, it doesn't look too flash, I'll admit,' the salesman conceded. 'It's been used by the water police for several years, and was always out in the open. But the fabric is military standard. Though it may look dull, it's tougher than any new boat you could buy at three times the price. The outboard motor is bigger than you'd normally find on this size inflatable, too, and it's in top shape. Just serviced. You even get a trailer with it, included in the price. What's more, we'll throw in the bird shit for free.'

Huang Bai looked sideways at the lanky salesman, failing to

understand Australian humour. He did, however, recognise good value, and after securing a small discount for paying in cash, he arranged to pick up the inflatable in two days.

Meanwhile, Wong Tao had also been visiting car yards in a rental hatchback. His specifications were a little unusual.

'So,' said one of the dealers, squinting at Wong Tao, 'you want a van, like a Toyota HiAce or similar, which can be a bit knocked about, but it must be mechanically good, and it must have a towbar. Did I get that right?'

'Yes, that's mostly correct. I want *two* vans of that description, though only one must have a towbar. And I want to pay in cash.'

Wong Tao made this same request to several different yards without any success. The vans offered were all too new and expensive, or so battered and old to be mechanically suspect. After hours of frustration as he struggled with Sydney traffic, he decided to retreat to the house and use the internet. There, on a website devoted to commercial vehicles, he located two that looked like they would meet his requirements. The next day, he visited their respective owners, whereupon he found both vans to be almost as good as they'd been described. He didn't haggle on price, which surprised both owners, but paid cash: $2500 for one, and $2750 for the other.

On the following day, Huang Bai took Lek Lin and Zou Ning with him to get the vans. Huang Bai used the van with the towbar to pick up the inflatable boat. Meanwhile, Lek Lin visited a boat chandlery in the suburb of Crows Nest, where he purchased two Garmin portable marine GPS units, both with local maritime maps already installed, as well as various safety equipment specified for small craft. Although the boat was to be used for a few hours only, he didn't want to be caught without mandatory equipment in a spot inspection by maritime authorities.

Zou Ning used contacts his father had made in Sydney's Chinatown during his days as a commercial fisherman to procure four 9mm Glock handguns. All had been stolen from a security guard company, and were expensive, at $1000 each. Although Zou Ning knew he was being ripped off, he had little choice but to accept the deal. He then went to the Roads and Maritime office in Hornsby, and sat for the simple boating licence required by NSW law. He'd downloaded the questions and answers the night before, so the test was easy. His last purchase that day was at a Bunnings store in Ryde. He bought ten tie-down straps of various lengths, for a total of $30.

On the next day, the four men checked they had everything they needed. Lek Lin had forgotten to bring a balaclava, although he did have the other black clothes he needed. A quick visit to a Target store just before closing fixed that omission.

The second phase of Operation Kangaroo began later that same evening. The four conspirators had Dave Pentreath's address in the Hills District from the copious records accumulated by the Chinese intelligence agency. When they zoomed in on that address on Google Earth, they saw that the Pentreath property was one of a row of several 2.5-hectare blocks bounded by Fenner Drive at one end and Sherman Lane at the other. They found it hard to believe that one person could own so much land, just for one house. On the computer screen, they saw that a tree-lined driveway ran from the entrance on Fenner Drive for about 100 metres, ending in a turning circle in front of a single-level brick house. From the left side of the turning circle, the driveway continued around the western end of the house to a double garage, then to a large workshop. All three buildings were surrounded by lawn and gardens, which mixed trees, shrubs and flowers. A strip of natural bushland had been left uncleared at the very end of the block, along the Sherman Lane frontage.

'We must watch both the back and front of the house,' Huang Bai said, as they prepared to enter the vans. 'But it'll likely be a quiet area, with only local traffic. If we sit every night in our vans watching, someone will notice.'

This concern was valid. Fenner Drive, while well-shaded by large trees, offered no hiding places for an observer. Its streetlights came on just before dark, and a vehicle parked for any length of time would attract attention.

Wong Tao said, 'I think the best we can do is drive past every so often, without stopping too long in Fenner Drive. Fortunately, it'll be much easier at the other end – Sherman Lane doesn't have any streetlights. One of us could hide in the grove of trees along it and watch all night if necessary.'

For the next seven days, one of the two vans cruised slowly along Fenner Drive hourly. One person drove, and another used binoculars. From the onset of darkness until midnight, they left a third man hiding in the bush at the Sherman Lane end. He could watch the main living area at the back of the house, with its wide terrace and pool. Despite only being able to catch glimpses of their quarry, they soon identified a pattern of behaviour.

Both Dave and Chloe Pentreath could be seen at around 6.30 a.m. through the floor-to-ceiling windows on this north side. Dave would eat breakfast, then spend a half-hour reading from a laptop, either at the kitchen table or in the sun just outside the kitchen. He devoted his days to his workshop, while Chloe spent much of her time at home with housework and gardening. She often drove out in her charcoal-grey Lexus sedan, and Huang Bai followed her several times. Once, she went shopping for groceries, and twice, she met with female friends over coffee or lunch. Both husband and wife were inside the house by nightfall. It was impossible to see any detail inside, because the curtains were always drawn at sunset. Lights were always turned off by 11.30 p.m.

After five days, this nightly pattern seemed so routine that Huang Bai and Wong Tao decided to risk closer inspection. The glow from a waning moon allowed them to walk carefully from Sherman Lane through the natural bush, over the lawn, past several extensive garden beds, to the workshop. They used a small torch with a pencil beam to peer through one of the side windows. They could see an aircraft fuselage sitting in a jig, obviously under restoration, as well as two cars under dust sheets and a small boat on a trailer. As they skirted the roller doors, a wall light came on without warning, starkly exposing them. They froze for a few seconds, before realising they'd activated a motion-sensor. After a few minutes, the light died.

From the workshop, they crept past the locked double garage, which they knew housed the two cars the Pentreaths used regularly, and along a path that led to the back of the house. Huang Bai was about to set foot on a wide expanse of travertine marble paving when Wong Tao caught his arm. He silently pointed to two motion-activated lights under the eaves of the house.

It was only 10 p.m., so the Pentreaths were still awake. Huang Bai and Wong Tao could hear voices, and sometimes laughter, but the curtains hid anything more. They stood in the darkness for some time, uncertain what to do next, until a door slid open and out walked a person Huang Bai recognised immediately. It was the man he hated so deeply: David William Pentreath.

In Huang Bai's mind, he had grown into an ogre of near-superhuman ability, strength, and size. However, here in the flesh was an ordinary man, around 180 cm tall, a touch under the ideal weight, with short grey hair and a slightly hesitant gait that indicated some sort of injury. Moonlight highlighted the lines on his face. Huang Bai knew that face, but he could see that it had changed in the last couple of years. He wasn't going to be taking revenge on the man he'd duelled with in the sky; it was too late for that.

As Huang Bai took in his old adversary, an unwelcome reality struck him like a physical blow. He had devoted so much of his life to seeking revenge on this old man, and suddenly, he knew that it wasn't worth the sacrifices he'd made.

Huang Bai tried to banish these thoughts and harden his resolve. He'd come this far. There was no backing out now.

Wong Tao also waited motionless in the shadows. He watched Pentreath look up at the sliver of moon, take a sip from a cup, then return to the house, sliding the glass door shut behind him. After ten minutes, he and Huang Bai silently retreated to the bush. An hour later, Lek Lin picked them up in one of the battered Toyota vans.

* * *

The trawler *Xie Xie* dipped and swayed in a long swell some 300 nautical miles off the southern NSW coast. It was ostensibly fishing, but in reality, it was just marking time before its master, Yang Da, judged it was time to make the distress call.

On September 10th, he did just that. He proclaimed by radio that he had technical problems and needed urgent repairs, although he was in no immediate danger, asking for clearance to head for the nearest shelter. Anyone who saw the boat wouldn't have doubted his story. The black hull was pitted with corrosion, and rust stains streaked from every hull and deck fitting. The once-white cabin structure was even worse. The smell of dead fish and fumes from a worn diesel motor followed the vessel all the way into Sydney Harbour.

Australian Customs had every reason to suspect unscheduled visits by Chinese trawlers. All too often, they were a ruse for criminals to land illegal drugs and firearms. However, a close examination of the *Xie Xie* showed that it was clean in that respect, if no other. The sight of the ship's engineer toiling to replace a propeller shaft bearing added to the authenticity of the emergency, and the master and crew received temporary visas to stay at a wharf in Sydney Harbour, valid for one week.

On the night of September 12th, Wong Tao led the discussion in the rented Eastwood house. 'It'll be easy,' he boasted. 'We'll wait until after 2 a.m. They'll be sound asleep, and won't notice the lights coming on, even if we do trigger them. We'll prise open a door, kill the woman, and tie up the target.'

'No,' said Zou Ning, 'it'll be easier to control the man if we have his woman too. By himself, he'll risk anything to escape – and if we don't deliver him alive, we don't get the two million.'

'What about the weather?' asked Lek Lin. 'Has anyone checked it?'

'Yes, of course,' Huang Bai replied. 'Minimum temperature at night is fifteen degrees, maximum for the day twenty-six, with light winds. Some moonlight early, but it'll be quite dark between 3 and 5 a.m.'

It was agreed. The date was set for two nights hence, and a phone call was made to the master of the *Xie Xie*. He was to leave Sydney Harbour in the early hours of September 15th, so he would be five nautical miles off the coast at 5 a.m.

On the chosen day, they carefully packed all their gear into the two vans. At midnight, Huang Bai, and Zou Ning drove away from the rented house in one van. Wong Tao waited an hour, then followed in the second, towing the boat and trailer.

The first van parked on Sherman Lane, outside the back fence of Number 10, at 12.40 a.m. The three occupants donned their black balaclavas, checked their pistols, and squeezed through the wire fence into the small area of bush at the end of the Pentreath property. Near the house, they paused for fifteen minutes. As expected, it was silent, so they crept to the corner furthest from the main bedroom. By hugging the wall, they tried to avoid triggering the motion sensors, but they stopped dead when lights suddenly illuminated the northern side of the house. Shortly afterwards, the lights went out, but they waited another ten minutes before Huang Bai inserted a small jemmy into the corner of the laundry window. It gave with a crack, and the three men climbed into the house.

Huang Bai and his colleagues were correct in assuming Dave and Chloe would be asleep. What they didn't know was that Dave was a very light sleeper, and the tiniest sound would wake him. He'd been disturbed by the automatic lights coming on, but he'd assumed that it was just one of the possums, foxes, or feral cats that occasionally visited.

The sound of the breaking window lock woke him fully, though he didn't know what it was. Perhaps it had been the neighbour's dog? That dog had tipped over their garbage can not long ago, leaving rubbish all over the paving. He decided to investigate. He didn't turn on a light, but Chloe woke as he searched for his slippers.

A floorboard creaked. Dave knew exactly what had caused that one creak in the entire house. Motioning Chloe to be silent, he stood behind the bedroom door, which had been pushed almost shut, leaving a gap for airflow.

The door began to swing open. Faint moonlight through the curtains allowed Dave to see the barrel of a pistol first, followed by the fist holding the weapon.

Dave slammed into the door with his full bodyweight. There was a crunch and a gasp. The pistol fell to the carpeted floor. He scrambled for it, but was knocked aside as the door flew open, and a torch blinded him for a few seconds.

Huang Bai scooped up his lost weapon with his left hand, pointed it at Dave, and raised his right hand to examine his bleeding and twisted fingers. Lek Lin and Zou Ning crowded into the room to study the man who Huang Bai hated so much.

'We meet again, Mister Pentreath,' Huang Bai spat, all compassion for the older man gone.

Dave stared. The voice was vaguely familiar, but the speaker's face was still in darkness. Quietly, he said, 'The war is long over, boys. Just leave the way you came in and let us all get on with our lives.'

Huang Bai scowled, and the other two laughed. They did allow Chloe and Dave to dress, keeping them at gunpoint, before tying their hands in front of their bodies with the straps. Dave couldn't resist, fearing what might happen to Chloe if he did. They were marched outside and bundled into the back of the van. They had no idea where they were being taken, as the rear of the van was windowless. All Dave could determine was that the last ten minutes of the journey were on a twisting road.

Eventually, the van lurched to a stop, and the back door swung open. Chloe and Dave were dragged out. Both knew immediately that they were at the secluded boat ramp in Berowra Waters, where they periodically launched their own small boat. The surrounding hills and thick bush made it unmistakable. The carpark lights provided just enough illumination to see that they were parked alongside a similar van, which had an empty boat trailer behind it. Otherwise, the area was deserted.

They were shoved towards the jetty on the left side of the tiny bay, where they saw a waiting black Zodiac inflatable with a fourth man already aboard. They both protested, but Huang Bai kicked Dave and whispered, 'Quiet, or we'll gag you both, and we won't be gentle with the woman.'

They were made to lie down on the wooden floor either side of the RIB's central driving console. The floor was already wet, and both shivered as their clothes soaked up dirty bilge water. For Dave, it brought back bad memories of the last time he'd been captured, but this was worse, because they had Chloe too. He was breathing fast, close to panic. He knew that unless he got a grip on himself, there was no chance of escape.

Huang Bai, Lek Lin, and Zou Ning sat in single file behind Wong Tao, who was driving, resting their feet on Chloe and Dave. The boat quietly pulled away from the jetty and into Berowra Creek. Once they passed the small marina situated on the right side of the bay, Huang Bai held a portable spotlight at Wong Tao's shoulder. They motored slowly downstream, past silent holiday cottages on their left and moorings holding small cruisers on their right. Barely visible in the darkness were the 40-metre-high rugged sandstone walls on both sides of the valley.

After about ten minutes, they cleared the four-knot speed zone, as the creek began to widen into a broad waterway. They increased speed to 20 knots, which was all the Zodiac could do. Here, the spotlight was useless, so they continued navigating the bends by looking for the red or green lights atop the occasional marker post, and by peering at a handheld GPS.

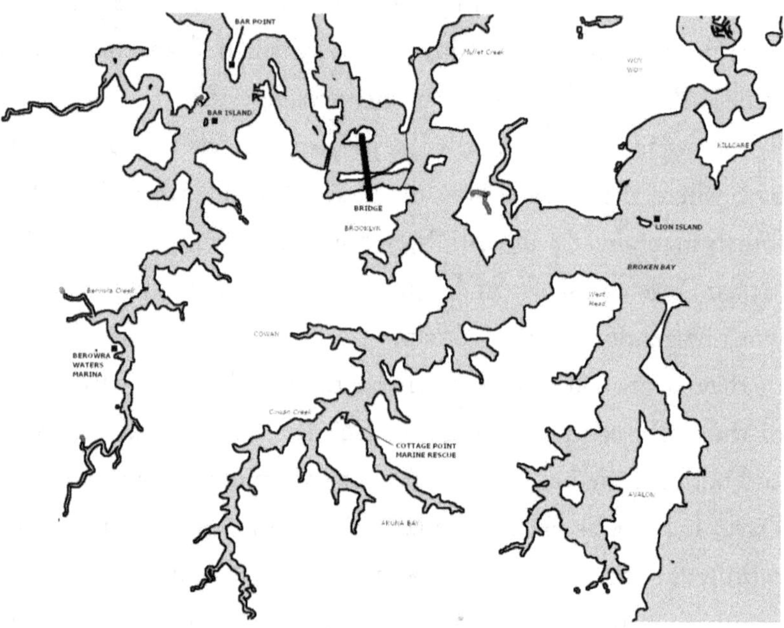

What they didn't know was that at the marina opposite the jetty, a security guard had observed their departure. He normally visited the closed marina two or three times a night, but a recent spate of burglaries from the luxury cruisers moored there had prompted management to install temporary extra security. The guard had a seat in the corner of the restaurant on the floor above the marina offices, and its panoramic windows gave him a 270-degree view of the carpark, jetty, and marina.

Sitting in darkness from 7 p.m. to 7 a.m. wasn't much fun for anyone, but this guard was diligent, and he observed the few regular fishermen who came and went at all sorts of odd hours. There was nothing very unusual about seeing six people departing in an inflatable boat in the early hours of the morning. What was unusual, in this case, was that four wore balaclavas and appeared to be manhandling the other two. When he used his powerful night-vision binoculars, he could see that these two had their hands tied.

The guard made two phone calls. The first went to the Marine Rescue office in Cottage Point, and the second to Sydney Harbour's water police.

* * *

While being pushed aboard the inflatable, Dave had noticed that the tide was at an unusually low level. For years, he and Chloe had used this ramp every month or so during the warmer months to launch their five-metre bowrider boat, and they knew their way along every part of the extensive and beautiful Berowra Creek-Hawkesbury River-Broken Bay system. Navigating its many twists and turns at night was a challenge for anyone, and it was obvious that none of their captors was familiar with the waterway. They were relying totally on their GPS and the occasional dimly lit port and starboard markers along the zigzag course to the sea. Dave was able to keep track of their progress, even from his position on the floor of the boat.

A glimmer of hope entered his thoughts. The maritime maps used by the GPS system were surprisingly inaccurate in a couple of areas. Approaching Bar Point, the recommended course line indicated by the GPS was displaced sideways by 100 metres or more, and could lead the unwary into very shallow water. With this night's very low tide, if the helmsman didn't watch the channel markers carefully, he could get into trouble just to the south of Bar Island, where Berowra Creek and Hawkesbury River met.

Dave called softly to Chloe, 'Be prepared to roll over the side. They might run aground at Bar Island.' He knew that the rowdy outboard would prevent the men sitting over them from hearing what he said. Chloe nodded.

Immediately after they passed the port marker where Berowra Creek entered the far broader Hawkesbury River, they should've made a 60-degree right turn, but the GPS course line indicated the turn almost 200 metres beyond. Wong Tao swung even wider than he should have, drawn further north by the distant lights of the few waterfront cottages near Bar Point. This mistake brought the inflatable much too close to Bar Island, which, invisible in the darkness, lay halfway between the port marker and Bar Point. A yellow and black shallow-water marker on the southern tip of the island was also lit by a lone, dim light, but it was easily lost in the brighter lights of the cottages further behind it.

Wong Tao thought he was safe in the middle of a wide waterway. Due to the Zodiac's very shallow draft, they would've normally done nothing more than stir up some mud. But in a recent storm, an old, dead tree had fallen into the river near the town of Windsor. It had ceased its downstream journey when its roots snagged in that mud, sinking just enough to be invisible, but not enough to prevent it from catching the prop shaft of the outboard motor.

Huang Bai and his colleagues were totally unprepared for the very sudden stop. Momentum carried all four forward, pinning Wong Tao against the console and its small windscreen. However, Dave and Chloe were ready. Chloe pushed herself up onto the side of the boat, hesitated for a moment, then flipped over face-first into the cold, dark water. Dave went to do the same, but Zou Ning, who was at the rear, recovered quickly enough to see what was happening. He yelled, and was about to leap into the water after Chloe when Dave grabbed his leg with his tied hands. Zou Ning fell onto the side of the boat, half in and half out. Dave hung on despite being kicked in the face. 'Go, Chloe!' he shouted urgently, and heard her splashing away.

It wasn't easy for Chloe. The mud was soft and deep, and the water was up to her waist. She found it difficult to balance with both hands still tied. But she was fit and strong for a woman in her mid-sixties, and she knew exactly where she was headed. The four abductors were in total confusion for long enough to give her a 50-metre head start.

Dave lost his grip when Huang Bai struck him just above his eye with the barrel of a pistol, knocking him momentarily senseless. Huang Bai aimed the pistol in the general direction that Chloe had gone, and fired several shots, but all went wide in the darkness. He leapt over the side, and began sloshing through the water after Chloe, yelling for the others to hold Dave down. They did.

Chloe could barely discern the outline of the 25-metre-high island against the setting moon and dim starlight. She knew where the jetty was, and she headed for the beach to the left of it, where she knew the water was shallowest. Huang Bai followed. He could hear Chloe, but couldn't yet see her. He went too far to the right and found himself getting into deeper water, so he stopped and listened again for Chloe's splashing.

Scrambling onto shore, she hurried along the narrow beach, then up the rocky path that wound through trees to the top of Bar Island. The path was difficult enough in broad daylight. She stumbled repeatedly over rough stone steps and tree roots, and grazed her knees more than once, but she made it to the old graveyard near the top of the hill. There, she scrabbled on the ground until she found what she wanted.

A few years earlier, some vandals had, for unfathomable reasons, broken every single headstone, all of which dated between 1876 and 1892. The Hornsby Council had repaired the damage, but Chloe had seen on a previous visit that there were still chunks of marble scattered between the restored headstones. She grabbed a sharp, solid piece, and felt her way further uphill through the trees, to the remains of the church that had burned down in 1892. Just past it was an old stone retaining wall, and beyond that, the ground fell away steeply to the southern shore of the island.

Chloe clambered over the wall and dropped down on her haunches behind it. Breathing deeply, she huddled with her back to the stone, held the marble between her knees, and sawed frantically at the strap holding her hands. It parted just as she heard a muttered curse. By chance, Huang Bai had found the path, but he tripped at every obstacle.

For minutes, she listened to his noisy approach. Then there was silence.

Panting from the excursion, Huang Bai stopped at the fireplace, the only remnant of the church still standing. He stared around himself. In the faint starlight, he made out the low wall, and saw the drop behind it. He began to creep towards it. Chloe was waiting, crouched low on the far side, struggling to breathe quietly. Holding the gun out in front of him, Huang Bai peered over the top of the wall, but didn't see her immediately. She stood and swung the chunk of marble at his head.

Seeing the movement, Huang Bai instinctively began to pivot away. He was too late. The solid marble caught him on the side of his mouth, breaking his jaw. He dropped the gun, howling, and staggered back with his hands to his face. The gun bounced off the top of the wall and landed at Chloe's feet with a thud. She groped for it, found it, and swung it towards Huang Bai. Spinning around, he ran back towards the jetty. He collided with the old fireplace, reeled away, and blindly stumbled back onto the path. Chloe followed the sounds of breaking twigs and his grunts of pain.

She'd never even held a gun before. She aimed and pulled the trigger, but the shot went wild. As she hurried further down the track, she heard Huang Bai blundering ahead of her, until he jumped into the water and begin swimming away. When she reached the jetty, she fired twice more in his general direction. He called out, and was answered by one of his colleagues. The outboard motor started and puttered uncertainly away downstream.

She screamed into the night. As the sound of the motor faded, she collapsed on the wharf. Wet through, she hugged her arms around herself, but the kind of chill she felt was impossible to warm.

* * *

The Cottage Point-based Marine Rescue staff had had a quiet night. The swell was low through the heads at Barrenjoey, the wind was light, and the night was cold and dark. Only a few very dedicated fishermen would be about.

When the call came from the night watchman at Berowra Waters, the two on duty had to untie their 15-metre power catamaran, warm its engines, and clear the moored boats that surrounded their base before they got underway. It would take them about thirty-five to forty minutes to reach the confluence between Berowra Creek and Hawkesbury River – more if they had to dodge fishermen in small boats who didn't bother to carry lights.

There was one such fisherman out there that night. None of the kidnappers saw the four-metre aluminium boat anchored in the deepest part of the channel south of Bar Island. The tinnie showed no lights, as its lone occupant relied on flashing his torch if any boat came too close for comfort. The old man aboard enjoyed the solitude of the river at night, even if he caught no fish. Jolted from his rambling thoughts by the approach of the inflatable, he readied his torch, but relaxed when he heard it swing wide, well away from him. He wasn't overly surprised by the following commotion as it hit the submerged log.

Damn fools, he thought. *Should go slowly if they don't know the river. Getting their arses wet might teach them a lesson.* He chuckled to himself, but was startled to hear the first shots, and positively alarmed when he heard three more some minutes later, followed by Chloe's scream.

He might not have bothered with lights or some of the safety gear that he should've carried, but he did have a small radio for emergencies. He'd never used it, and he spoke hesitantly. 'Marine Rescue, Marine Rescue, have I got the right channel?'

The radio crackled. 'This is Cottage Point Marine Rescue. Do you have an emergency?'

'No, I don't, but something fishy… er, I mean, something strange just happened. I just heard shots and a woman scream.'

'Where are you located, sir?'

'Just south of Bar Island. I'm not certain, but I think the shots might've come from the island, or a boat near the jetty.'

'We're actually on our way to your area right now. We'll investigate.'

The old man didn't want to be found by the patrol in a boat without lights, so he up-anchored, started his small outboard, and headed home.

* * *

Dave was still pinned by three men on the inflatable. He struggled when he heard Chloe scream, but with his hands tied, he was helpless. When Huang Bai returned to the boat, one hand still bloody from his encounter with the Pentreaths' bedroom door, the other clutching at his jaw, Dave was hugely relieved to see that he'd lost his gun. Clearly, Chloe had somehow bested him.

The abductors tied Dave's legs and strapped him to the centre console. Raising the outboard motor, they levered a large chunk of rotting wood from the propeller to expose a badly bent prop blade. The motor started quickly enough, but because of the damaged prop, it vibrated abominably and refused to drive the boat at more than half the speed it'd previously reached.

After about thirty minutes of slow progress downstream, Wong Tao saw the marine patrol boat emerge from Cowan Creek. They doused their navigation lights and hugged the northern shore. When the catamaran swept past 200 metres away, they weren't spotted.

The sky was slowly lightening. Dave noticed that the kidnappers kept looking at their watches, their rising concern obvious. They evidently had a meeting to make, and they were running late. It wasn't a meeting that Dave wanted any part of.

By the time the struggling Zodiac came abeam the bush-covered Lion Island at the Broken Bay mouth, the light had strengthened just enough for the open sea ahead to be visible. The Zodiac bucked as it hit the swell caused by incoming tide, and they had to slow further to avoid being drenched.

Huang Bai was shivering uncontrollably. His clothes were soaked, his hand and jaw ached intolerably, and he'd lost his gun. He feared that the delay caused by the bent prop might dash all his plans. They were already past the rendezvous time, and at their current speed, it would take at least another half hour to reach the rendezvous point.

Fifteen minutes later, they were through the worst of the swell. He urged Wong Tao to increase speed. Peering ahead, they spotted the old trawler, just about four kilometres further out to sea. They stood and waved frantically, but soon realised that the trawler couldn't see them yet.

They laboured on. With barely a kilometre to go, Wong Tao saw the white bow-wave of a boat behind them. He scanned it with his binoculars, and feared the worst. He shouted a warning to his compatriots. 'It's a twin-hull fast cruiser, and it's approaching us quickly.'

Dave didn't understand Chinese, but guessed what was happening. He grinned. 'It's the Marine Rescue boat, boys. The game's up. Untie me and throw your guns overboard.'

The four abductors began a heated argument. Huang Bai looked ashen, Wong Tao aggressive, the other two despondent.

The Marine Rescue catamaran came abeam the inflatable, then slowed to match its speed. A crewman standing on the open deck behind the cockpit called them with a loud hailer. 'Zodiac inflatable, this is Marine Rescue. Stop your engine.'

The four sat in stunned silence for a moment, then began arguing again. The command was repeated: 'Zodiac inflatable, stop engine, *now*.'

Wong Tao, Zou Ning, and Lek Lin responded by firing their

pistols wildly at the larger boat. The rolling of the inflatable made aiming difficult, but the two unarmed rescue officers ducked down. Engines roaring, the big cat pulled ahead and curved away to the right.

'The trawler, it's increasing speed!' Huang Bai cried, wincing in pain from his broken jaw. 'Go faster. We must catch it, or all is lost!'

Sure enough, black smoke was pouring from the trawler's exhaust. It wasn't waiting for anyone. On board the *Xie Xie*, Captain Yang Da jammed the throttle forward, cursing bitterly. He'd been given only $10,000 to come this far, and was expecting a one-fifth share of the two-million-dollar reward as well. However, he'd just spotted a second fast-approaching boat, and it was clear to him that the whole idea had been a big mistake.

This second vessel was the Sydney water police boat *Intrepid*, out of Sydney Harbour. It was capable of over 20 knots even in a moderate sea, and it carried armed police trained to board other vessels. It was heading straight for them.

With the outboard motor roaring and vibrating, the inflatable reached the stern of the trawler, where there was an open hatchway, just as the *Intrepid* came within 100 metres of both. Lek Lin could see that boarding the trawler, now at its full speed of ten knots, was going to be difficult. With any weight transfer forward, the Zodiac's nose would bury itself into the trawler's wake, kicking up sheets of spray and slowing them so that they'd fall behind. Having to manhandle the unwilling captive would make it even harder.

'Wong Tao, bring us alongside if you can,' Lek Lin yelled. 'Zou Ning, follow me. We'll board the trawler over the side, just ahead of the stern.'

With a few extra revs from the complaining motor, Wong Tao

manoeuvred the inflatable to the port stern quarter. They leapt onto the side of the trawler, clung precariously for a moment, then scrambled up and over its railing.

'Throw me the bow rope,' Zou Ning called to Wong Tao, who quickly complied. With the Zodiac tethered to a bollard on the *Xie Xie*, it bounced and bumped in the trawler's wake.

Wong Tao shut down the outboard and made the difficult transfer next, leaving Huang Bai and Dave in the inflatable, barely able to cling on. 'Huang Bai, get him standing up,' he shouted. 'Untie his legs. We'll throw a rope. Tie it to him and we'll drag him aboard.'

Even with the water police rapidly closing in, Dave feared that if he was dragged on board that trawler, he might be killed before his abductors were forced to surrender. He stood, swaying. Even with his arms tied, he could just reach Huang Bai's loose-fitting black pullover. He grabbed hold of it and threw himself backwards, taking both of them over the Zodiac's side.

They surfaced in the trawler's frothy wake, winded and spitting seawater. Huang Bai cried, 'I'll kill you!' He grabbed Dave around the neck and forced his head under. Kicking and writhing, Dave got his head above water, only to be dragged down again seconds later.

Both men were near exhaustion, but still fought with all their strength. Huang Bai was hampered by his injured hand and broken jaw. Dave had been kicked, punched, and struck by the pistol, and his arms were still tied. Neither was in great shape to survive, let alone fight.

It was Huang Bai's youth that gave him the edge. Dave couldn't break free of the grip that held him underwater. He was pinned, with Huang Bai's arms around his neck and legs around his hips.

Underwater, Dave's eyes locked onto Huang Bai's. Then, Huang Bai knew that at last, he had bettered his adversary. It was enough.

At the very moment Dave couldn't hold his breath a second longer, he felt the weight come off his neck. Instead, Huang Bai's arms were under his, lifting him. He gasped air and spat seawater.

The *Intrepid* manoeuvred ever closer, but the police aboard could see that they wouldn't reach the struggling pair in time. One aimed his rifle, trying to draw a bead on the captor. Even with the high-powered scope, it was a difficult shot, as the launch heaved in the ocean, and his target bobbed up and down.

Dave's lungs were burning, his eyes stinging. He was face-to-face with his adversary when he saw Huang Bai's eyes and mouth open wide in surprise. The grip under Dave's arms slackened. Huang Bai's head slowly slipped down below the surface, blood swirling from a hole just behind his ear. A wave broke over them both, and when Dave resurfaced, Huang Bai had disappeared.

Dave coughed and spluttered, fighting panic. By furiously kicking, he could barely stay afloat, but with his arms tied, he could do little else. He saw a man dive from the police boat.

Within minutes, Dave was safely aboard the *Intrepid*. He lay on the launch's afterdeck, wrapped in a blanket, shivering and heaving seawater.

Also wrapped in a blanket, Chloe watched frantically from the Marine Rescue catamaran. Once the police established that Dave was okay, they transferred him to the cat, freeing them to speed off in pursuit of the trawler.

Dave and Chloe huddled together. 'What happened after you jumped out at Bar Island?' Dave gasped, his voice still hoarse from being half-choked and swallowing salty water. She quickly related the events that lead to Huang Bai's return to the Zodiac with a broken jaw and without his gun.

'Then how did you get on this boat?' he asked.

'It seems that a night watchman at the marina saw them forcing us into the inflatable. It looked suspicious, so he rang both the Marine Rescue and the water police. The Marine Rescue cat was already on its way when a fisherman near Bar Island heard the shots and called them on the radio, so they pulled close to the jetty to investigate and saw me there. I was able to tell them about the inflatable, and they figured out it was probably meeting a larger boat offshore. They went at full speed to catch up – and, well, you know the rest.'

Dave frowned out at the brightening horizon. 'Chloe, I'm not certain, but I think that guy… Huang Bai… actually saved me in the end. I was just about done when he lifted me enough to get a breath.'

'Oh my God, Dave,' she whispered, 'and they shot him. They couldn't have known! You must never tell anyone, or the policeman will be pilloried.'

* * *

The water police caught up with the trawler, boarded it, and arrested all aboard. Under interrogation at the NSW Police Marine Area Command in Sydney Harbour, Captain Yang Da denied any knowledge of the plot. Wong Tao, Zou Ning, and Lek Lin refused to talk. All three were charged with attempted kidnapping, forced entry of a dwelling, holding unlicensed firearms, and resisting arrest, and were held in custody by federal police.

After two months of negotiation, the Australian and Chinese Governments agreed on a deal. All charges against the captives held in Australia were dropped, and the prisoners repatriated to

China. In exchange, China rescinded the reward on the surviving F-15 pilots. The trawler was confiscated, later to be emptied of fuel, towed offshore and sunk at the site of an artificial reef.

The US Government demanded return of the four F-15 Eagles that were still airworthy. At great expense, a team of contract pilots, all ex-USAF fighter jocks, were flown to Australia. They ferried the aircraft back to Guam, then on to the Davis Monthan aircraft 'boneyard' in Arizona, where the aircraft were promptly 'reduced to spares'.

Dave Pentreath's F-15, tail number 056, sat in the desert for many weeks, until a recovery team from the RAAF transported it to Canberra. There, in the Mitchell Annexe of the Australian War Memorial, it was put on display to the public. It retained its battle damage – its broken canopy and shrapnel-peppered fuselage. Dave's helmet, still scratched and bloodstained, was also displayed in a glass cabinet alongside the jet.

Huang Bai's girlfriend, Yuan Xue, discovered that she was pregnant two weeks after he'd left for Australia, never to return. She was granted what was left of Huang Bai's estate, and was able to buy a comfortable flat in a good part of Wuhan. Later, she met and married a young man who owned a small business, who matured into a dutiful husband and loving father to her child. Yuan Xue too was happy in the marriage. Before long, she ceased to ponder the troubled life of Huang Bai, and what might have been.

Chloe and Dave returned to their peaceful life on their property. They made no significant changes to their lifestyle, but they did upgrade their home security and adopt two frisky kelpie pups, who grew to be alert but friendly watchdogs. Chloe's gardens flourished, and Dave kept busy with helping her, walking the kelpies, and working on his P-51 Mustang restoration project. He had no interest in piloting an aircraft ever again, but loved the challenge of rebuilding one.

One year after the dramas on the Hawkesbury River, Dave could go for days without waking from a dream in which his F-15 was burning around him. Now, almost at the age of seventy, the worst of his memories had faded, and he'd come to terms with his own actions in wartime. He felt good to be alive, and to have contributed something to his grandchildren's future. He still, however, missed his regular chats with his old mate, Trevor.

Shawline Publishing Group Pty Ltd
www.shawlinepublishing.com.au